"SAY AGAIN?"

The air traffic controller at New York Center sounded understandably incredulous. After all, here I was in a single-engine Cherokee, requesting clearance for ascent to a flight level a couple of miles higher than any Cherokee had ever been.

That was nothing to the reaction when we got up there, right in with the commercial jets.

"Center, tally-ho!" came the call from one airliner. "American Six One Nine has the traffic. But I don't believe it. We're right under him now—and his prop is stopped dead! And . . . he's maintaining altitude!"

The skyhook was working perfectly—in front of witnesses nobody was going to argue with!

STAR DRIVER

A Novel by

Lee Correy

A Del Rey Book

BALLANTINE BOOKS • **NEW YORK**

Library of Congress Catalog Card Number: 80-80236

ISBN: 0-345-28994-3

Manufactured in the United States of America

First Edition: July 1980

Cover art by Atila Hega

TO:
THE REST OF THE CAT PACK:

W. O. Davis
E. L. Victory
S. A. Korff
J. W. Campbell
H. M. Coanda

Chapter One

"What do you mean, my project's been canceled?"

"Just that, Mike. The money didn't come through. NASA has been cut back pretty severely." Dr. Albert Halstead didn't look at me as he spoke, but averted his eyes as he fumbled with his ever-present pipe. "We've all been expecting it, and I'm sure it must come as no surprise to you . . ."

"It sure as hell does!" I didn't return to the chair I had been sitting in, but continued to pace in front of his desk. "How long have I been on staff here at Lowell? Three years, right? How many Mars papers have I published? Seven, right? Is NASA unhappy with my work? Has my research been trivial? Is my research no longer relevant? . . ."

"Mike, please sit down. It isn't that at all." Halstead wasn't a man to become emotional, but I could see that he was upset right then. He acted as though he didn't relish this meeting. "We've been hit with a real crunch here. The Lowell trust funds don't begin to cover the operating expenses these days. And the NASA funds just aren't there any more. So I'm afraid there's more to it than just your project being canceled, Mike. I'm sorry to say that I must ask you to take a temporary leave of absence . . ."

That was certainly a civilized way of telling me that I was fired. I just stopped dead in my tracks.

"Mike, I truly regret this," Halstead went on, still fumbling absentmindedly with his pipe. "I'm certain that it isn't permanent . . . at least as far as I am concerned . . ."

What could I say? I sat down, tore my eyes away

1

from Halstead's nervous hands, and stared out the window at the ponderosas surrounding the building.

"I've asked the business office to make out a check for an extra month's salary to sort of help you along . . ."

I don't remember too much more about that meeting, just platitudes and regrets and embarrassed comments from both of us. I walked out into the afternoon sunshine and didn't even look back at the domed building that had once been a shrine to me.

I stopped in the driveway and took a deep breath. Well, Mike Call, I told myself, you may now be a slightly unemployed astronomer, but there must be work around here somewhere for an astronomer and a teacher. I was still a commercial pilot. Surely I could find temporary work as a flight instructor, clenching my teeth while some student wallowed around the sky in a Cessna 152.

But, damn! Having to leave Lowell Observatory chewed at my insides! I was just beginning to get a handle on Martian meteorology, the surface wind patterns, and the genesis factors for the great dust storms. I'd have to leave that work now—and I hate incomplete work with loose ends hanging out all over it like festoons of moss.

I didn't need to get very much out of my office. My programmable calculator would come in handy whatever I did. But the drawings, the photographs, the Mars globe, and other paraphernalia that had to do with my former work were useless. I could replace them later if and when I got into astronomy again. I didn't even have the usual mementos that I would care to take with me.

I have always operated with the philosophy that I should be prepared to abandon my personal belongings at any time, so I've never collected much. When I was flying as an agricultural pilot—what you might call a "crop duster"—I lived with whatever clothing and personal belongings would fit into a small bag that would, in turn, fit under the pilot's seat in a Grumman Ag Cat or a Piper Pawnee. I have never lost that habit.

I left my office without closing the door. I didn't even say good-bye to Chick and my colleagues. Most of them were still in bed because they were scheduled on the various instruments that night. Well, they'd find out about me tomorrow, if they were still on the staff then themselves.

I began to lay some plans as I drove down Mars Hill in the White Whale, a four-wheel-drive Travelall that I had coaxed up that steep road on many a snowy night.

First of all, there are more astronomers and observatories in the state of Arizona than anywhere else in the world. When I got to my apartment, it took only one telephone call to the nearby Naval Observatory to learn that they, too, were in the midst of a "reduction in force." But Clive Thomas told me that things looked better down at Kitt Peak and suggested that I call Dr. Brad Johnson at the University of Arizona.

"Hell, Mike, I didn't think that you'd be one of those caught in the cut-back at Lowell," Brad Johnson said after I'd gotten him on the phone. "Listen, when could you come down for a chat? I don't know if there's anything here, but it might not hurt to talk about it."

"Can you meet me in about two and a half hours?"

"What? Mike, it's two hundred and fifty miles down here from Flagstaff! The cops have radar out all over interstates Seventeen and Ten!"

"Not at ten thousand feet!"

"Can you get an airline reservation that fast?"

"I've got my own airliner. Can you pick me up at Tucson International?"

Ten minutes later, I was at Pulliam Field undoing the tie-down chains on Piper Cherokee N1422T, affectionately known as *Two To Tango*. I had picked her up four years ago when I was still an ag pilot and had managed to get a good deal because her former owner had folded her nose gear in a cornfield outside of Norfolk, Nebraska. I also have my airframe and powerplant mechanic's license, so with that A&P ticket I put her back together, put a big 180-horsepower engine in her, fitted her out for instrument flight, and had a

$30,000 airplane to call my own for less than half that
sum. She was my personal magic carpet.

Sure, I know that my astronomical astronomer's salary of $15,000 per year doesn't buy a fancy airplane,
but I had made good money as an ag pilot.

Brad picked me up at the base of the tower at Tucson and took me home for supper. We didn't say too
much during the drive to his house.

Ginny Johnson was not only a computer programmer, but she was also a great cook. "Kitchen chemistry," Brad called it, which was a fair statement because
Ginny also had a degree in chemistry.

It wasn't until after supper that the subject of my
situation came up.

"I did some checking around after you called," Brad
began. "I've got a certain amount of clout with the department head, and we're somewhat short-handed. But
there is one big problem . . ."

I sighed because I had run into it before. In fact, I
think it was one of the reasons why I was one of the
first to go at Lowell. "Let me guess, Brad. It is because
I am Mike Call, B.S., M.S., but no Ph.D. Right?"

"That's the problem," Brad admitted. "To teach at
the university level in astronomy today, a doctorate is
mandatory. Without it, a person *might* become an associate professor after twenty years and a Nobel Prize.
But he would never make it to full professorship because of all the new astronomers getting their Ph.D. union cards these days."

Ginny Johnson, who is usually very quiet, spoke up
at this point as she loaded the last of the supper dishes
into the dishwasher. "Mike, why don't you try for the
astronaut corps? NASA is hiring some again. Seems to
me that you'd be a natural astronaut."

That really struck a sensitive spot with me. The only
reason I have maintained a current commercial pilot
license with instrument rating, a current first class medical certificate, and a certified flight instructor (Instrument) rating is that I really wanted to be an astronaut.
I'd make a good astronaut because I stand 5-foot-4 in
my stockinged feet and weigh almost 125 wringing wet.

There was only one factor that was keeping me out of NASA astronaut corps: I didn't have 1,000 hours of flight time in high-performance jet aircraft—just 4,500 hours of flying aircraft with big old propellers in front, sometimes inches above the ground or the telephone wires at the end of the field. Those 4,500 hours don't count, not a single one.

When I didn't say anything in reply, Brad spoke up, "What do you know about electronics, Mike? I need an electronics engineer up at Kitt Peak."

"Brad, I used to hire technicians to handle my own electronic telescope control equipment at Lowell." I was so rusty that I really didn't know what was going on in modern electronics technology any more. "I've been an R&D type when it comes to electronics. The only place I really like to get my hands dirty is on airplanes . . ."

"Brad, how about Bill Osbourne?" Ginny piped up. "Didn't he tell you that he was thinking of hiring a pilot-astronomer one of these days?"

The astronomer scratched his head. "When did Wild Bill tell us that?"

"Don't you remember? At the AIAA meeting at JPL last May."

"Oh, yes!" Johnson brightened. "But as I recall, he was a little vague about it."

"We were all a little vague at that WRT party."

"You're right. It was a little drunk out that night."

"Why don't you give him Bill's telephone number, dear? Mike could call him tomorrow and find out . . ."

"Excuse me," I interrupted, "but who is Bill Osbourne? I thought I knew everybody in the astronomy field."

"Don't tell me you never met Wild Bill Osbourne?" Brad asked. "Well, of course you haven't! That was before your time at Lowell . . . Maybe six years ago."

"Wild Bill left the Air Force five years ago, dear," Ginny reminded her husband.

"Uh, yeah, well, I haven't been keeping score over

on the Air Force side of the house for several years now," Brad admitted. "But Colonel Bill Osbourne used to be the chief space cadet in the Air Force Office of Basic Research." He took a sip of the coffee from the big mug he had to hold in both hands. "You might say that Wild Bill stepped on some toes at NASA when it came to the Department of Defense participation in the NASA space program. So he ended up flying a desk in some dying laboratory at Holloman Air Force Base before he retired after twenty-three years in the Air Force."

"They must have really put him under," I remarked.

"They did. I don't know whether or not I'd have the guts to quit after twenty-three years like Bill did." The astronomer finished off the contents of the huge coffee mug, got up, and started rummaging through the cluttered contents of a small desk in the kitchen. "Yeah, he might like to hear from you, Mike. Ginny! Where did you put Bill's address?"

"Stay the hell out of my desk!" his wife snapped at him. "Don't you know better than to go rummaging through a woman's drawers?"

"I'll overlook that remark," her husband muttered. "Why don't you get things organized in here?"

"What? Like *your* office, *Doctor*?" she taunted him. "It *is* organized!" Within a few seconds, she found a 3-by-5 file card with an address and telephone number on it. As she was copying it on her electric typewriter, she muttered, "When are you going to get me that terminal so I can use the computer down at the university? Then we can put all this data on disk and forget these ridiculous pieces of paper."

Brad didn't say anything. Ginny finally handed him the card, which he looked at and then handed to me. "Give him a call tomorrow, Mike," Brad suggested. "I really don't know if there's anything there or not . . . and it's a long way from here."

I looked at the card.

Dr. WILLIAM D. OSBOURNE
Director of Research

NEMECO Corporate Research Center
430 Factory Drive
Bridgeport CT 06603
(203) 784-7667

I must have had a big question mark on my face because Brad added, "I don't know anything about this NEMECO outfit. But I've known Bill Osbourne for more than ten years because he was involved in a lot of the Air Force basic research that I was doing then. I lost track of him after he retired. Ginny and I happened to run into him at JPL in May."

"I'll call him tomorrow morning," I promised. "I never heard of this outfit, either, and it sounds vaguely mysterious, which intrigues me. In addition, it may be a job."

Brad suddenly glanced at his watch. "Speaking of jobs, I'd better pay attention to mine. I'm scheduled on the four-meter at Kitt Peak in forty minutes!"

"Migawd, Kitt Peak must be a two-hour drive from here!" I blurted out. "Brad, I'm sorry if I caused you to miss your observing schedule—"

Brad did more than chuckle. He guffawed. "Mike, you guys up there at Flag must be nineteenth-century astronomers! I'll bet you even looked through the eye pieces of those telescopes! Hey, it will take me five minutes to get to my office where I've got remote controls rigged on the four-meter along with a TV screen and an image intensifier. Hardly anyone is needed at Kitt Peak for my program except two technicians to keep things working. We let a computer do it all, including image intensification. I haven't looked at a piece of photographic film since I left Las Cruces!"

"Progress!" I snorted. "Come up to Flag sometime if you want to learn how *real* astronomers work!"

"What? And freeze my ass off? The university listens to the Chamber of Commerce here, and they would never admit to the reality of a medical claim for frostbitten buttocks!"

Chapter Two

The next morning, after a somewhat sleepless night, I made a long distance telephone call to Dr. Osbourne at 7:45 A.M. Arizona time so I'd get the night rate.

"Dr. Bradford Johnson suggested that I call you," I told him when he came on the line. "My name is Mike Call. I'm in Flagstaff, Arizona, right now. We had a layoff at Lowell Observatory yesterday. I was involved in some planetary work there. I am also a current instrument-rated commercial pilot with an A&P and a CFII . . ."

"Hold it!" a deep voice with touches of Southern drawl came back over the phone. "Say again slowly, please. You caught me completely off guard."

So I went back through it in more detail.

Dr. Osbourne's voice came back over the 2,500-mile telephone link, "Doctor Call, frankly, I'm fascinated, but—"

"Just Mister Call," I corrected him.

"Sorry. Uh, I did have some rather vague plans down the line that might require a pilot-astronomer. I happened to mention it to Brad Johnson because I know there are damned few pilot-astronomers around. I figured it would be a long time before one surfaced . . ."

"There aren't very many of us," I admitted. "But I am one. If you need one, I'd like to set up an interview with you."

"Well, I couldn't justify bringing you all the way from Arizona right now . . ."

"I'm not asking for travel expenses. I'll fly my Cherokee there out of my own pocket," I told him. What

8

the hell? Sometimes, you've got to take a risk on your own! "If we have a pleasant conversation, you don't lose anything. If something jells, we'll worry about a couple hundred bucks for aviation gas then."

There was an immediate change in Osbourne's tone of voice. "Wait, this is your nickle. Give me your telephone number and let me call you back on our WATS line."

The conversation picked up two minutes later.

"I would like to talk with you, Mr. Call. My schedule is rather hectic for the next few days, but could you be in Bridgeport by Thursday morning?"

"No sweat. I'll plan to arrive at Bridgeport on Wednesday evening. Can you recommend a reasonable motel close to the airport or to your offices?"

"I'll do better than that. The company maintains rooms at the New Barnum because we get so many of our people in here from subsidiaries all over the country. If you're willing to fly more than two thousand miles to talk to me, I can arrange to put you up on the company."

"Well, that will help, although I am not exactly destitute."

"Okay. When you arrive at Sikorski Memorial in Bridgeport, ask Ground Control to direct you to NEMECO's hangar. Ask for Jake Stock, our chief corporate pilot, or Pete Kukowski, or Wimpy Winfield. I'll pass the word to them."

"Got a corporate air force, huh?"

"NEMECO's scattered all over the country, and so are our customers. We use our corporate ships not only for our executives, but also to get some of our stuff to our customers in a hurry. Every once in a while, I get to log some time if they are short a pilot and some of the executives have to get somewhere. Keeps me current. Nice fringe benefit." He suddenly brought the conversation to a close. "I'll see you here on Thursday morning. Give me a call from the airport when you arrive on Wednesday. I am looking forward to meeting you, Mr. Call."

It was only after I had hung up that it occurred to

me that it was one of the damndest telephone calls that
I had ever made. Osbourne had started out very cool
and cautious. But the conversation had grown rather
cordial. Was it because we each found out the other
was a pilot? I know that the aviator's camaraderie often
cuts through a lot of social ice.

Whatever was there was certainly worth looking into.

If for no other reason than to take a trip in *Two To
Tango*.

It suddenly occurred to me that, once on the East
Coast, why shouldn't I spend a little time there and
look around if nothing panned out at NEMECO? Why
should I think about coming back to Flagstaff at all?
This whole episode was over and there didn't seem to
be anything left for me here anyway. Why not pull up
stakes, get flexible, and be able to move as quickly as
Two To Tango would allow? Why not *really* look for
that pilot-astronomer's job if Osbourne had nothing?

It took me about an hour to figure it all out, then I
spent the rest of the day making it happen. I canceled
the lease on the apartment, paying a penalty . . . but
there was money in the sock for those contingencies.
The apartment was furnished, so I had to worry about
nothing but clothes, books, dishes, table and bed linens,
cooking utensils, and other housekeeping gear. I
packed those up and toted them down to a local mini-
storage. Then I swallowed hard, steeled myself, and
sold the White Whale at a used car lot—Cash For Your
Car; Buyer On Duty. I got something less than Kelley
Blue Book wholesale for it, but a couple of thou wasn't
chicken feed and would keep me going for a long time
if necessary. I took a cab out to Pulliam Field and
threw my two bags into *Two To Tango*. I fixed a couple of nagging little problems—a wing-tip light that was
intermittent, plus an upper door latch that had a tendency to pop open in flight. I made the check of my
two navigation receivers and got the ship legal for instrument flight rules operation.

I had planned originally to stay in a motel in Flag
that night and get started at dawn the following day
after a night's rest. But I had everything ready to go,

and I was eager and keyed up. The weather briefing I got by phone from Prescott Flight Service told me that the weather between Flag and Albuquerque was clear so that I need not fly IFR. As usual, visual flight rules were the order of the day in Arizona, so I filed a VFR flight plan and was on my way to Albuquerque thirty minutes before sunset.

Many flatland pilots do not like the idea of mountain flying at night in a single-engine airplane, but it never bothered me. Night flying in the West is better anyway because the air is a lot smoother then.

And it was a nice night to fly.

But, boy, I was sure going a long way!

Well, Mike Call, you have always enjoyed adventure, I told myself as we winged our way over Winslow toward Gallup. I talk to myself when I am flying alone. It relieves the boredom.

The old astronomical observatory was getting too staid and stuffy, anyway. After all, Martian meteorology *is* a rather abstract and academic subject that won't be very useful until somebody like myself goes flying through the atmosphere of Mars someday.

I stretched it to Tucumcari, refuelled, and went on to Tulsa where I had to sack out because I got tired even with my autopilot flying most of the time. I can sit in that seat only about eight hours without getting cramped. When I got up, it was morning, and I discovered that I had left the American West behind me. As the day wore on, I bored eastward over the Midwest, flying by instruments on an IFR flight plan because that was the only way I was going to get anywhere. I made an instrument approach into Alton, Illinois, across the river from St. Louis, flying down the invisible radio beam of the instrument landing system for a perfect ILS approach and landing. Then on toward Pittsburgh.

As I flew in the beauty of towering cloud masses with only an occasional glimpse of the ground in a never-never land that few nonpilots ever experience, I kept asking myself why I was going to Connecticut? What did I expect to find there? The end of the rain-

bow, maybe? I didn't really know. The shock of having
a professional career in astronomy shot out from under
me was beginning to take effect.

Maybe I *could* find some way to combine my education as an astronomer with my training and experience
as a pilot. I'm a good pilot. Never had an accident that
I didn't walk away from, which is saying plenty for an
old ag pilot! One of my instructors once told me that I
was a natural three-dimensional person. I have *never*
experienced vertigo, and I always know where I am,
even shooting the back-course ILS approach down to
minimums at a high altitude airport between two mountain ranges with blowing snow and a twenty-knot cross-
wind.

Maybe I should have gone after that Ph.D. instead . . .

But there wasn't time!

I was already over thirty years old. I felt the sands of
time running out on me because I couldn't find time to do
everything that I wanted to do.

What I really wanted were the stars . . . somehow
. . . any way that I could get them.

But how? When you want to do far-out things, you
can't plan a career. You move with the breaks, hoping
that the zigs and zags along the way will somehow find
a least-squares solution and end up pointing you in the
direction you wanted to go in the first place.

I felt very lonely up there at 9,000 feet in *Two To
Tango* heading eastward. I really don't mind loneliness.
No, let me put it another way: I have had to get used to
loneliness.

I reflected that at my age, most men had already settled down into a job, a career, or a profession. They
were busy raising families, paying off mortgages, and
clawing their way up the ladder. Was I missing something by not doing that?

I seriously doubted it. I had enjoyed myself doing
what I had done.

My introspection went to hell over the Alleghenies. I
had to go to 11,000 feet to clear icing conditions. Even
at that, I picked up some clear ice that didn't improve

the flying characteristics of *Two To Tango*. I was very fortunate that she was lightly loaded and had 180 horses in her nose. I ran into imbedded thunderstorm cells, and New York Air Traffic Control Center wasn't very helpful in radar vectoring me around them. I didn't rate with New York Center; I didn't have swept-back wings, four jet engines, and 400 people aboard.

The weather cleared over Allentown, and I could see the ground most of the time as I went over White Plains because I did not want to say howdy to any of the thick jet traffic around New York City. But I still had to fly an instrument approach into Sikorski Memorial Airport at Bridgeport under a cloudless blue sky because the haze over Long Island Sound had the visibility down to one mile with an indefinite ceiling.

If eastern pilots do not like to fly over mountains, I as a western pilot do not like to fly a single-engined airplane over water out of sight of land. Coming down the ILS runway 6 approach, I picked up the high intensity runway lights at about 400 feet out over the Sound and above the water . . . and that was my first sight of land!

I got it on the ground, got directions to the NE-MECO hangar from Ground Control, and taxied on over with their help in giving me the proper turns.

An ancient Douglas DC-4 was parked in the open hangar, and an Aero Commander sat on the ramp in front. As I taxied up, a lanky pilot who was doing a preflight inspection on the Aero Commander waved his arms violently, trying to shoo me away. I paid no attention to him, but taxied *Two To Tango* next to the Aero Commander and shut her down.

The pilot was over to my ship immediately. "Parking for transient aircraft is further down the ramp! This is a private hangar!"

"This *is* NEMECO's hangar, isn't it?" I asked as I climbed out onto the wing.

"Yeah, but you don't work for us."

"Didn't you get the word?" I asked politely as I bounced down to the ground. "Where's your rest room?"

At this point, a short, stocky, balding man in greasy coveralls came out of the hangar. He completed this Mutt and Jeff team. As he wiped beads of sweat from his face with a rag, he called out, "Pete, is this Mr. Call from Arizona?"

Well, somebody *had* gotten the word after all! The hostility vanished from the tall man's face and he thrust out a hand. "Sorry. I'm Pete Kukowski. This is Wimpy Winfield, our chief mechanic, who didn't bother to give me the word about you or I would have provided a warmer welcome. But Wimpy's okay . . . for an A&P."

"I'll remember that remark the next time you blow an engine on the Four!" Wimpy growled at Kukowski and shook hands with me. "Glad to have you here, Mike. Osbourne said to call him when you got in, and I'm supposed to take you over to the Front Office or the New Barnum . . . whatever."

"Thanks, but where's your bathroom? The last time I touched the ground was in Pittsburgh . . ."

"Follow me," Wimpy said. Over his shoulder as we walked away, he called to Kukowski, "Pete, let me know if that right engine pulls rated manifold pressure, will you? I had trouble timing those mags." The pilot merely waved and went back to his preflight inspection.

Wimpy Winfield was the talkative kind. "You flew that Cherokee all the way from Arizona, eh? How long did it take?"

"Sixteen hours in the air," I told him as he showed me the rest room. As I relieved my hydraulic pressure, I continued, "IFR all the way from Tulsa. I think I might have blown the exhaust gasket on number two cylinder. Is there a Piper dealer on the field?"

"You can get it right across the street from the company that made your engine in the first place," Wimpy pointed out. "Matter of fact, let me pick it up for you."

"Thanks, Wimpy, but I do my own work. It's my pink body strapped into that ship."

"You an A&P?"

"Yup. Also Inspection Authorized. Commercial ticket

with instrument rating, and a Certified Flight Instructor to boot."

"If Osbourne doesn't hire you, I can use you here!"

I called Obourne's office from the hangar lounge, which was pretty plush and belied the ratty exterior of the hangar—but everything looked raunchy and well-used here in the East.

A soft female voice told me, "Dr. Osbourne had to go into New York City on short notice, Mr. Call. He asked me to give you his apologies. Wimpy Winfield will take you to the New Barnum. Dr. Osbourne will be in his office tomorrow morning and looks forward to seeing you at nine-thirty."

I couldn't get upset over the polite and mannered way she put it. But it meant that I had the rest of the day to kill. It was still early afternoon but I hadn't had lunch yet. I mentioned it to Wimpy.

"Get your bags. We'll grab lunch before I drop you at the New Barnum. As a matter of fact, let's haul your Cherokee into the hangar for the night."

Wimpy asked Kukowski if he wanted to join us, but the lanky pilot said that he wanted to test-hop the Commander because he had to take it to Detroit tomorrow morning. I got the distinct impression that the NEMECO corporate air force was busy all the time. And Wimpy confirmed my suspicions as we drove off in the NEMECO airport vehicle, an old but clean van that was beginning to rust out along the quarter panels. "Yeah, we've got a DC-6B, too. She's out in Montana right now. The Bonanza's down in Raleigh today with some sales types."

Wimpy drove. It was a good thing.

I hadn't been to New England before except to Boston on a commercial flight many years ago. But I had *never* been *in* New England. The place seemed cramped and crowded. I got the feeling that it was old. Bridgeport looked dirty and well-used. I got lost because the streets were not square with the world the way they are in western cities, and I could not see the sun through the gray haze of smog and clouds. I had difficulty maintaining my sense of direction, which is unusual for me.

There wasn't a square foot of unused land anywhere. And the buildings on that land were right out of the First Industrial Revolution. A movie company could have shot a Charles Dickens script here with very little set trimming. And the place was *busy*, almost frantic.

Wimpy managed to find a place to park the van on one of the narrow streets. He took me into a cafe.

I haven't been in a place like Mama's since my ag pilot days. We sat down in a vinyl-upholstered booth with a linoleum-covered table. The menu was hectographed in blue on a single sheet of white paper enclosed in a celluloid folder trimmed in red plastic. Nothing fancy on the menu—chili, chowder, chicken-fried steak, hamburger, BLT, and a list of other basic dishes that I had not encountered in years.

The Special was liver and onions. "Take it," Wimpy suggested. I ordered a Special with coffee, pulled a paper napkin out of the spring holder on the table, and did not lace my coffee with cream from the little chromed pitcher on the table; Wimpy did.

"I could have taken you to a fancy place," Wimpy said apologetically, "but this is where all our pilots eat. None of the corporate types ever show up here, so we can talk. Mama's food has never caused any trouble in the air." He was right. The food was good. Nothing fancy, but it stuck to the ribs.

I got to know Wimpy Winfield. He didn't tell me much about NEMECO. Only about himself. "I'm chief airframe and powerplant man and spare pilot," he said. "I don't bother myself with corporate politics and all that stuff. It's my job to keep the airplanes flying and to fill in as pilot when needed. Good job. Been here two years. Got one other A&P, and I need a third. Come see me if Osbourne doesn't have a slot."

"How long you been at this?" I wanted to know.

"Too long. Got my ticket back in the war . . . the Big One, World War Two. Kept it afterwards. I got my A&P and did a lot of work for fixed base operators here and there, but I don't like to work for FBO's. I answered a classified ad in *Trade-A-Plane* one day, got hired by a small company in the midwest that had a fleet of eight Cherokees. I discovered that working for corporate outfits was the way to go. I can handle the big NEMECO birds okay, but I'm a Cherokee man. Guess I've flown just about every one of the three million different kinds they've made in Vero Beach. And you wouldn't believe some of the things I've done with a Cherokee. I know them inside and out. You have any trouble with that bird, you come see me."

He liked NEMECO. "They pay well, and they stay the hell out of my way and let me run my shop. The company seems to be run by people who know what they're doing. Never any panic. Never any hassle. The Front Office trusts me to do my job, and there isn't a one of us who's going to step out of line and screw up this good thing . . . Oh, sure, the comptroller gives me a hard time every once in a while, but that's his job. Company makes money. Always has. Wish I had some more stock, but I've got two in college."

Wimpy waited for me to volunteer my interest in NEMECO. When I didn't, he asked, "You joining Corporate Research?"

"That's what I'm here to talk to Osbourne about. But I haven't the foggiest notion what they're doing."

"Neither do I. They don't talk about it. I catch some rumors, but . . ." And he let it drop at that.

Wimpy left me at the New Barnum in the rejuvenated downtown area. I was left with the rest of the afternoon to kill in a typical All-American Plastic Hotel that looks like every other hotel in America so you have to write yourself a note telling yourself where you are before you go to bed at night.

I decided I would try to find out something about NEMECO.

I put on my suit and tie so that I looked like an Easterner. A stockbroker was located on the street floor of the hotel. There I settled down with Standard & Poor's. The broker even had recent annual reports because NEMECO was headquartered in Bridgeport.

"A good buy," he advised me. "Selling well below

earnings. Excellent cash position. Well-managed outfit. The stock doesn't move very much because it is still closely held by employees and the Cranmer family. It is an old and very respected firm."

That was the understatement of the hour.

The New England Mill Equipment Company had been founded in 1877 by the three Cranmer brothers. Two of them had gone out to Montana during the gold strikes and managed to lose what they had of their inheritance. But they learned about mining. They came back to Bridgeport with the knowledge that the way to make money was to make equipment that the mining industry needed. They persuaded their older brother to come in with them and find some venture capital. That came from England. Since the turn of the century, the firm had shown continuous growth and careful diversification into solid, industrially oriented products. The company went public in 1937 when the Cranmers managed to buy out the descendants of the original English investors. Then they went over-the-counter to raise additional working capital. Now they were listed on the New York Stock Exchange.

NEMECO no longer made just mining equipment. It made mill equipment, but "mill" is a New England word for "factory." The corporate name had been changed to NEMECO in 1963 in keeping with the rising wave of corporate image modernization.

NEMECO had six divisions scattered all over the country making specialized heavy construction equipment, marine equipment for large ocean-going vessels such as oil tankers, airborne controls and electronics, steel mill equipment, and special ceramics.

The most recent P&L statement and balance sheet were shining textbook examples of a well-run "small company." Gross sales in the preceding year were a shade over $74 million, and it paid $3.75 a share.

The broker thought he might be able to pick me up a hundred shares at 27 if I would give him a couple of days.

It occurred to me that there were probably thousands of successful "little" companies like this all over America doing good business, meeting their payrolls, paying their bills, providing a return on investment for stockholders, making good jobs available to skilled people, and being very quiet and professional about it. Everyone has heard of the *Fortune*-500 companies, and the spotlight is always on the fast-rising high-technology firms. Very few people pay much attention to companies like NEMECO.

Since I didn't have any plans for the evening and did not want to venture out into the Bridgeport streets alone, I borrowed the annual reports from the broker, grabbed supper in the hotel, and retired to my room to digest the contents of the annual reports.

I read the three-year-old annual report announcing that Dr. Osbourne had joined the firm as Director of Research. The following year's report announced the formation of the Corporate Research Center Laboratories in Bridgeport. And that was all. Period. No talk about new products, new research, nor new development work in progress. There was no possible way to tell from the balance sheet how much money was going into the corporate research effort.

I gave up in disgust because there was no way that I was going to find the data I was looking for.

If General Dynamics or Rockwell International had wanted to hire a pilot-astronomer, it would have been understandable. Even in a small high-technology company, a pilot-astronomer could provide a capability to cope in advance with the problems of an astronaut using the firm's Mark Umpty-Ump fully automated gizmoscope.

But here was a firm without a single visible NASA or Department of Defense contract. Its only connection with aviation was in the manufacture of jet engine control components and special switches to "original equipment manufacturers"—known as "OEMs" in the trade.

I ran into an inconsistency. The NEMECO Airborne

Controls Division was located in Tempe, a suburb of Phoenix. Osbourne had been unwilling to foot the bill for travel expenses, but why hadn't he suggested that I go to Phoenix and hop aboard the next corporate airplane returning to Bridgeport? It didn't make sense.

I put the annual reports away because they weren't telling me anything. I switched on the TV. It wasn't until later while I was watching a TV spy drama that it suddenly hit me.

Suppose NEMECO Corporate Research was being used as a cover-up for some top-secret scientific development project for the government?

Why not? The government could never again use the Manhattan District—or "Manhattan Project," as it was incorrectly known—approach; it would leave far too many tell-tale signs in this day and age. Even at Lowell I would have caught some rumors about it.

Something like the legendary Lockheed "Skonk Works" wouldn't be useful either. It's now too obvious.

But *nobody* would ever think of looking at NE-MECO!

If so, *why me*? If an outfit wanted a pilot-astronomer, where would they start looking? Not on the roster of the USAF or the commercial airlines, but among the astronomers who couldn't care less about secrecy! And things could be more easily arranged. Said pilot-astronomer could suddenly lose his job because of a "tight budget." One of his colleagues handling government research contracts on the university level could be asked to put said pilot-astronomer in touch with the covert operation. And the pilot-astronomer could be quietly transferred without getting in touch with the nearby corporate division.

The only people who knew where I was were the Flagstaff postmaster and the Federal Aviation Administration which had routinely recorded my various cross-country flight plans and radio communications. In thirty days, the FAA would wipe its tapes and computer records to save money. In six months, the Flagstaff postmaster would no longer forward my mail.

Something *very* interesting was cooking quietly at NEMECO Corporate Research Center.

I *had* to find out what was going on!

Tomorrow I would . . .

Chapter Three

NEMECO's corporate offices were housed on the fourth floor of a clean, unobtrusive office building in downtown Bridgeport. The building itself was not one of those flashy new aluminum-and-glass boxes, but a solid and respectable brick edifice.

I almost missed the door to the lobby of NEMECO because of the small Gothic letters announcing, "New England Mill Equipment Company—NEMECO."

Inside, the receptionist took my name and told me Dr. Osbourne was expecting me. Unlike some corporate receptionists I've seen, she was neither seductive nor dazzling. She was just all there.

I was led down a corridor past several doors, some open to reveal their occupants were absent, others that were discreetly closed, and still others that showed very ordinary-looking men working quietly at their desks. It seemed much too quiet and sedate with far too few people to be the headquarters of a corporation grossing $75 million per year. There was no hustle, just efficiency.

The office into which I was led was no flashier than the rest of the place. No door had had a name on it, and this was no exception. A short, heavy-set man with intense eyes, bushy black moustache, and short-cropped hair got up from behind the desk and thrust out his hand. "Hi, I'm Bill Osbourne. Glad you're here, Mike! Sit down."

The receptionist left, closing the door behind her. Osbourne leaned back in his chair and looked me over with a smile on his face. It was a rather handsome face, and I could not picture this man as the research director of a corporation. He did not have the pontifical bearing of the usual academic scientist. Nor did he have the ordinary, noncommittal appearance of a corporate scientist.

There were the usual scientific union cards hung in plain black frames on the wall behind him—Ph.D. from NYU, Phi Beta Kappa, membership scrolls from several scientific societies, scattered photographs of people whom I did not recognize, and a small plastic model of the old Saturn V moon rocket bearing the small label, "The Hard Way."

There was a framed motto lettered in engineering LeRoy style:

TRIVIALITY No. 43:
If you try, you will know;
If you fail, you will learn.

I indicated this motto. "Why do you call it a triviality? It seems reasonably nontrivial to me. And what are the other forty-two?"

"A conversation piece," Osbourne replied with a smile. "Many offices and labs have profound mottoes such as this tacked up on their walls. Most of them are trivial."

"The labs or the mottoes?" I wanted to know.

Osbourne looked pensive. "I've never really thought about that. The lab gang comes up with a new one every so often. We keep a book full of them down at the lab. Sometimes, they are not trivial mottoes at all . . ."

"For example?"

"How about: 'One cannot possibly begin to learn that which he thinks he already knows.' "

"Come on, now! That's Epictetus!"

"I'm going to have to watch myself around you, Mike. You know too much."

"Is that a threat or a compliment?"

"Neither." Osborne turned to the credenza behind his desk and flipped a switch on a piece of complex-looking electronic equipment. It began to buzz. Lights flashed. Every so often, it would make a little hop.

"Looks impressive. What does it do?"

"Just looks impressive," Osburne explained and shut it off. "That makes it very functional because it does exactly what it was designed to do. The lab gang came up with it one day in a fit of creativity."

I was beginning to become a little bit suspicious. The meeting was swinging far wide of where I thought it would be heading. "This came from a bunch of *research scientists*?"

"Nope. We are a bunch of technical con men. Frustrated inventors. Radio hams. Hot rodders. Freaks who have grown up with technology and like the things that can be done with it. People who want the Universe to work for them. Hard to find them these days, I'm afraid, and they are real individualists. But we must tag ourselves with socially acceptable titles or people won't know what we do . . . which means they will think we are practicing black magic . . . which we are anyway."

I was having a great deal of difficulty in getting the measure of Dr. William D. Osbourne. I began to sense that the man was complex, that there was a great deal of iceberg about him because only a small percentage of him was showing, and that he was exceedingly adept at playing whatever game he and NEMECO were engaged in.

"Well, I guess us rugged individualists have got to stick together these days," I remarked.

"I like that."

I decided to get right to the point. "Although I enjoy this sort of bull session, Doctor, I've come a long distance. I'm interested that you may want to hire a pilot-astronomer. If so, I'm your man. What's up?"

"I told you: magic."

"What?"

"Really! Remember Arthur C. Clarke's observation than any sufficiently advanced technology may be indistinguishable from magic?"

"Okay, so what sort of magic are you currently engaged in?"

"Well, the Department of Black Magic hasn't made

much progress because of the shortage of hellebore root, but we seem to have made significant controversial breakthroughs that may shed some light on some important aspects of white magic." Osbourne said it in a serious tone, but there was a twinkle in his eye.

"Does the sorcerer's union know about this?" I asked.

"Speaking of that, what does your sorcerer's union card say?" he suddenly asked, getting right down to the basics as quickly as I had tried to do.

"Star gazer and airplane driver. Actually, my present task involves finding a job that exists for both titles simultaneously."

I had managed to draft a resume in my best hand lettering in the hotel room last night. I gave this to him without apologizing for not having it typed. He took it without a further word and began to read it. I tried not to fidget.

"Well!" he finally exclaimed. He put down the paper and leaned back in his chair again, gazing silently at the ceiling. Then he straightened up, looked at me, and said, "I didn't expect to find a man like you this quickly. I can't use both of your talents . . . yet. I may never be able to. I can't accurately forecast if or when the requirement will really jell . . ."

Well, Mike, I told myself, at least you had a nice airplane trip and a good bull session.

"But, since my crystal ball is very cloudy and I cannot therefore forecast very clearly," Osbourne went on, "I sometimes have to operate opportunistically . . . or with gut feel, if you will. I know it's not very scientific or rational, but it usually works." He leaned forward and put his hands on his desk in front of him. "Mike, you've got precisely the credentials I was looking for. But let me ask you something that you didn't tell me in your resume. Why did you quit crop dusting? It pays pretty good, doesn't it? Better than astronomy, at any rate?"

I told him why. There was this hot, steamy morning in Kansas. I was bombing along in a Pawnee loaded with herbicide about one foot above the alfalfa. Two kids squatting between the rows tossed rocks up as I went past. The prop parted company with the engine. I got the plane over the wires at the end of the field, managed to pancake it into the next field, popped my harness, and got out just before the wing tanks blew. We never caught the kids.

Then I asked him, "Why did you quit the Air Force? I thought they paid fighter jocks pretty good."

Without batting an eye, Osbourne said, "I was making a run on a target drone in an F-4 at Indian Springs when my own Sidewinder chased me right up my tail pipe."

"I didn't think that could happen."

"Anything can happen, especially when it's not supposed to. Sort of took the tiger out of me. So I went the science route. Air Force paid for the Ph.D. from NYU. I thought it would help me talk to the scientists working for the Air Force."

"Did it?"

"Nope! The scientists distrusted me because I was an Air Force officer, and the Air Force distrusted me because I was a scientist. Q.E.D.: I couldn't win and I couldn't even break even. So I quit the game while I could."

"How did you come to NEMECO?"

"Well, one gets to know a lot of people in the sort of overview position that I had in the Office of Basic Research. Hayward Newcomb, one of our top research managers at Wright-Pat, full colonel, USAF Academy, Ph.D. from MIT, he got the message about two years before I did. He knew the President of NEMECO and went to work for the outfit. When I got out, he brought me aboard to set up a corporate research operation, the first one that NEMECO has ever had."

"NEMECO seems to have been around for a long time. Why did it suddenly need a corporate research lab?" I was trying to get to the bottom of this because it was sounding more and more like a new Skonk Works.

"True, NEMECO has been around for a century more or less. And it wants to be around for another century. Did you ever have a look at who the *Fortune*-

500 companies were twenty years ago and compare them to the *Fortune*-500 list of today? How many companies held their position? And why? I'll tell you the answer to that one because it answers your question. Only those companies who have managed to move with high technology have managed to stay in there. Those who kept right on making the same old saleable product slowly but surely slipped right off the *Fortune*-500 list. It's my job to keep that from happening to NEMECO, even though we are far from *Fortune*-500 material."

"So why do you need a pilot-astronomer?" I tried to press the point home.

"I told you: I don't. But if I did, I'd hire you. Come to think of it, I might anyway."

"What are you going to need a pilot for? Don't you have a hangarful over at Sikorski Memorial?"

"I don't need a pilot. If I did, I would be the one because I, too, carry a commercial ticket, Mike." He looked at me for a moment. "I may be able to use the scientist part of your astronomer's education. You're smart, bright, unafraid, and yet you've got the discipline of both an academic degree and a commercial instrument ticket. You're also sassy and suspicious and curious. You'd have to be curious to come more than two thousand miles to find out what's going on here. You are the kind of person I need." He paused for a moment as though he felt he had perhaps said too much, but then he went on, "I want you to meet the lab crew, Mike. I might have to share you with Jake Stock for a while if the pilot situation gets tight. But, before talking turkey, I must find out if you will be able to get along with the crazy crew I've got. Let's go to the lab."

I was totally unprepared for the NEMECO Corporate Research Center Laboratories. I guess I have been spoiled by seeing too many beautiful research centers of giant corporations—acres of lovely landscaping with modernistic buildings scattered around in a campus atmosphere to provide research minds with the artificial, quiet, pastoral, academic atmosphere in which to do their thinking.

The research center was smack between two of the

biggest, dirtiest, raunchiest factories that I've ever seen. There wasn't a blade of grass or a tree to be seen anywhere, just red-brick factory buildings jammed tightly together in an apparent random array. Trucks, cars, and industrial vehicles clogged the narrow streets.

I almost said, "Thanks, it's been a great gag, but I'll be going now." But then I thought, what better place to hide a Skonk Works?

Osbourne slid his TR-7 sports car into an impossibly small parking slot in front of the building, jerked on the parking brake, and advised me, "Don't let it throw you."

"Well, it sort of blows the image," I admitted.

"It's supposed to. Can you guess why it's here?"

"Sure. You want to hide it."

"Nope."

"Positive?"

"Positive. Look down the street. There's a good junk yard and the best machine shop in town. The other way up the street you will find the best electronic supply shop around. Across the street is a lab supply house. When we need something, we can get it in a moment. And when you're being technically creative, you *can't* wait."

He had a point there. But I looked around and observed, "Seems like one hell of an environment in which to do research."

"On the contrary it is the very best possible environment for doing industrial research. 'I am surrounded by the roar of the world; thank God for the roar of the world.' The joint jumps, Mike. There is an aura of accomplishment, of doing things, of making the world go, and of making money . . . literally *making* the stuff of money. Mike, I can afford only an occasional romantic program because every dollar of my research budget comes out of company earnings and means a dollar that the stockholders will not get as part of a dividend. In the long run, I *must* produce new ideas and new things to keep the company in business as technology progresses. I'll let you in on a secret . . ."

Here it comes, I thought.

"We don't do scientific research. We do technological research of the Edisonian type whose true end product must make money for NEMECO. Our output must eventually pay back every dollar NEMECO invests in us. And it will."

"How long is the 'long run' for NEMECO?" I wanted to know. "When do they expect the first pay-off?"

"Hayward Newcomb told me ten years."

"Do you really think you have ten years?"

"How much do you know about NEMECO?" Osbourne wanted to know.

"Only as much as you were willing to admit in the last three annual reports, Doctor. I do not go into things blindly. Never fly without getting a weather briefing, right?"

"Right!" Osbourne grabbed the door handle and opened his side of the car. "Let's go in and take the tour."

"You'd let an outsider go through your labs? Suppose I twigged to the competition?"

"You won't. Do you really think that I'd let you see anything that the competition doesn't already know about?"

The inside of the building didn't match the outside at all. It was reasonably new and up-to-date once we got past the door. I have seen more than a few research labs in my time, but this one was just slightly different.

The difference started with the first person we met in the small entrance lobby. She was an elderly woman, snowy-haired, with rimless glasses. She was surrounded by a telephone, a couple of intercom boxes, a microphone, and assorted pieces of electronic equipment whose purpose was not immediately apparent. She also had a typewriter and looked up from working on it as she saw us enter.

"Good morning, Dr. Osbourne! You have several telephone calls. Mr. Halden called, and Professor Korsinski called from Hoboken." She handed him two pink telephone call slips.

"Thank you, Ruth. Meet Mike Call who flew all the

way from Arizona to see us. Mike, this is Ruth Morse who is officially the Chief Laboratory Administrative Director . . . but that's too long a title, so everybody just calls her the house mother . . ."

Ruth looked the part, she acted the part, and I later found out that she was indeed the house mother of NE-MECO Corporate Research Center Laboratories in more ways than one. "Shall I bring coffee into the conference room for the two of you? I hope you'll stay for lunch; I've brought chili today."

"Whether we stay for lunch or not, we'll sample it," Osbourne told her. "Never mind the coffee. I'm going to show Mike around."

We started down a hallway, and I could hear the argument all the way. I didn't catch all of it because I didn't know what it was all about, but it sounded something like this:

"Hell, Len, why can't you throw it together out of stuff Mac has on hand in the shop?"

"Damn it, Vic! I don't like those numbers! If it works—which I doubt—the whole building will go . . ."

"There's nothing wrong with my equations! All you gotta do is put it together!"

"It cannot be assembled the way you've sketched it on the back of that envelope! Why the hell didn't they teach you MIT idiots to dream up stuff that could be put together in the first place?"

Osbourne stepped into the office first. "Who's winning?" he wanted to know.

A thin, sallow man with jet black hair, a trim moustache that contrasted with Osbourne's bushy one, and attired in a natty business suit looked up, grabbed a handful of papers from the desk, thrust them in front of Osbourne, and jabbed them with a pencil. "You remember that tensor I derived from the Hamiltonian? Well, the radiation term *does* work out! But I can't get Len to build something that would test . . ." He suddenly became aware of me and stopped short. "Who's this?" he wanted to know, suspicion sticking out all over him.

"This is Mike Call," Osbourne introduced us. "Mike, this vitriolic refugee from the Mid-East oil patch is Victor Aboud, my Assistant Director for Contracts and Analysis and, by his own admission, our resident mathematical genius."

Aboud stuck out his hand. "Howdy, Mike Call. And who in the hell are you?"

"You'll have to excuse Vic," the other man spoke up. "He's been in America only about ten years, and he still thinks his cousins own everything here, too. One of these days, we'll get him housebroken . . ."

"Len, get the hell off my back!" Vic was quick and sharp, all right.

The other man turned with a grin and also thrust out his hand. "I'm Len Marshall, the Laboratory Director." Len Marshall was a stout, puckish man who still wore his hair in the close-cropped fashion of the 1950s. He was obviously a technologist because he was in uniform: dark slacks, red tie, and clean white shirt with double breast pockets filled with pens. Just another hardware man, I thought, but my first impression was quite incorrect.

"Bill, we'll discuss this problem with you later," Vic snapped, picking up the papers and heading for the door. Obviously, he wasn't too happy about my presence. "I've got some data to massage. Len, I'll prove to you that I'm right! Good to meet you, Mr. Call." And he was gone.

Osbourne glanced at me, expecting some reaction, so I gave it to him. "He acts just like most of the math geniuses I've ever known . . . except for the introverted ones who are impossible to work with."

"Can you work with guys like Vic?" Osbourne wanted to know.

"Yes. It's difficult, but barely possible."

Osbourne laughed. "Mike, you'll do all right here!"

"Mike's joining us?" Len asked, plumping back into the chair behind the desk.

"Maybe," Osbourne replied, taking one of the side chairs and motioning me to another one. "Mike's an astronomer, so maybe he knows enough math to stay even with Vic. And he's a pilot and A&P mechanic, which means he's not afraid to get his hands dirty."

"Sounds like a combination I could use right now," Len said, tapping his pencil on the desk top.

"We may have to share him with Jake Stock."

"I don't see why," Len said. "I haven't had a chance to tell you, but Ron walked out yesterday afternoon."

"I was afraid of that, but I'm not sorry to lose him," Osbourne said, shaking his head sadly.

"This gives me two open technician slots, and I could fill both of them with one professional like Mike here on the Dynamics project . . . which I definitely need. Those calculations are a grind, and Tammy's getting behind. Think we could afford some more computer time?"

"Is it getting to be more than our microcomputer can handle?"

"Yes. But we can get a modem for a couple hundred and then tie in with Korsinski's big general-purpose machine in Hoboken."

"How much time might you need?"

"I'll find out." Len punched an intercom button and said into the device, "Tammy, this is Len. Can you drop in for a moment?"

In less than thirty seconds, the room seemed to light up. I turned to behold a real rarity: a beautiful woman who is shorter than I am. She couldn't have topped five feet. A lot of small women tend to be on the dumpy side—short on height, but not short on other dimensions. She was proportioned according to her petite height.

Len performed the usual introductions, and Tammy Dudley destroyed forever my mental image, gained from years of experience in grad school and at Lowell, that most women scientists and mathematicians got into the game because of what they lacked in appearance.

"Tammy, can you use some help?" Len asked.

"Oh, can I!" she replied in a sort of whispery voice that almost caused me to melt into the floor. "Len, I've got some of Vic's data reduction to do, and I've gotten behind on the Dynamics project . . ."

The lights went dim. The building shook slightly, rattling the old windows in their double-hung frames. I heard the cough of a fire extinguisher.

Len Marshall almost trampled over me, and he collided with Bill Osbourne as both tried to get out of the office door at the same time. Tammy Dudley managed to get out of the way of the onrush. "Come on!" Len shouted. "It sounded like it came from the dynamics lab!"

I followed them out the door and pounded down a corridor behind them. I guess Tammy was right behind me. I didn't know where I was going. I just followed Osbourne.

. Len stopped before a closed door. Wisps of smoke were curling from under it. He simply kicked the door open, and all of us burst in.

The room was jammed with equipment, and it was a mess. It was full of smoke and stank of burned electrical insulation. There was a large hole in the wall leading to the outside. Something had hit that double-bonded brick wall hard.

"Carl! Are you all right?" Len asked the blond-haired lab technician in the dirty white smock who was standing over some of the wreckage, an exhausted fire extinguisher in his hands.

"Huh? Oh, yeah! Yeah! I'm okay! I'm okay!" The man nodded, speaking in a high-pitched voice of shock. Then he snapped out of it and turned to Len. "It worked! *It worked!* Len, you were right! I adjusted the phasing and tapered the field strength the way we talked about . . . and it swung right out and went clean through the wall. It woulda kept going except the wires tore loose!" He was jubilant now.

"But are you all right?" Osbourne repeated Len's question. It is often surprising how people react in an emergency. They forget. They repeat. Somehow, the cerebrum becomes disconnected and all functions are programmed through the cerebellum.

"Sure! Had a little electrical fire, but I got that out." Carl was breathing heavily now as the room cleared itself of smoke through the gaping hole. "But the unit smashed on the ground outside."

Osbourne's face was radiant. His eyes sparkled. "Did you get the data?"

"You betcha! My lab notes are right on the bench over there. Fire didn't get to them."

"Hot damn!" Osbourne whirled to face me. "Mike, you're hired! As a pilot-astronomer! We're going to go a long way!"

"Where?" I wanted to know.

"To Mars! We've got a space drive!"

Chapter Four

"You've gotta be kidding!" was the most brilliant remark I could muster.

"On the contrary!" Osbourne shot back. He walked over to the gaping hole in the wall. "This is an open door to the Solar System." He looked down at the ground. "Carl, get out there and pick up the pieces right away! And make sure you get *all* the pieces."

The lab tech crawled through the hole. From outside, Carl's voice came back, "Doctor, it doesn't look like it was dinged up too badly. Hey, Mac, come out here and give me a hand!"

I hadn't noticed the tall, gangling technician who had come into the dynamics lab behind us. He too crawled out the hole, grumbling as he did so, "Damn it, Carl, I'll bet you bent those coils . . . and they're a bitch to make!"

"Hell, Mac, if you have to fix them, it will just keep you out of trouble!"

The two technicians lifted something long and slender and began working it back through the hole into the lab. It was a totally nondescript collection of parts with broken wires leading out of it at various points. There was some broken glass in the unit, but neither end seemed to be damaged. Carl remarked about this, "Doctor, I don't know how it happened, but it isn't badly damaged."

Bill Osbourne squatted down to inspect the unit closely as Mac and Carl set it on the floor of the lab. "How long to fix it up, Carl?"

Carl was poking at it. "Oh . . . maybe two days with Mac's thumb-fingered help."

"Speak for yourself, electron-pusher," Mac growled. "Three days at the very most. The coils aren't bent. They're the parts I was worried about."

Tammy was also inspecting the unit. "Carl, what did you do here in the middle with the phasing coil?"

"Made it like the drawing, Tam."

"But you didn't!" She stretched her hand alongside the unit, roughly measuring the parts with the span of her hand. "You made the coil about nineteen inches long. Vic's sketch said fourteen inches."

Carl stood up and took a sheet of paper from a nearby lab bench. "Here it is. It says nineteen point six seven five inches."

Tammy looked at it. "That dimension's *fourteen* point six seven five inches, Carl."

Carl squinted at it. "Vic's fours look like nines. I made it nineteen inches. I figured if it's too long, it's easier to cut it off to fourteen inches than to try to stretch it from fourteen to nineteen."

"Hold everything!" Osbourne interrupted them. "That may be why we haven't been able to get any action out of this thing!"

"Serendipitous lab accident," Len Marshall added. "Exactly!"

The discussion was interrupted by the arrival of a Bridgeport Police cruiser, siren blaring and red lights flashing as it pulled into the parking lot behind the lab and became visible through the hole in the wall.

"Great!" Osbourne sighed. "Somebody reported this as an industrial accident!"

Len peered through the hole in the wall. "That's Roger Catlin and Tom Baker. I'll go have a talk with them." The lab director ducked out through the hole and went over to the patrol car.

"I'm sort of curious, Doctor," I put in. "Little lab accident. Hole in the wall. You tell me it's a space drive and I'm going to fly it to Mars. What the hell is this pile of junk? It doesn't look like any rocket motor to me!"

"It isn't. It's a sky hook," the research director said. "What Carl did here today was to produce motion through space without the ejection of mass."

"A massless rocket? Come on now!"

The two technicians were looking at me, aware of my presence at last, and there was suspicion sticking out all over them.

Osbourne noticed it. "Sorry, gang. Meet Mike Call, star gazer and airplane driver. Mike, this tall drink of water is Mac Roston, our chief mechanical tech. Carl Curley here is our dynamics lab tech, an electron-pusher by trade because there are so many electronic gadgets connected with the sky hook." I shook hands with both of them as Osbourne went on, "Mike is practically aboard, and I see no reason to withhold information about this from him. After all, he's seen it, and he'll be working with it . . ."

"You mean, you're not afraid I'll run out of here and sell it to the Russians?" I quipped, still reaching for the reaction that would confirm for me that this was a government Skonk Works operation.

"No, I am more worried that you might take it over to Caterpillar or International Harvester," Osbourne told me levelly. He indicated the broken unit with a sweep of his hand. "And just because you've seen it doesn't mean that you know how it works."

"Uh, well, you're sort of right about that," I admitted. "But look, I'm a hardware type, and I can usually duplicate something after I've seen it, providing I have a basic understanding of how it works . . ."

"But you can't duplicate a fluorescent light tube after seeing one if you don't understand phosphors, plasmas, ballasts, and so forth," Len Marshall told me. He was right.

"Well, it's really pretty simple," Osbourne tried to explain. He pointed to the shattered remains of a glass tube. "This is—or was—a simple glass tube filled with neon at a fraction of a torr. There are other gases that might have worked better and given us a more efficient plasma, but neon is cheap and readily available. We established a plasma in the tube. Then we accelerated the charged plasma particles with a very high frequency saw-tooth wave shape. The sharp-rising leading edge of the sawtooth wave smacks the plasma hard, and it reacts by moving and accelerating. Before the system has time to react as a whole, the plasma is then socked with the trailing edge of the sawtooth wave at a much lower rate-of-change of acceleration. Now, if we hang the unit ballistically with the thrust axis horizontal, any thrust that shows up will displace the pendulum . . ."

"But if it does anything, it should just oscillate back and forth around its rest point," I argued.

"If we'd driven it with a sine wave, it would. But we're using an asymmetrical sawtooth wave to drive it. Different rates-of-change of acceleration in different directions. All the early experiments with this sort of system were made with mechanical devices working at a hundred Hertz or less, and they all tended to come apart once the reaction force was properly phased with the action force. So we went to electromagnetic, driving at several megaHertz . . ."

"You're getting 'way beyond me here," I objected, "and what you're saying doesn't make any sense from the standpoint of physics. Action and reaction are equal and opposite . . . and that's the way it's been since long before Sir Isaac Newton wrote the equation for the Third Law of Motion. This whole thing—if it does work the way you are trying to explain it to me—would violate most of the energy conservation laws, the principles of thermodynamics, and most of Newtonian physics that has been thoroughly checked out in practice for more than four hundred years!"

"And Newton worked fine until Faraday, Maxwell, Einstein, and Planck came along, Mike," Osbourne pointed out. "Give me thirty minutes at a chalkboard, and I'll explain it in mathematical terms that you'll understand perfectly . . ."

"Mathematics will only give you the logical consequences of your initial assumptions," I told him.

"But when you use the math to design working devices, wouldn't you say that the math bears a one-to-one relationship to the real Universe?"

"Well, yes, but . . ."

Osbourne stood up. "Carl, Mac, let's get this thing

swinging again. Rebuild it. Carl, let Len and me know when you get ready to turn it on the next time."

"Sorry, Doctor, I didn't mean to run an experiment without letting you know. I was just trying to adjust the phasing," Carl attempted to apologize.

Osbourne waved his hand. "Never mind! The fact that you misread Vic's rough sketch plus the fact that you were diddling around to get it to work gave us the keys to success. Congratulations on making it work!"

That accolade from Osbourne seemed to make the lab tech very proud indeed. He grinned from ear to ear as though it were the highest honor that anyone could pay him.

Len Marshall ducked back through the hole in the wall. "No trouble," he reported. "Roger and Tom were just responding to a call from United Telecom next door. Thought we might need some help."

"Good enough. Mike, let's go up front and get you signed up on the payroll right away."

"Uh, Doctor, could I talk with you privately first?"

Obviously, Osbourne thought that I wanted to discuss salary. "Mike, I don't haggle. But if you want to discuss it in private, okay by me." He turned to his lab director. "Len, let me borrow your office for a few minutes. Tell Ruth to bring in all the necessary employment forms."

Once settled in Len Marshall's office with the door closed, Osbourne said, "Okay, Mike, shoot!"

"I want to know exactly what's going on here."

"Fair enough. What's bothering you?"

"You've got a cleverly hidden covert research operation going on here, another Manhattan District or a new type of Skonk Works," I told him directly. "I must compliment you. It's very, very well done. But, if I'm going to work for NEMECO, I want to know who's *really* paying my salary. Is it the Department of Defense? The CIA?"

Bill Osbourne started to laugh. He laughed for almost a full minute.

"What's so funny?" I wanted to know.

"Mike, you're overly suspicious because of some incident in your background that you haven't revealed to me."

"Hardly. Look, everything just happens to fall neatly into place. Here's a well-run little industrial company with an impeccable record and a far-out research lab working on a gadget that hasn't a damned thing to do with the company's historic product line . . ."

"And that's where you're dead wrong," Osbourne cut in. He lit up another of his dark cigarettes in its long filter holder. "We have some far-out stuff going on here. You haven't seen any of it except for the sky hook. But every damned bit of it is related to the company's future product lines twenty years from now . . . I hope."

"Okay, then tell me what a basic industrial firm like NEMECO is going to do with a space drive? Are you going into competition with Rockwell or Thiokol in the space business?"

"Maybe we'll license that use. It could well be that NEMECO doesn't have the capital or the marketing know-how to properly exploit the space side of the sky hook," Osbourne admitted. "That remains to be seen. But it's really a sky hook, and our Heavy Industrial Equipment Division out in Roseville, Michigan, will probably end up making the units for industrial use."

"I don't follow you."

"You've just come from the milieu where all high-technology is government stuff. No wonder you have a tendency to think that we're a Skonk Works operation. Boy, I could sure use some of that kind of money if it weren't for the strings attached to it. Anyway, there are lots of applications in industrial and extractive operations where you have to lift something. So you get a crane, or a chain hoist, or a gantry, or a jack. But suppose none of those will do the job? Suppose you can't get a heavy crane into the site? Suppose the item to be lifted is in a mine tunnel with a seven-foot overhead clearance? Suppose you've got to cantilever the rollers on a rolling mill without taking the whole damned machine apart to do it? So you get a NEMECO sky hook, which will be the registered trade name of the unit. That is why Grant Halden and Hay Newcomb are backing the research on our dynamic systems project, the sky hook. I could *never* sell them on backing research on a space drive, as you know very well, having studied the annual reports of this company . . ."

"Then why do you want to hire a pilot-astronomer?"

"Because I am going to build a space vehicle for peanuts powered by the sky hook that will go to Mars and back with a pilot-astronomer on board. It will give us publicity that will let us license the sky hook for whatever the traffic will bear. It will also boost the price of NEMECO stock right through the ceiling . . ."

"And you've got stock options."

"You're damned right I do! And so will you, along with everybody else who works in this lab. 'Do not bind the mouths of the kine who tread the grain.' "

"The mouths of the what?"

"The modern word is 'swine.' And that's the way it's got to be done because the objective is to make money . . ."

"And to vindicate your career."

"Yes, that too. The reason I'm going to send a space drive vehicle to Mars on a shoestring is because I've fought tooth and nail against our overpriced, overengineered, overtested, and overrated space program for years. It's run by a bunch of Brahmin high priests who've set it aside as their own private preserve. Every low-cost, privately financed project that's come down the pike—things like OTRAG—have been killed by them. I'm going to beat them." Osbourne stopped for a moment, then snuffed out his cigarette and blew residual smoke out of his cigarette holder. "Yes, I'm thinking about my career too, because the sky hook is going to make it for me. As a matter of fact, anybody who's associated with our work here is going to have his career made. Now, knowing all this, do you understand why your suggestion that this is a covert government project was so hilarious? How would a government organization handle this, even if it were a covert operation?"

"It would be classified so high that nobody could exploit it," I guessed.

"Or it would be parceled out to a favorite aerospace company with a wad of million-dollar bills for additional development work to tide them over the transition from rocket propulsion to space drive propulsion, which might take as long as twenty years, or at least long enough to enable the lead managers and engineers to retire with successful careers in rocketry behind them and without having to learn new things. And long enough to legally write off all the tooling and other capital equipment associated with rocket propulsion work." Osbourne stuffed his cigarette holder in his shirt pocket. "No, Mike, there isn't one penny of government money involved in this work . . . and we could've had all the government money we wanted."

"Yeah, I guess that you and Hay Newcomb probably have some good contacts with the Air Force . . ." I observed.

"You bet we do, and we also know how they think and how they work . . . and we don't want a bit of it. We have even better contacts through the NEMECO Board of Directors to any government agency you want to name, but we don't want to suggest such a course of action to the Board . . ."

"Why not?"

"They might prefer to use somebody else's money to finance the R&D, even knowing that NEMECO might wind up holding the short and dirty end of the stick, but with enough of the action to make a few bucks anyway."

"Won't you eventually have to face that possibility?"

"Not if we do it right after you have flown to Mars and back . . . and then it's too late because the existence of the sky hook is public knowledge around the world."

I decided that Osbourne and NEMECO were for real . . . and I also decided that I wanted to be a part of it in the very worst way. "Doctor, I'll fly your gadget to Mars and back if there's a reasonable probability that I can make it in one piece. But I have to have a say in how the vehicle is designed and built. After all, I'll be the guy who's going to strap his pink bod into it . . ."

"Welcome aboard!"

Ruth Morse showed up with a whole pile of forms that I had to fill out. Len gave me a little office about six by eight feet, just enough room for a desk, a file cabinet, and two chairs. Fortunately, it had a window because I don't like being bottled up in the usual engineering cubicle found in aerospace plants.

It was right next to Tammy's office, but I didn't get the chance to talk to Tammy at all. I spent the rest of the day filling out forms.

It gets worse and worse to go to work for somebody. Not only is there the usual company employment form that lays one's personal life bare before some unknown (and probably uncaring) company personnel officer, but there are uncountable government forms as well—FICA, withholding tax, workmen's compensation, ad nauseam. Then there were additional lengthy company forms for hospitalization insurance, medical insurance, executive life insurance, retirement plan, stock option and stock purchase plans, and a "corporate information disclosure" form. I read this last one over and then went to see Len Marshall about it.

"Bill told me that you were to be brought aboard on the professional level, so that gives you some neat perks such as the stock option plan . . ."

"Yeah, that doesn't bother me, but it's this other one, the 'corporate information disclosure' form. It sounds very nasty," I said, looking it over. "It locks up everything that I do—all scientific and technical work, all patents and patent rights, all copyrightable material, everything. It says that I can't talk to anybody or write anything about what I do for NEMECO under any circumstances without prior written approval from the chief executive officer of the company. That's pretty broad and pretty restrictive, Len. And there's no time limit on it."

"Look, Mike," Len said quietly, "all of us signed that. It's a small thing to give up in order to do this kind of work for this kind of a company. NEMECO has to protect itself against body-snatchers who raid brain-power for the competition. We're in a competitive marketplace. I don't know of any instance in the history of the company—and NEMECO's been around for many years—that the company's gotten nasty about things like that."

"Yeah, but there's always a first time," I pointed out.

"True, but what sort of image would that give this company? This is no shlock outfit, Mike. Ask anybody here. They'll all confirm the fact that NEMECO treats its people right. This is a very paternal company. It didn't get to where it is by screwing its employees."

"I don't like it. Suppose I don't sign it?"

Len sighed deeply. "Then I'd have to show you to the front door, Mike. This is policy, and I've got to carry it out. It's part of my job. Just sign it. If any problem does come up, you can always discuss it with the legal department or, in the extreme, take NEMECO to court about it. Everybody's always got that right."

So I signed it. Len witnessed my signature. Ruth Morse put her notary seal on it.

Ruth gave me a time card. "I'll come by every Friday afternoon and pick it up so that the Payroll department up at headquarters gets it that evening. Then you'll get your check the following Wednesday."

"But this is a time-clock card!" I objected. "I don't punch a time clock. I never have, and I never will."

"Nobody at the lab does, so don't fret. We use it because it's a corporate form, and it makes it easier for Payroll. Fill it out anytime. Here's a list of charge numbers."

"Well, I guess I am assigned to Dynamic Systems," I remarked.

"You should put down G&A for today," Ruth suggested. "Actually, nobody really cares what you charge your time to, except don't lay too much on G&A or Administrative. The Front Office gets upset and questions it."

"So I should use G&A when I go apartment hunting?"

"If you want to save some time, why don't you have a look at the room at my place? Ron Miller just vacated it."

It turned out that Ruth had been left a large home by her late husband. Her own children were off on their own. So she rented rooms to "NEMECO people and other nice technical types." She also had a breakfast and dinner boarding deal available to "hold down the awful cost of food these days; I can buy things in large quantities down at the wholesale market, and all of us make our paychecks go farther."

When the lab doors closed at five o'clock, I found myself riding home with Ruth Morse in her old Plymouth to have a look at the room and to decide whether or not I wanted to take it. She car-pooled with Tammy Dudley and Carl Curley, both of whom also boarded with her.

Ruth chattered on in an almost absent fashion as we cleared the industrial and downtown area and drove out Park Avenue to the older, residential part of town.

Except for the modern automobiles on the streets, it was like returning to the early twentieth century. The homes were huge by modern standards, mostly big, wood-framed structures with porches and at least three stories, one of which was a windowed attic with dormers. These homes must have been built in the early 1900s, and they were in beautiful condition. It was comfortable, almost traditional American living of the sort one remembers with warm fondness from one's own youth.

Morse Manor, as Carl called it, was a big old brute of a place with white shingled siding, a bay window, a window-enclosed porch, and a genuine porte cochere. Green canvas awnings shaded the windows. A white picket fence surrounded the grassy front yard with its huge oak trees that shaded the house. Morse Manor had personality, and so did each room.

Mine was a corner bedroom with two windows, one of which faced the street with a small air conditioner in it. Its walls were covered with print wallpaper and there were honest pictures in frames on the walls—not some hack artist's impressionistic paint-two-per-day for the motel market. The bathroom was between my room—it was *my* room the moment I saw it—and Carl Curley's, and it was tiled with real ceramic and dominated by a huge enameled bathtub perched off the floor on cast-iron clawed feet.

I paid a month in advance, kicked in for a week's groceries, found out which bank I should open an account at, got checked out on all the light switches, was given a key to the back door, and learned how to hit the window whose sash weight would occasionally stick.

The rest of Morse Manor was just as comfortable because we were treated by Ruth as "her family."

I met Peter Wilding as Tammy, Carl, and I were sitting in the living room watching the six o'clock news on TV. He was an older man, bustling and stocky, with horn-rimmed glasses. A devout and confirmed bachelor, he worked for United Telecommunications Laboratories in Trumbull and told me that he was a specialist in vacuum tubes.

This sort of set me back. "Vacuum tubes? I didn't think there were any of those left around any more."

"That's why vacuum tube engineers are in such high demand," Peter Wilding explained, settling himself into a chair with a thump. "There are a lot of applications in electronics where the good old thermionic vacuum tube does the job better, cheaper, and more efficiently. After all, we're sitting here watching TV on a big vacuum tube!"

Dinner was family style. It had been a long time since I had had a genuine family meal. It was pleasant, like coming home.

Wilding volunteered to take me down to the New Barnum to pick up my things from the company room after supper. Carl said he wanted to go along for the ride. Wilding chattered and talked all the way. He wanted to know what I did and where I'd come from and what schools and universities I'd attended. I told him.

After we got back, I unpacked my things and began to hang them up. There was a discreet knock at the bathroom door, and I opened it to see Carl Curley standing there.

"Hi! Come in!"

"Not for long. Gotta get to bed," Carl said quietly. "I just wanted to tell you to be careful."

"Why?"

"Peter Wilding is one of the best industrial spies we've ever run up against."

Chapter Five

I bounded into the lab the next morning with Ruth, Carl, and Tammy, all eager to go to Mars.

Osbourne wasn't there. It was Friday, and Len told me that the research director usually spent the day writing up weekly reports and briefing the NEMECO executives.

I wanted to find out more about the sky hook. So I asked Len.

"According to Bill's instructions, you are assigned to the dynamic systems project," Len told me. "I've been handling the experimental aspect of it. Vic is the theoretical man and the math shark."

"Let me get something straight," I said. "Who's running the show? If Vic comes in and tells me to do something, do I tell him to shove it?"

"No, at least not that way. Do it gently and diplomatically. Vic has a short fuse. So use t-a-c-t tact. Remember, he comes from a different culture where he was part of the elite who could order everyone else around. Basically, he's a nice guy and wants to get along."

"I've worked with other mathematicians. I'll cope. But you're the boss, and that's what I wanted to find out." I had been working in the strict pecking order of scientific academia where the important thing is to find out who's boss and, equally important, who has the ear of the Top Man.

Len went on, "We'll more or less work together for a while as you become familiar with the theory and the hardware. You know of Bill's long-range plan for the sky hook . . ."

"We discussed it . . ."

"Good. Don't talk about it." Len paused for a moment, then added, "And be careful of Peter Wilding."

"Carl warned me about him."

"We are pretty sure he was planted at Morse Manor, although he's been a for-real vacuum tube engineer at United Telecom Labs for years." Len paused and looked thoughtful for a moment. "Ever been associated with any classified government programs?"

"No. Astronomy was an open field."

"Then you won't have to unlearn things. Around here, we don't talk to anybody except the lab gang concerning anything that we do here. I'll give you some cover-up false data that is intended to lead industrial spies down the garden path in the opposite direction."

"That's fine, except I don't even know where we're going, and I work here now," I told him. "I'd like to find out about the sky hook."

Len got up from his desk and went over to a file cabinet. "That's the next order of business," he said as he opened the second drawer. He pulled out several large documents bound with orange plastic spines; the covers were an innocuous blue. "If you ever see a report like this with an orange binding and a blue cover lying unattended on a desk or lab bench, pick it up and bring it to me immediately. We don't put big SECRET stamps all over our sensitive stuff. That'd tell people what's the most important stuff to steal. You'll see a lot of cover-and-binding color combinations here in the lab, but this combination of orange binding and blue cover means that the information's hot-hot-hot. It's never left unattended except in a locked file cabinet or in the locked lower left hand drawer of your desk. What I'm telling you isn't written down anywhere. It's passed to each employee by word of mouth only. Just remember it."

"Gotcha!"

"Although Carl could probably use some help back in the dynamics lab cleaning up and rebuilding the unit, you can more profitably spend your time coming up to the same level of ignorance and confusion that the rest of us enjoy." I was beginning to get a feeling for this stocky laboratory director who spoke so seriously and yet interlarded his talk with unexpected bits of humor delivered with a straight face. He was obviously dedicated. He was not a leader, but a very good Number Two Man—an executive officer, so to speak. I guessed that he used his humor to maintain his sense of perspective. Some people might consider Len to be flippant, but I understood that he was using humor as a tool for handling people. He went on, "I'm not enough of a mathematician or theorist to give you the full dog-and-pony show that Osbourne and Vic can put on. With your background, you'd be asking me embarrassing questions that I couldn't answer, so I don't care to be put on the spot, thank you. It's quite likely that Bill will have Grant Halden and Hay Newcomb down here for a full briefing within the next few days, and you'll get the full treatment. But you won't be able to keep up with the show unless you've got the basic background."

"As I told you, it seems to me that you're violating a lot of basic conservation laws."

"That's the first reaction most physicists have," Len said with a smile. "You should've heard Serge Korsinski and Ted Mayan try to tear Bill apart that first time!"

"Pardon me, but who are they?"

"Professor Serge Korsinski is from the Engineering Physics Department of Stevens Institute of Technology in Hoboken, and Dr. Theodore Mayan is with the Physics Department of the State University of New York. Korsinski is one of the world's top authorities on the photon and attacked Bill pretty strongly when Bill gave the first paper on this at a New York Academy of Sciences meeting about a year ago."

"I didn't think you were talking about this work."

"Back then, we were. Bill was using the NYAS paper to convince the academic types that NEMECO had a legitimate corporate research effort going here. Unless you've got the recognition of academia, you aren't going to get papers published and you can't attract good research people as the effort expands."

"Tell me all about it!" I muttered.

"Huh?"

"Never mind. I've been down that road."

"Oh. On the other hand, Ted Mayan was Bill's thesis advisor once . . . Top-notch man, probably the world's greatest authority on hyperstrength gravitational fields. Both men are on our consulting staff. Bill brings them up here about once a month to look things over, to ask embarrassing questions, and to keep us honest." He pushed a pile of reports across the desk at me. "Here's something you can start on, a collection of papers on the theoretical background beginning with copies from Bill's research notebook and including the landmark NYAS paper—which has been forgotten, by the way. There are also a bunch of internal reports and unpublished papers. They should give you the theoretical background."

He then pushed another stack of documents across the desk to me. "And here are the regular monthly progress reports. They'll tell you all about the blind alleys we went down. Should keep you from inventing the square wheel." He then pushed a third volume toward me. "And this is the far-out stuff, the implications of the work assuming that certain portions of the hypothesis are correct. You should take this last report with a very large dose of salt. It's pretty far out, maybe something our grandchildren will be working on."

I groaned under the load that I carried back to my office, got myself a cup of coffee, sat down, looked out the window at the gray New England sky, and started to read.

I was looking forward to a boring day or two reading dry, dull, uninspiring scientific documents filled with page after page of partial differential equations and tensor calculus—"banjo music," *Physical Review* stuff.

I was dead wrong.

The first volume I opened began with a photocopy of Osbourne's research notebook written very carefully in a round, legible script as though he were thinking at the time that perhaps a lot of people might be reading it someday. He started off:

"It has occurred to me, based upon my own observations of the behavior of real systems and upon a great deal of information of both classified and open nature which I have had occasion to obtain during the past twenty-seven years, that the basic principles of both classical (Newtonian) and modern (relativistic) physics have never been compared with many of the empirical findings and know-how of the engineering arts. This is not to say that either the physicists or the engineers are wrong, but only that their views of the Universe are different. Physicists use the ubiquitous 'Constant K' while engineers use various 'finagle factors' in order to make their math match the reality of the Universe. Of great interest to me in this regard is the behavior of real systems when subjected to sudden change.

"The very nature of the relativistic space-time concept, the quantum nature of matter and energy, and the reaction of real systems leads me to a postulate that both physicists and engineers will generally agree to without argument:

"The characteristics of any given system cannot be changed in zero time, and a definite period of time must elapse between the instant of onset of a change and the moment at which the entire system responds to the change as a total system. In a period of time less than this, the system does not and cannot behave as it does with constant inputs.

"If one accepts the hypothesis that one cannot change a given system in zero time, a number of fascinating consequences follow.

"Let us go back to the classical Newtonian equation of motion . . ."

It *was* fascinating! At that point, Osbourne began to investigate the logical consequences of his initial assumption. I had observed and used some of them for years. His mathematical analysis and development were quite straightforward. In several places, I could see where his logic started to lead him down a blind alley. But the notebook pages showed that he brought himself up short with his own realization that he was on the wrong path. He backtracked, picked up the train of logic again, and followed it down another path.

The reprint of the NYAS paper was an innocuous little monograph presented at one of the NYAS mechanical engineering symposia. It was entitled, "Some Characteristics of Transient Phenomena in Real Systems." Obviously, it had been intended as a landmark to indicate to those who might follow, "I was here first!" The paper was a more concise and technical treatment of the speculative and experimental rationales of Osbourne's notebook.

I borrowed a pad of ruled paper from Tammy and began to make notes. On several occasions, I had to work through the derivations of the equations just to satisfy myself that Osbourne was following the proper rules of mathematics.

It was obvious as the writing proceeded that Osbourne realized he was getting beyond his depth in mathematics. I could begin to see the abilities of Victor Aboud enter the picture.

I forgot lunch until Tammy stuck her pretty face in the door and asked, "Do you want a sandwich? Mac is going down to the corner deli."

"Huh? Well, I guess so. What kinds of sandwiches are available?"

"It's Friday, so the Special is hot pastrami on a hard roll with cole slaw on the side."

"Sounds good. I'll take it."

I put the reports away in the lower left hand drawer of my desk as instructed, turned upside-down the paper with my math, and wandered out into the lab.

Government regulations require that an employer provide a separate eating room with tables and chairs for all employees, and there was indeed one such room in the lab. It even had a sign on the door that said, "Employee Lunch Room." But nobody was in there. The tables were stacked high with piles of trade journals, technical magazines, and newspapers.

Where was the lab gang if they weren't in the special room that had been set aside for them? I found them in

Mac's machine shop next to the coffee maker. Carl had spread a drop cloth over the horizontal bed of the milling machine. Others were gathered around the big granite leveling block.

Mac showed up with a paper sack full of big sandwiches wrapped in waxed paper and paper cartons of cole slaw. Ruth Morse dug out a supply of washed plastic forks and spoons, plus a roll of paper towels for napkins. And I got initiated to the NEMECO lab-gang lunch hour.

Today, the subject was me. They wanted to know where I had come from, what I had done, and why I was here. I tried to tell them as best I could. In the process, I met Wendell Stone, a gaunt and acerbic engineer from the "Northeast Kingdom of Vermont" who spoke in the clipped, concise accents of the region and possessed an astringent sense of humor.

"Pray tell," I asked Stone, "what is a lowly mechanical engineer such as yourself doing in the midst of this gang of wild researchers?"

"Done a bit of research myself in my time," Stone replied casually. "But I'm a development engineer. In the old days back on Stone Hill in Vermont, they would have called me the local fix-it man. I'm on loan from the Mill Equipment Division in Trumbull and working out the final bugs of the shot-alloying process so we can eventually get the pilot plant set up . . ."

"Providing we can get all the bugs out," Len Marshall added.

"There are always bugs in anything," Stone pointed out. "The closer one comes to full production, the fewer bugs there are, but they are bigger and nastier and more expensive. And even when in production there are bugs . . . and it bothers me more than a little bit when the newspapers make a big thing about automobile recalls, airplane crashes, minor nuclear plant accidents, and all the rest. There comes a point in development where the engineers with calculators must turn a gadget over to a person like myself who can diddle with it, tune it, and make it run in spite of everything. Real engineering has always been an art. It disturbs me when universities give engineering degrees that are really scientific union cards. At the same time, they down-grade honest engineers to a level they call 'engineering technologists,' who are in reality the hands-on engineers."

"I thought you called yourself an inventor," Mac Roston interjected as he poured himself another cup of coffee from the big urn.

"That was last week," Stone replied.

"What's the difference?" I wanted to know. I was beginning to like this Vermont engineer who appeared to have his feet solidly on the ground with a pragmatic approach to the application of technical know-how.

"Between what?"

"Between an engineer and an inventor?"

"Inventors lead technology. They figure out something that works and leave it to the scientists to explain why and the engineers to make it bigger, better, faster, and cheaper. Invention is the bridge between research and engineering. Except it sometimes doesn't work out as neatly as I've indicated . . ."

"Wouldn't the sky hook blow a huge hole in your hypothesis?" Len Marshall asked.

"Not at all. Bill and Vic think that Carl made it work because of the equations and calculations. Carl and I know better," Stone said quietly.

"So you've had your heavy hand in that project, too?" Len said.

Wendell Stone looked back at him. "Len, stop thinking that it's possible to partition off the projects in this lab by Sheetrock walls or special rules. That's a fiction for the Front Office."

"I know that!"

"Which is why I enjoy working over here. Bob Destry's shop in Trumbull runs like a militarized production outfit."

"That's what it's supposed to be," Len pointed out.

"Yup, guess you're right. Somebody's got to put product out the back door to pay for our hobbies over here."

"Which Destry doesn't like at all," Len added.

"You are very correct. This whole lab is the target of

a great deal of envy on the part of some divisions who would rather have the budget divided up among themselves for their own in-house work."

"But that would involve only development work on their own product lines," Tammy objected. "Our job here is to come up with things that are different from their current products and yet in line with their capabilities."

"Tell Destry that," Stone growled. "You're all very fortunate in having Bill Osbourne to hold off Destry and the rest of the division managers . . . with no small amount of help from Newcomb."

"And don't forget Halden," Len commented. "He loves the stuff we're doing here."

"Great until he stumbles. Just let earnings drop for three quarters in a row, then start to sweat," Stone warned. "I've been through it before. The minute things get tight, the controller will start yelling for economy moves . . . And what are the two things that always get cut in a corporate economy move?"

"Research and advertising," Mac Roston said.

"You bet!" Len Marshall added to that. "I'd hate to have to stop work on the sky hook right now! Speaking of the sky hook, how's it coming, Carl?"

"Not bad," Carl replied in between bites of his sandwich. "Busted the glass tube, but I blew a new one this morning and got the electrodes sealed in. I'll have it filled with neon-argon today, and she should be swinging again early next week."

"I'm still having trouble believing that it'll work," I put in.

"Not difficult when you think about it," Carl Curley replied in an offhanded manner as though he were privy to all the secrets of the Universe. "Think of it as a version of the old rope trick."

"What do you mean?"

"Take a piece of rope and throw it into the air. Before it has a chance to fall back down, climb it in one hell of a hurry. Then as it starts to fall back, throw it up again and climb like hell. If you do it fast enough and keep at it long enough, you'll end up in the strato-sphere."

"If it were that easy, somebody would have done it long ago," I snapped.

"But it isn't easy, and we're conditioned to think that it's impossible. But it would work perfectly well on a low-gravity planetoid, wouldn't it?" Len put in gently.

"I don't know about that," I mused. "I'd have to check the math."

"And that's the problem with modern engineering," Stone observed. "Too much dependence upon science."

The back door to the shop opened and Bill Osbourne strode in with a big grin on his face. "Howdy, gang!" He was greeted by a chorus of voices. "Carl, can you have the sky hook swinging by Monday afternoon? Halden, Newcomb, and Sanatella want to see a demonstration as quickly as possible."

Carl groaned. "There's a lot of work there, Doctor. Maybe by Wednesday. I've got about two days' work just to rebuild it, plus about a day to hang it and get it tuned up."

"I hate to push you, but this is important. Can you possibly get it ready by Monday afternoon?" Osbourne wanted to know as he stepped to the coffee cup rack and took down his cup.

"It would mean working all weekend," Carl pointed out.

"Carl, can I help?" I wanted to know. "I'll spend a little time this afternoon going over some of the nuts-and-bolts stuff in the reports, then I'll give you a hand if it'll do any good."

"Extra hands are always a help," Carl said.

"I've got family plans tonight," Stone put in, "but I'll be here tomorrow if you need another ten fingers to stir the pot."

"Well, with help from Mike and Wendell, I might be able to make your deadline, Doctor," Carl told the research director. "But it'll mean a lot of overtime."

Osbourne looked at Len. "How's the budget?"

"Tight, but Carl would be the only hourly person involved. Mike and Wendell are salaried."

"Oh, the woes of a professional salaried engineer! The company owns us body and soul twenty-four hours a day and seven days a week," Stone remarked.

Osbourne said, "Keep track of the time and let Len know. You and Mike can take off compensatory time . . . provided you don't tell Destry about it, Wendell."

"I'm an engineer, but that doesn't mean I'm crazy," Stone observed.

"Okay, Carl, go to it! Overtime authorized. This is important, so anybody else who's involved and who can work on it this weekend is also authorized to come in," Osbourne announced. "R&D is not done on a nine-to-five basis . . ."

Chapter Six

I went back to reading and going over the equations. I had a hard time satisfying myself that the basic theory was sound. However, I began to make some sense out of the mathematical banjo music of Vic's tensors and field equations after it dawned on me that Bill and Vic had taken the basic Maxwell equations that tied together electricity and magnetism and had extended the analogy of the Maxwell electromagnetic field equations to gravity and inertia. I hoped that they were right because it was so mathematically *neat*.

Out of their analogy came the hypothesis that a gravitational field was a consequence of a *moving* gravitational charge as opposed to a *static* electric charge producing an electric field. The analogy to the magnetic field produced by a moving charged particle was the *accelerated* gravitational charge producing an "inertial field." And when a gravitational charge was subjected to a change of acceleration, a "surge" or a jolt—such as when a gyro is precessed—a new form of radiation should be produced analogous to electromagnetic radiation of charged particles. Osbourne labeled this new radiation as "gravito-inertial radiation," or GI radiation for short.

It was a logical consequence of Osbourne's unassailable basic assumption. But I couldn't get into the field equations deeply enough to grasp the basic characteristics of GI radiation. It was a whole new concept.

But I began to see how a sky hook could be built. On a basic level, it was somewhat like encountering the theories of alternating electric current for the first time after you've worked for years with direct current.

Back in the nineteenth century, it was generally believed by scientists that alternating current couldn't do any work because the positive and negative cycles averaged out to zero. It took Steinmetz to get out of that cul-de-sac and introduce the use of a purely imaginary number that does not exist in the Universe at all and without which alternating current won't work: the square-root of minus-one or "i." And he introduced such concepts as "capacitance," "inductance," and "impedance."

There were analogies to AC theory in Osbourne's work, and I began to see where it might be possible to utilize an alternating or cyclic force to produce work in an unbalanced system that was properly tuned so that the reaction force was out of phase with the action force.

A quick look through the lab reports showed that Osbourne had quickly given up on mechanical devices and gone to experimental units that were driven at very high cyclic frequencies in order to get above mechanical resonance points. To get high frequencies required electromagnetic devices operating in the megaHertz range, and Osbourne, Vic, Len, and Carl had gone to oscillating plasmas which, at first, expended all their radiant energy into the electromagnetic spectrum, that being the easiest path for excess energy to leave the system. To make the sky hook work, Len and Carl figured out the sawtooth wave concept that drove the system asymmetrically. The unit then also radiated into the electromagnetic spectrum as before, but had so much excess energy to get rid of that it had to escape the system as GI radiation, or so Bill and Vic surmised.

What really surprised me was the small amount of input energy required to make the sky hook perform at all. I should have expected it because there was no mass being expelled. Some clever gadgeteering by Carl and Wendell Stone produced a system in which nearly all of the electromagnetic radiation was picked up and fed back into the system through a positive phase-shifting feedback loop. A small amount of electromagnetic radiation from unshielded parts still leaked out.

The sky hook was supposed to displace itself by emitting GI radiation. But nobody in the lab had yet figured out how to measure or even detect GI radiation.

By the end of the afternoon, I was in the dynamics lab with Carl. It's rough when you step into somebody else's lab or workshop. You don't know where the tools are, you don't know where the spare parts are kept, and you don't know what spare parts are on hand.

I simply told Carl, "I've soaked up all the theory that I can manage. Use me as somebody with a strong back and a weak mind."

Carl did.

But he explained as we went along.

It didn't take me long to find out where everything was. We broke for supper, rode home with Ruth, then came back to the lab after dinner to work some more.

Basically, the sky hook looked like something right out of a Hollywood science-fiction movie: the planet-busting death ray gun with all the coils, adjustments, cooling fins, flashing and flickering lights, and glowing neon tubes. It was about four feet in length with a one-meter glass tube. Osbourne had suggested the one-meter tube to simplify some of the data reduction and calculations. Maximum diameter over the coils was about six inches. The whole unit weighed about twenty kilograms.

But the electronic gadgetry needed to make the sky hook operate filled a whole lab bench with pulse generators, amplifiers, buffers, phase-lock units, and assorted power supplies.

I noticed the Federal Communications Commission radio transmitting license on the lab wall. "Yeah," Carl explained, "we get some leakage of about two or three watts up around nine hundred megaHertz when we're running. So we had to get an experimental scientific radio station license."

"Does the FCC know what you're doing?"

"We stated that we needed it for legitimate scientific purposes, the end product of which was proprietary information . . ." Carl remarked in an offhanded manner as he took a meter measurement of one of the sky hook electrical circuits. "They don't seem to care; they just want to make sure we're legal . . . and it seems Newcomb has some friends in Washington," he said, reading the digital display of the voltmeter and entering the numbers in his ever-present laboratory notebook in a careful fashion. "I'm a ham, and we could have worked this unit in one of the ham bands . . . except that it didn't want to work at anything except nine-hundred megaHertz with these dimensions."

That evening amounted to just plain hard technical work. I didn't learn much. I helped with assemblies, helped stringing wires, helped make a few measurements, and held tools. By midnight, we were both worn out and went back to Morse Manor.

Saturday was not much different except that Wendell Stone was there. The engineer wasn't as good at electronics as Carl. I might have been Wendell's equal in that area myself. But when it came to out and out engineering, the Vermonter was indeed ingenious with mechanical things. He was right out of the old sealing wax and string days of 1890 physics. His favorite phrase was, "That's close enough for government work!"

"But this isn't government work," I reminded him.

"Okay, then tighten that bolt to a Curley fit."

"Huh? What's that?" Carl Curley wanted to know.

"The famous Curley fit, used by all and sundry around the NEMECO Corporate Research Center Laboratories. I am surprised that you don't know about it, Carl, since it bears your name." Stone was kidding him, and we both knew it. "The famous Curley fit: finger-tight, then back-off half a turn!"

This sort of banter went on constantly as we worked. It was interspersed with technical jargon while we checked this, measured that, and connected something else. If someone had bugged that lab with the idea of learning something about the sky hook, it would have sounded a lot like this:

"Throw me that seven-eighths open-end box . . . On second thought, just hand it gently to me . . ."

"Goddam miserable gawdforsaken lousy no-good . . ."

"Hit it with a bigger hammer!"

"Yeah, force to fit, file to hide, and paint to cover . . ."

"You sound more like Mac Roston every day!"

"Slide in there, you no-good lousy forking . . ."

"Now, now! Temper, temper!"

"Eyeball this and tell me how well you think it lines up . . ."

"Want me to get the theodolite and give you an honest answer?"

"Naw, just eyeball it."

"Excuse me while I put in my calibrated eyeball . . ."

"Okay, looks good! Nudge it a little more. Little more! Little more! Whoa, too much! Back it off an R-C-H! Easy! Okay, make it a half R-C-H!"

"Best I can do is one R-C-H. Can't expect much better than that without micrometers."

"Okay, turn it on and see if it passes the smoke test . . ."

"Power on!"

"I'll get another fuse from the electronics lab."

"Never mind! The power transistor protected the fuse by blowing first!"

"Think we ought to file for a patent on that one?"

"Naw, it happens all the time. The function of transistors is to protect the fuses in the circuit!"

By late Saturday afternoon, the three of us had the basic sky hook unit back together and checked out.

"Let's call it a day," Carl sighed. "I'm plumb tuckered out and I don't relish having to hang that mother tonight."

"I propose that we hit it with a great exuberance tomorrow morning," Wendell Stone suggested.

"It's still hard to believe," I remarked, glancing at the unit on the floor with wires festooned all over and around it where we had been making electrical checks. "It will never fly!"

"It had better not!" Wendell Stone added. "One hole in the lab wall was enough."

"Aw, we've got a good line item in the dynamic systems budget for bricks and mortar," Carl put in.

We locked up and I drove home with Carl.

I was worn out at dinnertime, and apparently both Carl and I showed it because Peter Wilding remarked, "Gee, you guys look tired. Did you work down at the lab all day?"

"What ever gave you that idea?" I asked.

"You've got solder splattered all over your pant legs, which means that you were working on electronic gear."

"Mike offered to help me trouble-shoot the new ham rig I'm building down at the lab in my spare time," Carl lied.

Nothing more was said about our whereabouts that day. Conversation was the usual small talk around the dinner table. Afterward, it was Carl's turn to wash the dishes and Peter Wilding had the task of drying them. I collapsed in the living room with Tammy and Ruth.

I looked at Tammy. She was just as attractive as she had been yesterday . . . and the day before that, too. I took the plunge and asked her, "Hey, Tammy, let's go see a movie."

She smiled and said, "No, thank you, Mike." And that was that. It sort of shocked me.

"Why not, Tammy?" Ruth popped up. "You've just been sitting around the house all day. Do you good to get out."

"I think I'll just take a hot bath and read in bed," Tammy said, getting up and starting up the stairway. "Ruth, will you yell up when Carl and Peter have finished using the hot water on the dishes?"

"Certainly, Tammy." Ruth shook her head and clucked sadly as Tammy disappeared up the stairs. "In all the months she's been living here, I still haven't been able to figure that girl out. She is very attractive, but she never goes out on dates. And practically every bachelor at the lab has asked her. So don't feel badly, Mike."

"Thanks for the consolation, Ruth. Maybe I'll ask her to go flying with me. She might find that different and interesting. I don't imagine there are many people around here who fly."

"Tammy does."

"Tammy's a pilot?"

"That's what she told me once." Ruth reached down to pick up her sewing basket. She extracted needle, thread, and a few items that needed mending. This was unusual because hardly anybody I knew mended modern clothes any more; once they were worn out, they were thrown out. Then I remembered that I was in parsimonious New England.

"What's Tammy's background, Ruth?" I knew that Ruth, in her role as laboratory house mother, would have access to all the personnel records.

"She has a degree in math from some little liberal arts college in the Midwest," Ruth said absently as she began sewing. "I guess she's also some kind of photographer because she's got a lot of camera equipment in her room."

"Has she been married?"

"Yes, but she doesn't talk about it. A very strange girl."

I let the whole thing drop at that. Just because I couldn't get a date with Tammy Dudley on the first try didn't make me feel that this Saturday night was the loneliest night for the weak. I sat around reading until Carl and Peter had finished the dishes.

"How about a rubber of bridge?" Peter Wilding suggested as he bustled into the living room.

"I'm not very good at bridge," I told him.

"Then how about a hand or two of poker?" the vacuum tube engineer suggested.

"I'm in," I told him. Carl nodded, too. Tired as I was, poker was something that I wouldn't pass up. It relaxed me and got my mind off other things.

But Ruth, when asked, said, "My husband used to play poker, but I never learned because he always played with cronies. Why don't the three of you go ahead and use the dining room table?" She got up and resurrected an ancient set of poker chips from a closet along with a few old decks of cards. But Wilding produced a new deck of Bicycles.

"Dollar ante?" Wilding asked as we sat down.

"They must pay better over at UTL," Carl remarked. "I'd say dime ante and limit. Payday isn't until next Wednesday. Go ahead and break the seal, and we'll cut for deal."

I ended up with the deal. "Five-card draw," I announced as I shuffled. I threw a chip and passed the deck to Carl to cut. Poker was one of the games I had played when we sat around in the evenings after a day of ag flying. I liked poker;-it was an aggressive game, and I knew the odds pretty well.

First hand was piddling. I won a pot worth all of sixty cents. But it wasn't hard work. Carl shuffled, Wilding cut, and I ended up with a pat hand.

"Incidentally, welcome to the club," Carl remarked as he dealt two cards to Wilding, but he was talking to me. "I'll take three," he added and flipped three cards off the top of the deck onto his hand.

"What are you congratulating me for?" I wanted to know. "Fifty cents." I threw chips on the table and glanced down at three jacks, a trey, and a ten in my hand.

"The club of them who has been spurned by Tammy Dudley," Carl announced. "I'll see you and raise you fifty cents."

"I'll see your raise and call. Yeah, Carl, what's with Tammy?"

"Two pair! Sorry, chaps!"

"Beats three of a kind any day, damn it! As I said, what's with Tammy?"

"Your deal, Peter. One day Vic and I were working and Vic bitched about the fact that he could never get a date with Tammy. He was wondering whether or not she was a real girl."

"Let's make a change just for the hell of it. Seven-card stud," Peter Wilding said, rippling the cards through a shuffle. The older man was very good with cards. It warned me that he was probably as shrewd as they came. That evaluation may have been correct for poker, but it didn't necessarily hold for industrial espionage because Wilding had thoroughly blown his cover. But his bumbling bumpkin style would certainly put people off-guard.

"Gawd, Peter, what a mess!" I sputtered as I looked. Deuce showing. Seven showing. And a mess of garbage underneath. But I decided it would be worth the money and the fun to see if I could bluff it through. It would at least help me psych Wilding and get a better handle on the man.

But I couldn't do it. Wilding out-bluffed me on the hand. I got the deal and we went back to five-card. As I shuffled, I asked Carl, "Well, what did any of you find out about it?"

"Tammy's been married once before."

"That's what Ruth told me." I let Carl cut. Sweeping the cards back, I started to deal. "What happened to turn her off?"

"I don't know. Apparently her marriage left a great deal to be desired because it didn't last very long."

"And it soured her on all men, is that it?" I wondered.

"You could sort of say that. I guess her husband was an airline pilot . . ."

"That tells the whole story," I remarked with a sigh. Airline transport pilots have a notorious reputation, most of it unearned and undeserved, as macho men of the sky because of those layovers with the stews.

"Not really. Ante-up, Mike! I'm standing."

"You're standing pat?" I asked incredulously, looking at my own outstanding hand. I threw in a buck's worth of chips.

"Give me two," Wilding put in. "I'll see you, Carl, Mike deals better hands."

"Well, I'd expect an ATP to adhere to their tradition of 'anything goes if more than fifty miles from home,' " I observed.

"I guess it was more than that," Carl told him. "The guy wasn't good enough to make the passenger flights and ended up flying cargo. He'd come home full of frustrations, get drunk because he didn't have to fly again for three days, and beat the hell out of Tammy . . ."

Wilding exploded with an expletive I had heard only occasionally among migrant farm workers who were often coarse in their language. "I hope that I never meet up with him!" he went on.

"You won't. Tammy walked out on him, and he flew into a cloud full of mountains two days later."

I had almost forgotten my poker hand. "Well, that certainly explains some of it. I fold!"

"Read 'em and weep!" Wilding laid out his hand, a diamond flush. He started to rake in the pot when Carl laid down his hand.

"How about that?" Carl chuckled. "Four queens!" He reached for the pot himself. As he stacked chips and started to shuffle, he looked around to make sure that Ruth was out of earshot in the living room. "No, that doesn't fully explain it, Mike."

"Huh? Why?"

"Well, this is a little lab gossip," Carl admitted, throwing a very quick glance at Wilding. I knew damned good and well that all of this was going into Wilding's obviously excellent memory for possible later use. "I don't know whether you've been aboard long enough to know that Bill Osbourne goes into New York City at least once a week . . ."

"He was in the city when I showed up."

"It's a very strange thing," Carl went on as he passed the deck to Wilding to cut. "Tammy usually isn't in the lab on most of those days, either . . ."

That set me back. "Kind of circumstantial, isn't it?" I had trouble believing that Bill Osbourne would dally with one of his laboratory employees. He had a great deal riding on the success of the laboratory and its programs. Although I didn't know the corporate officers yet, I had the feeling that NEMECO might not look favorably upon such carryings-on. "If he's ever caught, there would be hell to pay up at headquarters," I pointed out.

"Not only at headquarters. Osbourne's got a wife at home and three kids in high school . . ."

Chapter Seven

Personal indiscretions don't bother me the way they used to. I was brought up in Roswell, New Mexico, which is a small town where everybody knows what everybody else is doing. I've been taught and have always believed that I shouldn't go messing around in a way that fouls up other persons' lives. One thing for certain: if I were Bill Osbourne, I would definitely *not* do something as transparent as the rumors indicated. There are a lot slicker ways to get your kicks so that nobody knows at all.

Therefore, I don't think that my actions betrayed any belief in the rumor when Bill Osbourne dropped into the lab on the following day as Carl, Wendell, and I had just completed hanging the sky hook as a ballistic pendulum.

"Hey, it looks good!" Osbourne bubbled as he walked into the dynamics lab. "You guys have done a really fantastic job!"

"Thanks. It will show up on my time card," Carl remarked with a grin.

"Well worth it, too," Bill added, surveying the installation. The drive unit was hanging horizontally, supported at both ends by cotton cord attached to the ceiling twelve feet above. The cord at each end was in a "V" shape with two points of attachment on the ceiling; this kept the unit from swinging from side to side. It was a common arrangement used in the freshman physics laboratory experiment where momentum is measured by how far the pendulum is displaced by an impacting force. The unit could swing back and forth, and it maintained its horizontal attitude as it did so.

"Excuse me, Doctor," Wendell asked, "but why did you specify that the sky hook be supported this way? Why not put it on rollers and let it push against a spring or a strain gauge to measure its thrust?"

"Because this sort of arrangement completely eliminates any possibility of rate-dependent frictional forces such as 'stick-slip' phenomena that we *might* get if we used rollers or ball bearings to support it," the research director pointed out. "Any horizontal force produced by the unit will displace it from the vertically hanging rest position. As long as it produces thrust, it will maintain itself displaced from the rest position. Knowing the weight of the unit, the length of the pendulum supports, and the local gravitational force, we can calculate how much thrust it's producing by measuring how far it displaces itself."

Wendell nodded. "I recall doing something like this in my physics courses at the University of Maine."

"Precisely. By using this method and by leading the power into the unit with wires along the pendulum supports, we've got a free suspension," Osbourne went on. "I don't want any supercilious scientist trying to shoot us out of the saddle by claiming we're the victims of stick-slip or mechanical resonance phenomena. In addition, attaching the sky hook to any external measuring system such as strain gauges will probably change the tuning of the system . . . and that's something we don't know very much about yet."

"Uh, boss, I think I'd better go a little easy on the power input when I try to tune it up this time," Carl suggested. "Can you give me any indication of just how much power input we should use to get about a foot of pendulum displacement in the horizontal direction?"

"Not off the top of my head," Osbourne admitted. "I can give you a good estimate in about fifteen minutes."

"Okay, because we're about ready to begin tuning . . . and I don't want to have to patch that wall again," Carl told him.

"Take five when you get to the point of putting power to it. I'll see what I can get the computer to tell me," Osbourne said and disappeared in the direction of

Tammy's office where the microcomputer was located.

Thirty minutes later, we were ready to go. But Osbourne wasn't back yet. I went up to Tammy's office and found him seated before the microcomputer terminal, quietly cursing to himself.

"Problems?" I asked.

"Can't get the program to run."

"Let me try," I suggested. "I've had some experience out at Lowell. What language are you using?"

"BASIC. We bought this thing so we wouldn't have to learn how to program in exotic languages."

"Where's the program?"

"On this minifloppy."

"Have you listed the program to check the steps?"

"No. I hardly ever work this thing," Osbourne admitted. "I've got other people to do it."

"Okay, let me give it a try." I got to work as he relinquished the chair to me.

A half-hour later, no luck. The program would not load properly. By this time, Carl and Wendell were looking over my shoulder.

"Something's locking us out of that program," I pointed out. "It should boot-strap into working memory, but it doesn't."

Osbourne got up, saying, "I'm going to see if I can reach Vic or Tammy on the phone."

"Tammy said she was going out this afternoon," Carl remarked.

"And you'll be lucky to find Aboud unless you know the telephone number of his latest girl friend," Wendell pointed out.

I sighed. "Well, back to Square One. If you've got the equations, Bill, I'll run them by hand."

"That'll take hours!" Osbourne objected.

"Not exactly. I'll run them on my programmable."

I had almost as much computing power in my hand programmable calculator as in the microcomputer except I didn't have the memory capacity. As I was writing a program, Osbourne got on the phone to call Vic or Tammy. He acted as though I might not even get to first base with my little programmable. But I had the program written and debugged by the time he came back, shaking his head. "You were right. Tammy is gone, and Vic is nowhere to be found. Damned frustrating!"

"Well, it's Sunday afternoon," Wendell reminded him.

My program checked out. "Okay, Wendell, stand by for numbers," I told him.

In fifteen minutes, we had our answers.

"I'm glad I hired you," Osbourne admitted.

"At least I'm good for something around here," I replied, turning off my calculator.

"I don't believe your numbers," Carl said, looking at what Wendell had written down on the quad-ruled pad. "I'm not even sure that I can cut the power that low. Vic told me to have lots of power available just in case."

I scrooched the pad around so that I could get a look at the numbers. In technical work, I can get a feeling for "ballpark" numbers. If I slip a decimal point—a difficult thing to do these days with floating-point pocket calculators—it can be very obvious.

"These numbers say we should start out with about twenty watts of drive power," Carl explained, indicating the sheet. "Vic told me we'd need about two hundred watts."

"He must have assumed a much lower efficiency," I told him, "because it got away from you the other day. So I assumed a hundred percent efficiency as a point of departure. We're not going to *get* one hundred percent efficiency. But if we measure how far it swings with twenty-two watts on it, we can then calculate the actual efficiency."

"I'll buy that. Good experimental procedure," Osbourne said and turned to Carl. "Vic said two hundred watts?"

"He said that's what his equations indicated."

"But you didn't wind the front phasing coils the way he designed them. So you got better efficiency than Vic was counting on," Osbourne observed. "It begins to make sense now. But Vic will have a hemorrhage when he finds out he was wrong."

"We were all wrong," Wendell Stone pointed out. "Carl made a serendipitous mistake and mis-read the numbers."

Osbourne sighed. "Well, that's what happens when you plow fresh ground. You never know what the plow is going to turn up. Let's go give her a try."

"I'd suggest somewhat more stringent safety procedures because of what happened Thursday afternoon," I added.

"What do you mean?" Carl wanted to know.

"When you're operating a complex machine, it's a good idea to have a check list just to make sure that you don't forget something. If we make out a check list of what to turn on, when to turn it on and how it should be set, we may prevent this monster from going through the wall again . . . or worse."

So we sat down and worked one up. It covered twenty-three items to be checked in sequence. Later we could modify it as we learned more about it, but it was a start.

Back in the dynamics lab, Carl began switching on equipment. "I've gotta admit something to you all," he said as he was powering-up. "When Vic said to build it powerful, Len suggested that I should double Vic's estimate just in case. And I ended up doubling that because I wanted to be absolutely certain that we had enough power to make this thing work. So we've got about four times the actual full-power capability here than we really need . . ."

"Did you ever work in the Air Force space program?" Osbourne asked. "That sounds like the way they do it."

"If we've got that much power lurking around, let's run with dummy loads first to see if we can throttle it down to the level we need," I suggested.

"You're quite an experimentalist," Osbourne observed.

"What do you think astronomy is all about? And have you ever repaired ag planes in the field?"

A dummy electrical load is usually just a resistance element like the heating unit in an electric toaster or a hot plate. It turned out that we couldn't use such a simple approach because some of the equipment operated at very high frequencies. No resistance element is a pure electrical resistance at very high frequencies. There are inductance and capacitance to consider as well, and these factors can screw up a system by presenting some very wild loads to the equipment in terms of phase shift, for example. By the time the four of us got through making several lash-ups, it was late afternoon.

I was amazed at Wendell Stone's simple approaches and elegant solutions to many of the complex problems. For example, we needed a very large heat sink to dissipate some of the electrical power that was converted to heat by one of the dummy loads. Wendell simply ran tap water through the hollow ceramic tube on which the big resistive load was wound.

It took some time to get all the equipment adjusted. We had a lot of redundant stuff on that first sky hook because it was a very crude first unit. Even as we began to set things up for the first test run, I could see where it would be possible to combine several pieces of equipment and where several controls could be converted into one adjustable lever or knob.

It was about six o'clock when we decided we were ready to make the first test run at very low input power.

"Just to make damned sure," Osbourne said, "let's run it with only about ten watts to start."

Carl made some adjustments. I used my calculator to recompute some voltage settings.

"To paraphrase Lord Kelvin, 'When you measure, you *know*!' Hand me that roll of paper tape, Wendell. I am going to make a simple measurement. Carl, let me have that pencil." Osbourne taped the pencil to the side of the sky hook in a vertical position so that it just cleared the floor under the device. He taped a wooden meter stick to the floor so that when the apparatus swung, he could use the pencil as a pointer indicating how far the unit had swung.

"Is everybody ready?" Carl asked.

"Everybody get out from behind the unit . . . and from in front of it, too!" Osbourne warned.

We gathered on both sides of the sky hook. It hung there on its strings, forty-four pounds of the wildest-looking scientific gadgetry imaginable. Each of us had some knob to twist, some switch to throw, or some meter to watch. Bill Osbourne acted as commander-in-chief of the experiment.

"Main switch on?" Osbourne called, reading from the check list.

"Main switch on!" Carl called back.

"High voltage on?"

"High voltage on!"

"Drive plasma energized?"

"Plasma on!"

"Thirty-four-thousand volts on the plasma," I reported.

"Check! Front phasing coil on?"

"Front phaser on!" Wendell called back. "I read thirty-four volts peak-to-peak."

"Rear phasing coil on?"

"Rear phaser on! Eighteen-point-seven volts peak-to-peak!"

"Main drive frequency on! Check wave shape and frequency!"

"Drive frequency on! Nine-oh-seven megaHertz! Nice sawtooth! Lemme check rise time . . . ten nanoseconds! Looks good!" Carl's voice was excited.

"E-M radiation feedback coils?"

"E-M feedback loop on!"

"Check phasing!"

Carl busied himself looking into the black plastic hood of an oscilloscope. "Mike, give me about ten degrees positive shift on the front phaser."

"Ten degrees positive!"

"Wendell, readjust that peak-to-peak front phaser voltage."

"Okay, she's back where she should be."

"Ready to energize?" Osbourne sang out.

"Ready!" Carl replied.

The sky hook was just hanging there, the neon plasma tube giving off a bright orange-red glow that threw shadows on the walls of the brightly lit laboratory. There was no noise, no hum, no vibration.

"Okay, let's have ten watts on it," Osbourne ordered.

"Ten watts!"

Nothing happened. The unit just hung there.

"Something's wrong! How about your readings, Mike?" Osbourne wanted to know.

"Everything copasetic here!"

"Wendell?"

"Looks fine!"

"Carl?"

"It should be swinging out."

"What the hell? . . ." Osbourne wondered out loud.

"Uh, Carl," I ventured, not wanting to take my eyes off the instruments in front of me, "let me diddle with the phasing just a shade. It acts like it might not be tuned."

"Go ahead! When we rebuilt it, we might have changed some component just enough to throw her out of tune," Carl replied. "I'll hold ten watts. You diddle."

"Don't take forever," Wendell warned. "This feedback circuit is getting pretty damned hot . . ."

"Let me know if it starts to smoke," Carl told him.

I made a couple of delicate adjustments, trying to phase the reactive force generated during the trail-off slope of the sawtooth so that it reinforced the input jolt. "A little on the front . . . Check it . . . Looks good here . . . A little change in back . . . Whoops! Went the wrong way!" I talked out loud as I worked. "Phasing on the front and back coils are not the same. Acts like the ends are behaving differently. Okay, something's peaking on the phase voltage . . . It acts like it's coming up on some sort of resonance point . . . adjust the voltage there . . . Hey, it's coming into phase fast now! Wow! Just like tuning into resonance . . ." Everything peaked.

I turned and looked.

The sky hook was hanging away from the vertical!

I looked down at the pencil and meter stick. The unit had swung about four centimeters away from the vertical, and it was staying there . . . silently, with no noise or vibration.

The four of us just stood there and looked at it.

It was a puny force that was holding that forty-four-pound unit about two inches away from the vertical on its suspension. But it was a force that had been generated only once before: on Thursday when it had gotten away from Carl and gone through the wall. Now we had it tamed.

"I suppose," Bill Osbourne said, breaking the silence, "that I should make some sort of profound historic statement. And I can't think of anything profound to say. But I believe we've got it, gentlemen!"

"Let's find out for certain," I suggested. "Carl, run it up to twenty-two watts. I want to see if my calculations are right."

"Okay! Coming up . . . fifteen watts . . . twenty watts . . . twenty-two watts right on the nose."

Osbourne was down on his knees, watching the pencil in reference to the meter stick. "Stabilized just short of eight centimeters!"

I grabbed my calculator and began punching numbers into it. "Would you believe seventy-two-point-one percent efficiency?"

Over all the intervening years, the image of that strange glowing unit hanging only three inches away from the vertical in that laboratory with four of us clustered around it remains indelibly engraved in my mind. I was there. I saw it. And it was just the beginning.

Chapter Eight

In the car pool the following morning, we brought Tammy up-to-date. We hadn't breathed a word of it at Morse Manor on Sunday evening after Bill had taken us all out for a steak to celebrate. But Tammy and Ruth knew that something had happened. It's hard to hide enthusiasm. So I suspect that Wilding also got the drift that something big had occurred, although we maintained that we were just working on new amateur radio gear that Carl had built.

Tammy was very quiet as Carl and I explained what had happened. Then she asked, "You couldn't get the microcomputer working?"

"Nope. You and Vic have some sort of lock-out on the program," I told her. "But I managed to work it out on my small programmable."

"That's remarkable," Tammy said. "I thought more computer power would be required."

"I sort of simplified a few equations and linearized them where I had to," I admitted. "We were looking for ballpark numbers anyway. What really surprised me was the efficiency of the sky hook."

"What did you measure?"

"About seventy-two percent."

"Oh, that's very good! Vic had anticipated only about twenty percent." Tammy smiled, brightening up the entire car. Then her face got somber. "But Vic will have a fit. He convinced Osbourne to buy that microcomputer to run the programs for the sky hook design. We'll have to be very careful not to tell him that your hand programmable did the job just as well."

"Osbourne already knows it. He watched me do it," I

admitted. "If Aboud is in hot water, it's his own fault."

"He'll also be upset about the higher efficiency," Tammy remarked.

"For God's sake, why?" I wanted to know.

"Vic gets upset when anything doesn't work according to the Word of Aboud," Carl explained from the front seat.

"It's good for him," Ruth interjected. "Vic needs to have somebody like you around, Mike. He's been able to snow everybody with his math, including Dr. Osbourne."

"Well, I'm a better programmer than Vic," Tammy said.

"I know that, dear, but don't let *him* know," Ruth pointed out.

When we got to the lab, I went to Len's office to report to him. When he arrived, cursing the Bridgeport traffic, he told me, "Good morning, Mike! Nice work yesterday!"

"Oh, so Osbourne called you."

"Yes. Let's wait until Vic gets here, then I'd like to have you give us both a brief rundown on what happened. And, Mike, please let me handle Vic."

"Len, I appreciate your concern for the tranquility of personal relationships in the lab, but sooner or later I'm going to have to face up to Victor Aboud and have it out with him," I said. "If it happens to be this morning, I will not let you shoot my dog for me."

Len looked at me, then just grinned.

Vic did not show up for another thirty minutes. In the meantime, Len and I got coffee and had a look at the sky hook. Ruth finally called over the intercom that Vic had arrived.

"Hi, Vic!" Len greeted him as we walked back into Len's office. "Hey, Bill and Mike had a big breakthrough here yesterday."

"Why didn't you call me?"

"We tried. We couldn't get an answer at your home phone," I told him.

Vic grinned. "I thought I heard the phone ring late in

the afternoon, but I was otherwise occupied at the time."

"New girl friend?" Len asked.

"New carpet."

"I don't get you," Len admitted.

"I got a new carpet for my apartment living room," Aboud explained. "We have a tradition that requires a new carpet be properly broken in."

"I thought they did that by driving a Rolls-Royce over them for a month," I remarked.

"They do. But when you put the carpet down where you live, you must properly initiate it with your very best woman right in the middle of it. Sorry, but I was breaking in a new carpet when you called."

"How was it?" Len wanted to know.

"It's a great carpet," Aboud fired back with a straight face.

"Okay, then who was it?" Len persisted.

"Remember Joyce?"

"The dancer with the New York City Ballet?"

"Right! All muscles and limber as a willow wand . . ."

"I thought you liked them plump," Len said.

"Not when I can get an odalisque."

"How come you're so oversexed?" Len asked.

Obviously, this was one of Vic's favorite subjects. "I have some similar questions about American men: How come you're so undersexed? Don't tell me; I've had many Americans try to proselyte me into their sexually sinful religions. On the other hand, it's part of our religion. When I turned fifteen, my father gave me a credit card to the best whore house in the city and instructed the madam to have me properly taught . . ." Then, as rapidly as if he had never been bull shooting with us, he changed the subject and was all business. "What happened yesterday?"

So I started at the top and went through a rather complete verbal report on rebuilding the sky hook and getting it hung. I told them about rebuilding the phasing coils exactly as Carl had mistakenly done earlier in the week.

"I can't figure that one out," Vic mused, doodling on a pad of paper. "There must be something there we didn't anticipate."

"It could be due to the fact that the plasma dynamics are different at opposite ends of the tube," I tried to point out.

"Probably." Vic began jotting down equations. "Okay, tell me about setting it up for the low-power test."

So I gave him the details on that.

"How did you get the microcomputer to run your numbers?" he wanted to know. "We've got a lock code on that program."

"We found that out," I told him. "So I made a lot of simplifying assumptions and ran the ballpark numbers on my programmable."

Vic looked up. "You managed to do it on a hand programmable?"

"Only with a lot of linearization, and with considerably less memory than if I'd used the microcomputer," I pointed out, trying to be diplomatic. "Had to use pencil and paper as a memory register occasionally. Took Bill and me together to work the problem after I managed to write and debug a program."

"Why did you set the values so low?"

"Since it had gone through the wall on Thursday, I decided we'd better start out at very low power and increase by incremental steps until we got measureable deflection. At that point, we could make some crude measurements, figure the actual efficiency, and determine the power level that would give us a definite and convincing deflection without having to repair the wall and the sky hook again."

Vic looked at Len and remarked, "At last we've got a good experimentalist who understands the analytical side."

Len looked aside at me and I just smiled.

"Mike, I want you to work with Tammy and me today on the analysis of the rough data you got yesterday," Vic went on. "We need to know exactly how much power to put into the sky hook for various thrust levels and how we should go about tuning it for various loads."

"Vic, we've got Halden and Newcomb coming in right after lunch to see the sky hook in action," Len put in quickly. "Since Mike was primarily responsible for working out the test run yesterday, don't you think it would be a good idea to let him get everything checked out in the lab this morning and maybe make a few dry runs? After all, you've only got one computer terminal to work with . . ."

Len was right. If you handled Vic properly, he was a pussy cat.

With Len watching, Carl and I spent the rest of the morning checking out the sky hook and making additional tests and dry runs.

By doing a certain amount of fine tuning that we hadn't had time to carry out yesterday and didn't know how to carry out at that time, we peaked the unit and were able to increase the efficiency to slightly more than 79 percent. The displacement went out to about 67 centimeters, which displaced the entire length of the sky hook from the vertical rest position with the rear end well ahead of the rest point. I particularly wanted to get it to swing that far because it proved beyond a shadow of a doubt that we were creating a true thrust force. The electromagnetic feedback circuitry began to get hot at that power level, so we couldn't hold it out there for more than three minutes before having to shut it down to let things cool off.

Carl told me that he could beef-up that circuitry because Vic's computer had given a power level dissipation for the feedback circuit that was in error. I quietly reminded myself not to tell Vic about it; we'd just go ahead and beef it up. It wasn't Vic's fault. In any experimental design calculation where you can't get a firm grip on all the numbers, there are bound to be errors that creep into the equations from assumptions. That's why you build an experimental gadget.

Carl began to think about miniaturizing the circuitry. Since things were under control in the dynamics lab, I went up front to see if I could give Vic and Tammy any help with the analytical work. I found the two of them at loggerheads . . . which was not totally unanticipated.

They were arguing over programming, and Tammy was the better programmer. On the other hand, Vic was the better mathematician.

"Damn it, Tammy!" Vic was shouting. "Step 1130 is *wrong*! That's where you've got to GOSUB 5600 and start the integration loop."

The way Vic treated Tammy sort of grated on me, but I tried to hold my own temper. Tammy seemed to be in control anyway. "Run it that way, and you'll see that we'll get an error message at 1130! Just go ahead and try running it! Here! Sit down and type RUN!"

"Would a third party help?" I asked from the door. "Why don't you let me check the program?"

"No need to do that!" Aboud maintained.

"Okay, I'll input RUN," Tammy snapped and did so.

"ERROR 1130" flashed on the screen.

Vic reached down, reset, reloaded from the diskette, typed RUN . . . and watched while "ERROR 1130" flashed on the screen.

Tammy glanced up at Vic with a look that said, "I told you so!"

It was time I got into the loop. "Tammy, turn on the printer and list the program for me. While Vic's fighting it, maybe I can debug it."

I got the print-out, and Vic himself left the console to go over it with me on one side while Tammy stood on the other. At step 1130, everything was okay, but I found two problems in step 1110 and 1120 where both Vic and Tammy had overlooked a basic command. I corrected the program and turned to Vic. "Five bucks says it'll run now!"

"Come on, let's be sporting!" Vic snorted. He withdrew a slim wallet and extracted a crisp one-hundred-dollar bill.

I did not want to get into the habit of high-roller betting with a guy from the Mid-East petrol patch. So I made a suggesttion: "If I'm wrong, it's a free ride in my airplane so that you and a girl friend can join the Mile-High Club."

"What's that?" Vic wanted to know. Tammy had a trace of a smile.

"To be initiated into the Mile-High Club, you and your favorite girl have to do it in an airplane one mile above mean sea level."

Vic brightened. "How about it, Tammy?"

"Forget it! I'm already a member," Tammy told him icily.

"Okay, you're on!" Vic chortled. "A hundred bucks against that special airplane ride!"

"It's your money if you really want to throw it away," I sighed.

"No, it's your money, but we filter it through an oil field."

I inserted my program, booted-up, and ran it with only one minor correction in syntax in the next to last step. So Vic insisted that I'd lost and that he was due an airplane ride. Tammy tried to mediate but was unsuccessful. The controversy was broken when Len stuck his head in the door and announced that Mac was going to the deli for sandwiches as usual.

I was keyed-up over the afternoon's demonstration coming up and elected to stay in the lab. But Vic talked Len into going out. As Tammy and I walked back to the machine shop, she remarked to me, "Thanks."

"No sweat," I replied. "I didn't like the way Vic was treating you when I walked in. In spite of his cultural background where women are treated like dirt beneath his camel's hooves, I don't think anybody should treat a woman that way. Especially you."

"Bully is the proper term," Tammy said. Then, totally unexpectedly, she asked, "Would you check me out in your plane?"

"Uh, well . . . sure! Ruth told me you were a pilot."

"Sometimes Ruth talks too much."

"Not about you she doesn't."

She looked askance at me. "Mile-High Club, indeed!"

"I understand the latest federal air regulations require that a member get an annual review."

"I don't need to get current right now," she told me flatly as we walked into the shop, bringing an end to our conversation.

Bill Osbourne showed up at two o'clock with Grant Halden, NEMECO president and chief executive officer; Hayward Newcomb, the executive vice-president; Robert Destry, the division vice-president of the NEMECO Mill Equipment Division in Trumbull; and Phil Sanatella, the corporate marketing expert. Osbourne introduced us all as we met in the lab conference room.

The president of NEMECO struck me as a man who was completely at home with and enjoyed all of the authority and responsibility that went with the job of chief executive of a small corporation. He had a hawk-like face with a gentle smile and an extremely cultured manner. He was also a very large man . . . large all over and proportioned accordingly. Because of my own diminutive stature, a person's size always seems to be the first thing that I notice about them. But Grant Halden made me feel as big as he was. That's the sort of man he was.

Dr. Hayward J. Newcomb, on the other hand, was a balding middle-aged man with horn-rimmed glasses and a very broad mouth. He was polite, but not elegant the way Halden was. He spoke precisely with deliberate slowness as though he were constantly thinking out and evaluating each sentence before he uttered it. He had a preoccupied air about him as though he were partly present but partly somewhere else as well.

I didn't quite know what to make of Robert Destry. He was a handsome middle-aged man with wavy hair and an air of relentless drive about him. He was cordial when he spoke, but he seemed to have a no-nonsense air about him that bothered me.

On the other hand, I didn't like Phil Sanatella the moment I met him. He was about my size, but he wore elevator shoes to increase his height. This told me a great deal about him: he didn't like himself, and therefore he didn't like other people. And it showed. He was obnoxious to everyone except Halden and Newcomb, and only a trifle obnoxious to Destry. He was making up for his small size by noise and bustling action. I knew that Sanatella was very vulnerable, but I didn't know where. Only a person who is totally insecure will act as Sanatella did.

I was introduced to the four men as the new project director for the dynamic systems program. Osbourne told them about my background in physics and astronomy, but said absolutely nothing about my experience in aviation, which I thought was strange. "Mike is sitting in on the briefing today to help him get up to speed on the project, although he spent this last weekend here in the lab helping to get the sky hook in shape for the demonstration today. As a matter of fact, he has come up with a large number of outstanding experimental procedures for it already, and he has the sort of background in mathematics that will give Vic Aboud the help he needs."

Whereupon Bill Osbourne launched into a semitechnical briefing on the sky hook, much of which I had already read in reports and other papers in the lab. However, Bill added his own brand of enthusiasm and advocacy of the sort that was not evident in the written materials. He was also a bit more venturesome in what he said. "It appears that we may have identified a whole new type of radiative energy although we have not yet been able to build a detector to sense or measure what the theoretical equations tell us must be there. Vic has worked out the equations describing this type of energy. Both Dr. Mayan and Professor Korsinski have checked them over and found no place where our logic or methodology is faulty. By proper definition of the field vectors, we've found it possible to apply Maxwell's equations to predict the behavior of this new type of radiation. But we have a lot of work to do in this area. The potentials are mind-boggling, and we're certain to end up with a whole series of completely new proprietary products. It's too early yet to be able to describe these products in any detail. I don't want to give you the impression that we are working on a far-out project that has no immediate applications in the classical product mix of the company, but we may have something more than a mere lifting device here. If we do indeed have a new form of radiation, we should be able to figure out how to direct and focus it. We might be able to transmit mechanical power over great distances with no mechanical connections; this includes the possibilities of energy beams that will push or pull. Obviously, there will be many commercial applications . . ."

"And military implications," Hayward Newcomb interjected.

"We recognize that, Hay," Osbourne told him.

"Why don't we go after some military R&D money to pay for this research? Why should we spend the company's money on R&D that may eventually benefit the Department of Defense when they've got millions waiting to be put to use for this sort of thing?" Destry wanted to know.

"We want to control all of the patent rights," Hay Newcomb pointed out. "If we go to DOD too soon, they'll slap government security on this whole thing and put out a security directive to the Department of Commerce that would prevent us from obtaining any patents."

"Besides, the costs involved at this stage are very small," Osbourne commented. "It's not as though we were ready to go into direct product development as we're doing with the shot-alloying process. When development toward a product begins to overshadow the research, we bring in development engineers from the relevant corporate divisions to work with the people here."

"That appears to be successful," Destry remarked. "Stone reports that he has very good relationships with your people."

"I would like to keep this sky hook work here as long as possible," Halden said quietly. "Bill hasn't mentioned a lot of the implications of the work, probably because they would sound unbelievable. Matter of fact, I don't even want to let the other division vice-presidents know about it. Bob, you're in on it because your division will probably be working on the first products. But, in any event, this is to be kept absolutely quiet and must not go beyond this room."

Osbourne then turned the conference over to Vic who stepped to the chalkboard and began by saying, "I'll not bore you with all of the mathematical details." He then proceeded to do so, quite unaware of the fact that his corporate executive audience was probably un-acquainted with any mathematics higher than college al-gebra, with the exception of Dr. Hayward Newcomb. Or the whole show may have been for the benefit of Newcomb.

I could follow Vic. It was a brilliant display of eru-dite mathematical logic, and I learned a great deal more about the Dynamics Systems project.

Vic thundered onward until he had to stop to catch his breath, and Bill brought him up short with, "I think you can all see that we appear to have developed a rea-sonably good theoretical foundation for the work. Thank you, Vic."

Vic started to give Bill a dirty look and opened his mouth as if to remark that he wasn't finished yet. Then he shut his mouth, nodded formally to his audience, and sat down.

Osbourne got up and began, "I'd like to bring you all up-to-date on what has happened in the past few days here. Some of our highly speculative speculations no longer look quite as speculative . . ." He went on to describe what had happened on Thursday and Sunday. Then he invited everyone to come down to the dynam-ics lab for a demonstration.

Carl was waiting with everything warmed up. I stepped in to give Carl a hand on the adjustments, re-marking to the corporate people, "I hope you all realize this is strictly an experimental proof-of-principle de-vice. Anything that would be developed out of this in the form of a product would be quite different . . ." Halden seemed to understand this. I am not sure that Destry or Sanatella did.

We put the sky hook through its paces, and it per-formed exactly as we predicted that it would.

"The unit is now seventy-six percent efficient in conversion of input energy into energy required to maintain its position displaced from the vertical rest position," I explained. "Carl, let's show them how much control we've developed over the performance of this device. Let's give it enough energy to swing it out to sixty centimeters and hold it."

And we did.

Osbourne put in, "We're developing this quite rapidly. Our calculations are very predictive. I think our work will pass the Schwartzberg test."

"What's that?" Sanatella wanted to know.

"A simple test developed by Harry Schwartzberg at RCA many years ago," Osbourne explained. "It states that the validity of a science is its ability to predict."

Grant Halden and Hay Newcomb were greatly excited. I am not sure that Destry was impressed at all. It was Phil Sanatella who asked, "Okay, so what else will it do?"

I was greatly taken aback at this remark. "What you're seeing is the production of a force without a reaction force or the expulsion of mass. There is no other way that pendulum could be displaced from its rest position without . . ."

"So?" Sanatella interrupted. "It pushes itself. Will it push a load?"

"Probably."

"Then let's see it do it!" Sanatella demanded. "It's no good if it can just push itself. It's got to be able to do useful work . . ."

Bill stepped into the breach at this point. "We're not to that point yet, Phil. What we've managed to accomplish here is highly unusual and completely new. There's no other device on Earth that will do this . . ."

"Doctor, I realize that this may be a scientific miracle," Sanatella said. "But I'd like to see it push a box across the floor."

"I'm not sure that we are ready to do that sort of thing yet," I put in. "It'll require that we retune the unit and . . ."

But Bill Osbourne acceded to Sanatella's stupid request. "Carl, grab that cardboard box over there and stick about twenty pounds of junk in it."

Carl fired back, "Doctor, that'll change the characteristics of the system, and it takes a long time to retune this unit."

"Yes, I know that, but let's just give it a try to see what might be involved," Osbourne replied. "We're going to have to do something like this sooner or later. So let's treat it as an experiment."

I helped Carl fill the box with assorted electronic components and some of the damaged parts from the previous sky hook unit. We both estimated that it weighed about twenty pounds. Carl set it on the floor in front of the deenergized sky hook so that the front face of the unit was against the side of the box. "Bill, this isn't going to work!" I warned.

"It may not. Uh, Grant and Hay, I want you to understand that the sky hook unit here wasn't designed to push things. When we try to push the box, we will have changed the system and its reaction times and tuning . . ."

"I realize that this is just an experiment," Halden said.

I ran some quick calculations which Vic verified, but I could see that Aboud was upset, too. "Give me about seventy-three watts on the drive," I told Carl. "I'll try to keep an eye on the phasing here. Maybe we can tune it as we come up to power."

Carl powered-up as Bill read off the check list. But I couldn't get the phasing to adjust properly. "We're way out in left field!"

"Try it anyway!" Osbourne told me.

"Okay, full power on the drive. I'll do my best to adjust phasing as we come up to full power . . ."

"Coming up!" Carl called. "Forty watts . . . forty-five watts . . . fifty watts . . ."

Nothing happened. My phasing was getting completely out of hand.

Then the sawtooth drive circuit went up in a cloud of smoke.

Chapter Nine

"Screwed by Murphy again!" Bill Osbourne remarked.

I was about to say something a lot more pithy.

"What do you mean?" Phil Sanatella snapped.

Bill sighed. "Phil, this experiment wasn't designed to do what we just tried."

"Well, I don't see that it's anything except an interesting toy," Sanatella griped. "I can't see a single market for it!"

"There isn't any market for this. It's a test instrument to prove out the foundations for lots of new products," Osbourne tried to explain.

"Well, how soon will you have a working product that I can get my teeth into?"

"That was not the purpose for bringing you along, Phil," Grant Halden reminded him with considerably more diplomacy than I was capable of mustering at that moment. I hoped that he would follow up as a good manager should and have some very private words with this marketing jerk. The NEMECO president turned to Bill. "In spite of the fact that something burned out, I understand perfectly that you were trying to oblige Phil by attempting something that you weren't prepared to demonstrate. But I am very encouraged by this work, Bill. I want you to keep it up."

"Thank you, Grant."

"Bill, what's your next step?" Hay Newcomb wanted to know as Carl began turning off electronics.

"First of all, we've got to get on with the usual work of an experimenter: rebuilding equipment that failed and analyzing why," the research director explained.

"As Triviality Number Fourteen says, 'Experience gained is directly proportional to the amount of equipment ruined.' We'll get this working again in a matter of days. Then we'll make some more measurements and either modify the sky hook so that it pushes loads or build another one that will."

"When do you think you might have a sky hook that will push loads?" Bob Destry wanted to know.

"We don't invent on schedule, Bob," Osbourne explained carefully. "It could be weeks or it could be months."

"What seems to be the basic problem with hitching it to loads?" Hay Newcomb wanted to know.

Vic stepped into the fray at this point. "The nature of the load changes the nature of the system." He grabbed a pad of paper and began writing equations with Newcomb looking over his shoulder. The rest of us stood around for a moment and tried not to look bored. But Newcomb was following what Vic was doing and was nodding his head and grunting in agreement as Vic's pencil flew across the paper.

After about a minute, Bill broke in with, "Vic, why don't you continue to explain this to Hay up in the conference room? Let's let Carl get busy cleaning up and repairing things."

The corporate types left about thirty minutes later. Hay Newcomb was either satisfied that Vic was on top of the theoretical reasons for the failure of the sky hook to push the box of junk . . . or he was covering his lack of understanding of Vic's math.

I guess I looked completely defeated because Bill slapped me on the shoulder and said, "Mike, it all went beautifully!"

"But we shouldn't have tried the experiment that Sanatella suggested! One should never, *never* run a demonstration experiment without testing it beforehand . . ."

"I know that!"

"Then why did you tell us to go ahead?"

"Many reasons, most of them having to do with corporate politics that you don't see from here in the lab

. . . but I'm involved in them every day at the Front Office," Osbourne explained. We were in the quiet of my office now, and Osbourne lit up one of his stinky brown cigarettes in his long holder. I didn't have an ash tray in my office, but Osbourne didn't seem to care. Well, if the corporate research director wanted to flick his cigarette ashes on the floor of my office, he was welcome to do it! "Ah, that's better! Halden doesn't like people to smoke around him."

"Neither do I, but in this case you're the boss," I remarked quietly.

"I know. Sorry, but rank has some privileges, Mike."

"Can you clue me in to some of this corporate politics?" I wanted to know. "I might not make a complete ass of myself someday or hurt our work here if I was briefed a bit . . ."

"I thought most of it would be pretty obvious," Osbourne said. He took a blank sheet of quad-ruled paper from a pad on my desk and proceeded to fold it origami style until he had manufactured himself an ash tray. "Did you watch Grant Halden's face when he saw the sky hook swing out from the vertical?"

"I was sort of busy watching my meters and the unit."

"Halden was like a kid with a new toy! He may have to be a hard-nosed bottom-line executive to run this company, make a profit, and pay a dividend to the stockholders. But inside, the man is an incurable romantic. Do you know anything about his background?"

"Not very much," I admitted.

"He comes from a very old and well-off New York family of lawyers, and he was the second son. He got his B.A. and M.A. from Yale in English literature with his graduate thesis on the work of the nineteenth-century romantic poets."

"How did he ever get to be president of NEMECO?" I wanted to know.

"When his father died, most of the estate went to his older brother who was a lawyer, following in the old man's footsteps. Naturally, the older brother got the majority of the estate because of the way he worked

things with Father. Halden discovered that he couldn't
get much of a job with a specialty in romantic English
poetry. So he took what he had of his inheritance plus
the considerable clout that he couldn't help but inherit,
and he went through Wharton, sometimes working
when his cash ran low. He got an M.B.A., his key to
executive management ranks." Osbourne snuffed out
his cigarette in his origami ash tray, folded it up, and
tossed it into my wastebasket. Blowing out his cigarette
holder, he replaced it in his shirt pocket and continued,
"So we've got an unusual man running this company,
and he is doing very well at it."

"I guess so!"

"Right now, Halden's mind is preoccupied about
what he's going to do with the sky hook . . . which he
fully understands is a major scientific breakthrough.
He knows we'll get the bugs worked out! And Hay
Newcomb is congratulating himself because the basic
research policy he's always championed is beginning to
pay off. Both of these men are on our side, they are the
top people in the company, and we gave them encour-
agement today."

"Yeah, Bill, but I'm worried about Sanatella," I told
him.

"Why?"

"Phil Sanatella is out for Phil Sanatella. In the long
haul—or even over the short haul if he can figure out
some way to do it—he's out to scramble up the greasy
pole of management and to hell with who he steps on
or the company he happens to screw in the process.
NEMECO's only a stepping stone to further his career
. . . and the only way he is going to further his career
is not by success but by his track record advancing
through corporate ranks. When I was an ag pilot, we'd
run into his kind all the time. They've got beautiful re-
sumes that appear they've really got something on the
ball . . . until you look into the companies and find
out that these guys never really did anything at all. In
fact, they go through a company wreaking havoc." I
stopped for a moment, then added, "Believe me, Bill,
Sanatella doesn't give a damn about us, and he'll side

with anybody in the company who doesn't like Corporate Research and wants to economize by disbanding this operation."

Bill Osbourne scratched his bushy moustache for a moment in reflection, then added, "Pretty shrewd evaluation, Mike. But I wouldn't worry about Sanatella. Both Halden and Newcomb knew good and well that he was showing off. Sanatella didn't make any points here today."

"Maybe. Maybe not." I tried to convince my boss. "But he's up in the front office. He can get the ear of anybody in the company or its divisions because he's marketing manager. He's got a lot of clout. He calls the shots on how much of what can be sold to whom and when. The company treasurer and the controller are going to listen to him, and they sign the checks. And he obviously has some clout with the division managers like Destry who are also bottom-line men."

"I think you've put your finger on the man who should worry us most," Bill Osbourne pointed out. "We started this operation sharing some of Destry's plant space up in Trumbull even though he flatly opposed a corporate research outfit because he wanted to control it himself. Destry came to us from General Electric, and he's been thoroughly trained by GE. GE's R&D is divided among its divisions. Destry knows the GE system works. He wants it implemented in NEMECO. Furthermore, if it was, he would get his percentage of the current corporate research budget to plow into his own division's product development work."

"But, Bill, he's got his engineer down here right now working on a new industrial process that he's going to take over in a couple of months . . ."

"You don't understand the man," Bill told me. "He wants to be the next president of NEMECO."

"That makes sense."

"But the ladder is blocked by Newcomb. The only way Destry can get to the presidency is to get Newcomb out of the way . . ."

"And the best way to do that is to discredit Newcomb's corporate research policy," I added.

"More than that," Bill said. "If Destry can get Corporate Research discredited, it may also affect Grant Halden who has supported it . . . and it might mean that Halden would be eased out by the Board."

"You know, Bill, from the external appearance of NEMECO, I wouldn't guess that all of this political maneuvering was going on. NEMECO gives the appearance of being such a stable, well-run company."

"It is stable and well-run, and the Board will see to it that it maintains that image for the sake of the security analysts," Osbourne pointed out. "The corporate image isn't there for the sake of customers; they only care whether or not NEMECO products work. The image is there for the boys on Wall Street who can make or break the stock of the company . . . and the majority of the stock is held by the Cranmer family plus the executives and employees of NEMECO." Osbourne got up and stretched. "Rough day! Afternoon's just about shot to hell, so it's not worth it for me to go back up to the Front Office. Good time to go down to the chandler's and get those fittings for my boat . . ."

"Yeah, I'm bushed, too," I admitted. "I've been four solid days on that sky hook, and I can't face it right now . . . not after what happened."

"Take the rest of the day," Bill told me. "And tomorrow, if you want."

"No, I don't need that much time. I have to buy a car."

"Why don't you get Mac Roston to go with you?"

"I don't want to take somebody away from their work here."

"In astronomy, did you always work an eight-hour day?"

"Well, no, but . . ."

"Mac was trained in Stuttgart and Wolfsburg," Bill explained. "He runs Formula Vee cars as a hobby. Mac knows every car lot between Greenwich and New Haven. Have a good time, and get a good car!"

Mac Roston not only acquiesced to my request but seemed to thoroughly enjoy doing it. When it came to automobiles, Mac Roston knew what he was about. He had the same involvement with cars that I did with planes.

"I'd suggest a VW Bug if you can find a good one," Mac suggested as we tooled out on I-95 toward Milford where he knew of a "reasonably honest used car dealer."

"How about mechanics that will work on them? I've had mechanics in Arizona flatly refuse to work on any foreign car."

"Just bring it to the lab on Saturday."

"That's right! You were trained in Wolfsburg."

"And Stuttgart," Mac reminded me.

We chatted as Mac drove, and he surprised me. His father was a top corporate executive in one of the large multi-national conglomerates headquartered in Greenwich. He was raised in Westport in an environment of achievers . . . except that he found out he liked cars. Mac had turned down a chance to go to Harvard. "I'm not the type who likes to run people. I much prefer working with good machinery and getting it to run right."

"Yeah, Mac, but the world is run by people who run other people," I pointed out.

"I don't want to run the world," Mac said flatly. "Unlike a lot of other people, I think the world's being run better than it ever has been in history. I'm content to live in it . . . Okay, here is a reasonably honest lot. I've had fair dealings with the Hungarian . . . not that he is any more honest than most other used car salesmen. Let's look for a Bug about six years old; they were the best that Wolfsburg ever turned out for the American market."

I left the Hungarian's used car lot driving a light green VW Bug with a sun roof. Furthermore, Mac got Harry the Hungarian to agree to a conditional sale provided we did not put more than 100 miles on the car. Mac could check it over completely and had a week in which to do it.

Mac didn't take that long. I bought him supper, and we spent the evening with the VW pulled into the delivery entrance at the back of the lab that just "happened" to be a double garage door at grade level. There just "happened" to be a hydraulic jack, a drip pan, and a few other necessities right there, too. I recalled what Bill had said about binding the mouths of the kine who tread the grain.

Mac told me he didn't want to take chances because his reputation with me was riding on the line. Actually, I think he wanted to get that VW apart to find out for himself if it was really as good as it appeared to be.

It was. I learned a lot about my new car that night, and it pleased me because I don't like to ride around in any piece of machinery of my own unless I am intimate with it. More than once, this idiosyncracy has saved my life.

When I got back to Morse Manor, Ruth fretted that I hadn't gotten a good supper. She offered to warm up left-overs, but I declined and munched on a couple of oatmeal cookies she had made that evening.

Peter Wilding was excited about my VW. He drove an ancient Porsche that needed a lot of work. "Do you think Mac Roston would be willing to work on my Porsche? It needs new brakes, and there's something that goes *clunk clunk* when I down-shift from third to second."

"Why don't you take it to a Porsche shop?" I wanted to know.

"Thieves and con artists! Liars!" Wilding exploded. "Why, the last time I took it in for work, do you know what they did to me and what they charged me to do it?" This led to a long and rambling diatribe on how much it had cost for them not to fix it.

As Wilding rambled, I thought that Mac would know better than I about how to handle this situation. Although we had spent the evening in the NEMECO Corporate Research Center Laboratories fixing my car, and although I knew that there was no prohibition against doing such a thing as long as it was not done during working hours when somebody from the Front Office—say, the controller—might happen to drop by, I strongly doubted that it would be okay for Mac to work on the car of a known industrial spy there.

With great pride, I drove the Morse Manor lab car pool the following morning.

I found Wendell Stone sitting in my office making sketches on a couple of sheets of my quad-ruled paper.

"I heard about yesterday," Wendell told me in his clipped nasal manner. "Got to thinking about it last night. My eldest issue, Lowell, knows more than I do about electronics although he's only in high school. Got his ham license. Gear all over the place, and the roof covered with antennae. He suggested something that might work . . ."

Wendell Stone had absolutely no theoretical grasp of Osbourne's work, but he had an intuitive feel for the sky hook concepts. He couldn't work the math, but he could design things with a ballpark feel for the size, speed, and so forth.

He'd come up with a concept for automatically tuning the system for changing conditions! What he sketched out on my desk that morning was incredibly crude. He didn't specify the electronic circuits, but outlined them by using a functional flow chart diagram. He didn't know what should go in each box to make it do its job, but he certainly knew how to make his whole device operate. I didn't even know what should go inside some of the flow chart boxes, but I felt sure that Carl would.

Basically, Wendell's device was a feedback system that compared the desired characteristics of the sky hook against the moment-by-moment actual operating conditions, and then proceeded to change the operating values to bring the sky hook back into the desired range. It sounds complicated to describe in words; the equations make it much simpler to understand.

"Wendell, let's write this up as a patent disclosure, and I'll witness it," I told him as I studied it. "This is undoubtedly going to be one of the key aspects of getting sky hooks to work."

"Only on one condition, in spite of what the yellow-dog patent rights contract says," Wendell muttered.

"What's your condition?"

"The company gets the patent rights under the agree-

ment we all sign when we come to work for this paternalistic outfit," Stone explained. "I'll get the usual
hundred-dollar check so that there have been tokens of
value exchanged to make the contract binding. But I
demand and I get the ribboned patent document. It
should be mine because I did it. The company has only
the rights to it."

"Has there been some problem with this in the past?"
I wanted to know.

"Yes. John Whiteside, the legal eagle in the Front
Office who handles patent matters for NEMECO, likes
to frame the ribboned copies for his office wall."

"That sounds like an ego-trip."

"I agree."

Wendell and I worked over the concept for about an
hour and then went back to the dynamics lab to let
Carl look it over. The technician suggested several
changes because of his special expertise in electronics.
"Hell, yes, it'll work! Let me get a photocopy of this,
and I'll get busy with catalogs to figure out what I can
get that's already built."

Once Carl had his copy, we took the papers up to
Len's office to discuss it. Vic and Tammy were there.
This gave us the opportunity to bring everyone but Bill
up to date. Vic managed to get in his early-morning
licks.

"Where the hell have you been?" Aboud wanted to
know in no uncertain terms. "I've been looking all over
for you! I want you to help Tammy run the numbers on
the phasing matter."

"We've been working on the phasing matter," I reported. "It's not a matter of phasing at all. Wendell
came up with the answer at home last night."

"You did?" Vic asked in disbelief, pointing at Stone.

"I did . . . with some help from Lowell."

Vic snorted. "Rubber bands and staples again?"

"Now, don't start with that sort of a bias, Vic," Len
warned him. "What have you got, Wendell?"

We explained it. Tammy and Len nodded in understanding as Wendell and I presented the details. It became patently obvious that Vic did not believe in the

empirical approach. And it was also obvious that Wendell Stone did not believe in the theoretical approach. I could sense that there was very little love lost between the vitriolic mathematician and the desiccated Vermont engineer. The thinking processes of the two men were so enormously different that understanding each other was almost impossible.

"How in the world did you manage to come up with this concept, Wendell? It's a brilliant piece of work." Len told the engineer.

"Flattery will get you everywhere; keep talking."

"Seriously, how do you manage to keep coming up with these elegant solutions to the complex problems we always run into around here?" the lab director wanted to know.

"Common sense plus a lot of ESP."

"Come on, now! Extra-sensory perception?" Len asked with a grin.

"Nope. ESP stands for exaggeration of system parameters," Wendell explained. "It's a very useful trick in development work. Ask yourself such questions as, 'What happens if I make this part very big . . . or very small . . . or very fast . . . or very slow?' When you take one part of a gadget and blow it completely out of proportion, you can usually get a good idea of what to do and in what direction to proceed. I just asked myself what would happen if we wanted to build a sky hook that would push the whole world."

"Oh, that's easy enough to do!" Aboud snapped. "Given enough time, we could move the world with the sky hook hanging in the lab . . ."

"Maybe in a couple of million years," Len pointed out. "But I see what you mean, Wendell. When you make the load very large, it will drastically change the response time of the system. So you don't change the phasing. You change the driving frequency . . ."

Tammy squinted at the rough sketches. "This is simple! I should be able to write a program for this in thirty minutes or less."

"But you're neglecting any possible GI radiation effects," Vic objected. "Those field equations are not easy to program!"

"We don't need field equations for this," Tammy told him. "We're working with an operating device, and the GI radiation is something totally theoretical. We can't measure it. In fact, we can't even detect it. If the equations will work without the radiation terms, I'd rather use them because they're simpler."

"You mean you want to go back to the simple transient theory that Osbourne worked out last year?" Vic asked.

"If it works, why not?" Len put in.

"I'd expect that out of you!" Vic snapped at Len. "Well, go ahead if you think it will speed things up. I'll work it through on the microcomputer using the field equations."

"Hold on, Vic!" Len put in quickly as Tammy started to object as well. "I can't let you monopolize the micro for theoretical work when there's an urgent requirement that it be available for experimental design work!"

Vic got to his feet. "That microcomputer doesn't belong to the laboratory department. It's *mine*!" He tapped himself in the middle of his chest with his forefinger. "It was purchased for the use of my theoretical department. I proposed getting the micro, and I came up with the justification that resulted in the purchase approval! I'm going into Tammy's office, sit down at the terminal, and run my field equations for the design. Len, if you want to pull Tammy off my work and put her on lab work, that's your privilege. She's on the lab payroll. But that microcomputer is here in the lab only because there isn't room for it in my office up at corporate headquarters. I'll let you know when I am finished using it!" With that, he stomped out the door.

Nobody said anything. Tammy, Wendell, and Len just sat there for a moment. Then Len quietly remarked, "Mike, will you let Tammy use your hand programmable?"

"Sure! I'll even help her out because it's sometimes short on memory, and we'll have to resort to pencil and paper recording of some data. Besides, I'm also handy at programming it."

"Okay, we'll make do," the lab director said.

"I'll give Carl a hand on the nuts-and-bolts end of things," Wendell volunteered.

"Uh, Wendell, I appreciate that, but can you do it without neglecting the shot-alloying project?" Len asked. "Your paycheck comes over from Bob Destry's division. If Destry ever suspects that you're spending time on some of our research programs here, Osbourne will have a lot of explaining to do."

"I can take care of my boss," Wendell assured him. "I am making very good progress, the process is working well, and we are well ahead of schedule. In any event, Destry has other problems that are keeping him occupied right now, so I'm the least of his worries because I'm not adding to his G&A expense over there with a desk, a drawing board, and all the rest."

"Okay, Wendell, please keep it that way," Len advised him. He sighed. "Let's get to work."

Tammy and Wendell got up to leave, but I remained seated and leaned across Len's desk. "Hey! I don't object to having to use my hand programmable. But are you going to let Aboud get away with what he just did? We could really use the micro! It would speed things up enormously. But that's beside the point. Aboud just walked all over you on a matter that should be brought up to Bill Osbourne for a decision. Aren't you going to call Bill?"

"No, I'm not," Len Marshall admitted.

"But *why?*"

"Who has the office next to Bill Osbourne at corporate headquarters?"

"What do you mean?"

"I mean that Victor Aboud and I are supposedly both on the same level of the Corporate Research totem pole when you look at the organizational chart," Len went on to explain. His hands were quietly folded on the desk in front of him. "Aboud not only has Osbourne's ear, but also Hay Newcomb's . . . and Aboud has Newcomb convinced that Aboud is one hell of a research scientist with his MIT degrees and fancy footwork with mathematics at the chalkboard."

"So?"

"So Bill Osbourne is going to find out about this, probably when he comes down later today to see how things are going. I won't go running to him like a little kid whose brother has taken candy away. I'll wait for Bill to find out for himself and see that we did our best here to keep things working on a level keel in spite of it. In other words, I'm giving Aboud all the rope he is capable of taking."

"Why are you giving him rope?" I wondered.

"Don't you know that the only thing you can count on in this world is change? This set-up isn't going to last forever. As I said, I will cooperate with Vic to the utmost *except* for cooperating with him toward one goal."

"Keep talking. I am beginning to get the picture."

Len Marshall looked at Wendell Stone, Tammy Dudley, and me in turn. "I don't want Victor Aboud to be my boss as the Director of Research someday."

Chapter Ten

The intricacies of NEMECO corporate politics were no less complex than those of the various ag aviation companies that I had flown for, and certainly different only in kind and not in degree from academia and the astronomical observatories that dotted the mountains of the world. I wanted to ignore these ins and outs of NE-MECO corporate politics and just do my job, but that was impossible.

Tammy and I spent the rest of that day plus half of the next working with my programmable and a pad of paper. I kept waiting for Bill Osbourne to show up, but he didn't. I worked out an excuse to call him at corporate headquarters to ask him a question about an equation, but Helen, his secretary, told me Osbourne was in New York City.

That certainly blew a huge hole in Carl's rumor. Osbourne was in New York City and Tammy Dudley was sitting right next to me crunching numbers on a computer.

Vic stuck his head into my office where we were working. "Aren't you finished yet?" he asked.

"Thanks to you, no," I told him.

"Well, I've got my data, and we've got to add some additional equipment to Stone's glue-and-tape system," Vic reported smugly. "I want to check a couple of these figures with you."

I looked up at him. "Vic, when we get some numbers to compare with yours, we'll do so. In the meantime, please get the hell out of here so that we can go back to work."

"I thought your approach was so simple?"

"It would be if we had the microcomputer to work with."

"Well, I'm finished with it now, so you can go and use it if you need to." And he was gone.

Tammy sighed. "And just when we were ready to run some of these tables!"

I looked at her. "We could rewrite this program, but it would take another couple of hours . . ."

Tammy looked pensive, then said, "I think I can do it faster directly in machine language. We've got an awfully good assembler-editor program. Anyway, let's try! It's better than having to write everything down every time we want to go around the loop in the feedback system again!"

We had missed lunch, and I felt my blood sugar level going down. Tammy produced a box of cookies from the lower drawer of her file cabinet, and we munched cookies while the microcomputer crunched numbers.

It took us longer than we had figured. So we went home to Morse Manor in the car pool for dinner. Afterward, I asked Tammy, "Are you game to go back to the lab?"

"Yes. I won't be able to sleep until we've run the program a couple of times and know that we've debugged it."

Peter Wilding noticed the two of us leaving Morse Manor. "Two of you going out, eh?"

"Yes," Tammy told him. And then she went on, "Going to a movie."

"Oh, really? Can I get Ruth and join you?"

"No," I told him.

He looked at me over the top of his horn-rimmed glasses with a sly smile. "Have fun, kids!"

Tammy laughed as we drove away from Morse Manor in my VW. "And *this* is driving Wilding bananas!"

"I'll bet you," I said, "that Peter Wilding will drive past the NEMECO lab in about an hour to see if my car is there . . . just checking. Of course, it won't be there."

Tammy looked quickly at me and started to say something.

I went on before she could speak, "Oh, don't worry! I'll park it alongside the equipment supply house across the street after I drop you off . . . just to make good our story. I'm aware of the fact that you want to keep your relationship with me on a professional level. I think I know why, so it doesn't bother me . . . much. I'll respect your wishes, Tammy, because you've got reasons for them."

"But, you . . ." she began, then fell silent.

I let her out in front of the lab. It was lit up because somebody was working there this evening. Then I parked the VW in the darkened lot next to the supply house. I let myself into the lab and found out that Mac Roston was working on Wilding's Porsche . . . but without Wilding's being present!

We got through the program, debugged it, and ran it twice with the same variables. Got the same answer both times. So we ran several variables and got a handle on the parameters of the load compensator system. After that, it was a matter of minutes until the microcomputer had it all laid out for us.

"Beautiful!" I chortled as I looked over the printout. "Carl should be able to begin putting this together tomorrow morning. Nice piece of work, Tammy."

"You certainly deserve some of the credit," she said.

I put the hard copy print-out down. "Incidentally, you should have bet with me; you would have won."

"What are you talking about?"

"Wilding isn't going to drive down here to check on us. Mac's working on Wilding's Porsche in the bay right now. I never thought Mac would work on any car except one belonging to the lab gang."

"Oh, Mac works on almost anybody's car down here. Besides, I enjoyed fibbing to Wilding. He's such a blustery old bumpkin who's far too nosy for his own good. It was fun to see his expression when I told him I was going out to a movie with you."

"It was a nice cover, Tammy, but I didn't get my water hot over it." I sighed, pushed my chair back, and got up to put the hard copy in the locked file for over-night security. Looking over my shoulder at her, I told her, "Tammy, you're a sexy woman, but you don't have a social life. You won't go out with me, even though I've asked you."

"Once," Tammy reminded me. "And you forget that I asked you to check me out in your plane."

"Yeah, but to be honest with you, I didn't pay too much attention because of . . . because of . . . well . . ."

"Because of the lab rumors?" she put in.

"Well, yes," I admitted.

Tammy got up, shut the door to my office, and came over to me. She looked up at me, put her arms around my neck, and told me, "Mike, kiss me."

So I did.

I put my heart into it and some body English as well. It was about a quarter of an inch off-center, but we rec-tified that quickly. I was gentle with her . . . very gentle.

She finally buried her head on my shoulder and whis-pered, "I've been so afraid . . ."

"Nothing to be afraid of . . . not now," I told her.

"You don't know . . ."

"Probably not. Maybe someday you'll want to tell me . . . in your own good time. There's no rush, Tam."

"My God, it's been so long . . . and you're so different and so careful." She looked up at me. "Mike, do you ever get angry, frustrated?"

"Sure I do. Who doesn't?"

"But you're not violent about it. I have never seen a man as angry as you at both Phil Sanatella and Vic. I thought you were going to hit Vic."

This woman had obviously seen far too much vio-lence in her life. "Look, Tam, I'm a little guy . . . and a lot of people in the world try to push us small types around," I explained, although I really didn't think I needed to. Anyway, it would serve to reinforce some things and maybe help give Tammy back her confi-dence. "When I was thirteen and knew that I wasn't going to get any bigger, I got tired of being pushed around. I went out for Tae Kwan Do, Korean self-defense. Good thing I was still a rookie when the guy who first pushed me hard after that lived so I didn't get a manslaughter charge on my record. Then I took up judo and karate because I had to temper my self-defense. So I've got a strong built-in restraint against anger accompanied by violence . . ."

Tammy smiled . . gorgeously, lighting up the whole room. "Well, Mike Call, you can forget the stories of the rumor mongers . . ."

"I don't really pay too much attention to people who mong rumors. There are too many other things to do."

"Such as?"

"Such as this." I kissed her again.

The second time was even better . . . and longer . . . and much more fervent.

She finally broke it off and pushed back to look up at me. It's refreshing to be with a woman who has to look up at me. "You're impossible!" she whispered.

"What do you mean?"

"Never mind. Do you know how difficult you're making things for me?"

"I think so."

"No, you don't. You couldn't." She sighed and disentangled herself from me with great reluctance. "Mike, we'd better get back to Morse Manor, please. Things are . . . Things are sort of getting out of hand for me . . . and it's not really your fault . . . except for being you . . ."

"Tammy, you'll work it out . . . And I'll help you, if you'll let me."

"Dear Mike!" She caressed my cheek. "You don't have the foggiest notion of what's involved. And I *cannot* tell you."

"However you want it, Tammy."

We went to the front door, and I called back to Mac on the intercom, "Hey, Mac, you still working on Wilding's car?"

His voice came back with the echoing resonance of

the rear shop, "Yeah, I'm about finished. Wilding said he'd pick it up in about fifteen minutes."

"Okay, Tammy and I are going back to Morse Manor. Lock up when you leave."

"Will do!"

I turned to Tammy. "You wait here. I'll get the car out of the lot across the street and bring it by."

Tammy looked uncomfortable. "I'm not afraid of the dark!"

"Well, I'd rather not have you walking into dark parking lots in the middle of Bridgeport at night," I told her.

I went out of the front door of the lab. The street was deserted. There wasn't a car moving. I sauntered across, walked around the lab supply house to the lot, and started to unlock my Bug.

I heard a noise behind me. I didn't stop to think about it. I moved fast, turning as I did so.

There were two of them, and they were big. I don't remember what they looked like. It was too dark. But they were coming at me.

Some people believe they can describe blow-by-blow what happens in a fight. I can't. In fact, I don't even remember what I did. Tae Kwan Do was so thoroughly indoctrinated in my mind that I didn't have to think about what I did. That's one of its principles. You don't have time to think.

I *do* recall one of them saying, "That's him!"

Then I was standing next to my VW and looking down at two big men who were sprawled on the ground. One of them had a right arm that was strangely bent. The other was either bleeding or had landed in a puddle of oil; in the darkness, I couldn't make out the color of the puddle.

My left forearm hurt where I had apparently warded off the swing of the cast-iron pipe that now lay on the ground at my feet. I didn't think my arm was broken.

I wasn't even breathing hard.

I unlocked the VW, climbed in, started it, and drove across the street to park in front of the lab where there was some light. I got out, rubbing my forearm which now had an ugly red bruise rising on it.

Tammy noticed it. "Mike, what happened?"

"Couple of goons tried to get me in the lot. They'll keep until the cops arrive." I went right to the phone and dialed the police.

Tammy got cold, wet towels for the bruise, but it was still hurting when the police showed up. I told them what happened and went with them to the parking lot.

Both men were gone, and so was the cast-iron pipe.

"You been drinking, sir?" one of the officers asked me.

"Not at all. I've been working at the NEMECO labs all evening. Look at my arm here! And I *know* I laid those two slobs out cold enough that they shouldn't be gone by now. It was only about fifteen minutes ago . . ."

One of the officers was shining his flashlight around. "Well, they're gone now, but you were right. Here's a puddle of blood. What did you do to them?"

"I don't know. They came at me, and I reacted. I'm black belt plus Tae Kwon Do," I explained.

"Well, that tells the story. Not much we can do at this point. Let's go back over to the NEMECO lab so you can answer a few questions for the report we have to file on this. How's your arm? Need to go to the hospital?"

"It hurts, but it isn't broken. If it isn't better by to-morrow, I'll see a doctor."

Tammy was upset. She was almost in tears as we sat there, answering questions for the two police officers. They finished and one of them snapped the metal cover back over his report board as he admonished me, "Mr. Call, Flagstaff, Arizona, was probably a well-run town with a pistol-totin' sheriff to keep law and order. But I'd suggest that you don't go alone into any dark areas in this part of Bridgeport at night. You were lucky . . ."

There was a knock on the front door. I got up, opened it, and saw Peter Wilding standing there. "Come in, Peter," I told him.

Wilding turned and waved to the taxi that was

double-parked next to the police cruiser. The cab sped off, its driver obviously anxious to get out of this part of town at this hour. Wilding looked at the two police officers. "What happened, Mike?"

"Couple of guys tried to mug me across the street."

The police officers were mildly interested in Wilding and asked him a few questions, requested identification, then left.

"You all right? Can I drive you home?" Wilding asked.

"Arm hurts like hell, but I can make it okay," I told him. "Let me call Mac on the intercom and tell him you're waiting up here. He'll drive your car around. I don't want you walking around outside the lab. Somebody might try to mug you, too."

Mac didn't answer the intercom.

Instead, he walked through the front door and handed Wilding the keys to the Porsche.

Tammy was very quiet on the way to Morse Manor. Once there, she insisted on tending to my arm . . . and I didn't object because she was taking some of the hurt out of it. I tried to tell her what had happened, but kept running up against the block of not remembering my every move.

"Tammy, I didn't go berserk or anything like that. It's like flying and having an emergency. I react without thinking when emergencies happen."

"But you put them both out cold!"

"Apparently not as cold as I wanted. They were gone when I went back with the police fifteen minutes later. I must be out of practice. But I'm damned sure I broke one guy's arm. I'm surprised that they could get up and move out of there that quickly."

"Maybe they didn't," she observed. "Maybe they had somebody waiting in a car nearby."

"That could be. I think I heard one of them say something like, 'That's him!' " I stopped for a moment. "Tammy, I wonder if they were after more than just mugging me and lifting my wallet?"

"What do you mean?"

"I wonder if they were after *me*?"

"There's no reason why they might want you," she pointed out.

I was bushed, and the reaction of the mugging had finally set in. I went up and went to bed.

My arm hurt. I lay there in the dark for what seemed an interminable time, unable to sleep with my throbbing arm. If I hadn't broken the radius, it was certainly badly bruised. I got up, went into the bathroom, took two aspirin, came back to bed, turned out the light, and tried to get to sleep.

All sorts of psychological fantasies were running through my mind. My memory played back what I *knew* one of the goons said: "That's him!" They weren't out to mug just anybody in a darkened parking lot. They were out to get somebody specific: me! Why? The sky hook? Who knew of it except the lab gang and some people at the corporate offices? And why me?

I lay there in the dark, trying to puzzle it all out.

I heard the door to my room open very quietly.

I couldn't see who it was.

I didn't move, but I was ready, tensed and prepared.

Then I smelled the perfume.

"Tammy?" I whispered.

"Shhhh!"

There was a rustle of a garment falling to the floor.

Then she was there next to me, warm and soft. Her hair brushed across my face.

"Tammy? Wh? . . ."

"Do you have a compulsion to talk while making love?" she whispered.

"No, but . . ."

"Then be quiet so the others don't hear us!" She didn't whisper but blew the words softly into my ear.

"Look, I'm . . ."

"I don't need to look. I can feel."

"You change your mind? Why?"

"You turned me on, Mike! The way you handled yourself tonight did something to me! I liked that . . . and I like this!"

I was not in top condition, but the fight had pumped me full of adrenaline and hyped me considerably. It started slowly, carefully, gently. It was as though she were releasing years of pent-up emotions. But she was responsive, eager, exciting, and enduring.

My arm didn't hurt a bit the rest of the night. But I really didn't have an opportunity to think about it.

Chapter Eleven

Len Marshall sent me over to see his family physician. My left forearm was not broken, but it was badly bruised. The doctor prescribed fifty milligrams of meperidine to take at night if ordinary acetamenophen, which I was to take during the day, didn't kill the pain. He also prescribed some sleepy pills and told me to check back in three days if things hadn't improved.

I never had to use the sleepy pills. And I took only one of the meperidine capsules.

Bill Osbourne was at the lab when I got back, and he wanted a full report.

"What do you make of it?" I asked him when I had wound it up.

Osbourne blew a cloud of smoke from one of his long brown cigarettes. "Park in front of the lab at night after this, regardless of whether you think Wilding may come by to check you out. I'd rather that he knows some of us are working late at night than to have you or any of the lab gang get mugged."

"Do you really think it was just an ordinary mugging, Bill?" I wondered. "After all, one of those guys said, 'That's him!' "

Bill thought about that for a moment. "Mike, we've got the industrial espionage types spotted. Frank Weldon, the controller, handles counter-intelligence quietly on the side. I'll report this to him, but I'm sure that he'll tell me that it was just the usual sort of thing one can expect in this part of town at night . . ."

Apparently, I looked unconvinced, because the research director went on, "If I had any indication or even the slightest suspicion that last night's incident was connected in any way with industrial espionage, I would be the first to tell you because you deserve to know . . . especially when you're involved."

I sighed and looked down at my sore arm. "Bill, if you say so . . ."

"I do. I would rather have you thinking about the sky hook than about industrial spies. Now, I understand that you and Tammy got it together last night . . ."

"Huh?" I looked up quickly at him, thinking that news travels very fast. Who had heard us?

"You got the load compensating system worked out."

"Oh, yeah, we did! Sorry, I haven't gotten it to Carl this morning yet because I had to go to see the doctor."

"Well, Tammy did after showing it to me. Nice work."

"Thanks."

"How come it differs from the one Vic worked up?" Osbourne wanted to know.

"Tammy and I were using your old transient approach."

"We thought that was pretty well out-dated. How come you used it?"

"It was easier to work out on my hand programmable."

Bill didn't say anything for a moment. "Why didn't you use the microcomputer?"

"Vic has priority on it because it's part of his Analysis and Contracts department, and he wanted to run out the design with the GI radiation equations. So Tammy and I had to use my programmable instead."

Bill looked at the end of his cigarette stump, snuffed it out, and dropped the remains in the waste basket. Blowing the smoke out his holder, he said, "Didn't you talk to Len about it?"

"Len was there when Vic preempted the microcomputer."

"I see . . ."

"And I didn't want to make waves. Someday I'll have sufficient reason but I didn't think this was it."

"Where did you learn all the diplomacy, Mike?" Bill Osbourne asked rhetorically.

"I save my violence for when I need it."

"Yeah, I guess you do. Okay, I've approved the system that you and Tammy designed. Both Len and I feel that it is closer to being in the ballpark than Vic's."

"I hope you don't tell him that . . ."

"You let me worry about it. How long will it take you and Carl to put the load compensating system together so that the sky hook will push a load?"

I ran through some mental calculations. I had explicit faith in Carl's ability, but I didn't know exactly how long it would take. I finally made a guess. "We might have it ready by the middle of next week. It might be sooner if we worked through the weekend again . . ."

"I won't ask you to do that. You worked all last weekend and most of the nights this week. If you think you might have it in operation by next Thursday, I want to ask Dr. Serge Korsinski and Dr. Ted Mayan to come up."

"Good! I want to meet them!"

"You may not feel that way after you've tangled with Mayan!"

I didn't get to see Tammy except at lunch in the lab that day. It didn't make any difference; I had been with her a lot in the last twenty-four hours. She was working on some of Vic's stuff, and I was trying to steer clear of the situation with Vic.

Carl and I got busy on the load compensator, and things progressed slowly.

During lunch hour, I had to recount my encounter of the previous night in vivid detail. I have been liberally educated in the fine art of hangar flying by some of the best aeronautical raconteurs in the world: American ag pilots. What else do you do when the weather is foul and you sit around the hangar all day? "There I was, flat on my back, thirty feet above the cotton field, nothing between me and the ground but the farmer's daughter . . ." I think that has come down through the decades of aviation, being changed from time to time depending on whether or not there was a war on at the time. I didn't tell any outright lies because that is considered highly unethical by the Association of American Hangar Pilots. But one is permitted to stretch the truth as far as one thinks one can without breaking something. In any event, I utilized my hangar flying training to its utmost and stuck in a lot of violence . . . but I left out the sex.

Tammy was very quiet that evening as the two of us sat alone in the living room at Morse Manor. Carl and Peter were doing the dishes, and Ruth was downstairs in the cellar.

"Want to go to a movie?" I asked her.

"No, Mike, not tonight. But thank you for asking."

"If it will make you feel any better, I can give you the old cliché."

"Pardon me?"

"You know, the one where I say, 'But I still respect you!' "

After a moment's hesitation—I think it was difficult for her to realize that my sense of humor is sometimes a little wacky—she laughed. Then, with mock seriousness, she replied, "Oh, you don't know how relieved I am to hear you say that!"

"I've never met anyone like you," I told her.

"I have the same feeling, Mike."

"I haven't figured you out yet, but that doesn't bother me."

"Someday, I hope that I can tell you all about it." She paused for a moment, then added, "Do you love anyone, Mike?"

That was very surprising. "Uh . . . Tammy, I'm not sure that I know what love really is. I've experienced puppy love as a teen-ager. But I haven't had anybody to 'love' for more than half my life. Just airplanes and astronomy. What about you?"

"I loved somebody once. It turned out that he wasn't a real man; he was a beast. But I loved him . . . and it hurt a great deal. I'm not anxious to fall in love again," she admitted softly. "I like you, Mike, and I enjoy being with you . . ."

"I'm patient."

"Oh, Mike, there're so many things that you don't know . . ."

We broke it off because Ruth came up from the basement. She was concerned about my arm. "Let me see how it is tonight, Mike. Does it still hurt?"

"A little."

"What did that doctor tell you to do?"

"Take aspirin and call him in three days. Gave me some pain killers to use."

"That's what I thought! You should soak it in epsom salts. I found some in the basement."

It helped. House mother Ruth played her role very well.

But I felt stupid as hell sitting in the kitchen with my left arm soaking in a dishpanful of hot water and epsom salts. Inconvenient.

Saturday morning, I just *had* to go flying. In the first place, it helps keep a plane in good running order if it's flown at least thirty minutes a week at 75 percent power. Cleans the rust off the cylinder walls and boils the water out of the engine oil. I crawled into my grungy old coveralls and headed for Sikorski Memorial.

Wimpy Winfield was in the hangar. "Got the word you'd come aboard," he told me, "so I stuck your Cherokee back in the corner there. Jake Stock raised hell about it until I told him that this hangar was my turf."

"Cripes, Wimpy, I'll go rent a tie-down. I don't want to get you in trouble," I told him.

"Don't tie-down this plane outside . . . unless you want to end up with a pile of corrosion. We got plenty of room in here, and your Cherokee's a little bitty thing off in one corner," Wimpy replied. "Tell you what might help, though. Jake Stock took up cigar smoking back in the days when all hot pilots chewed stogies when they flew . . . like Joe Foss and Curt LeMay. 'Win' a box of panatellas at a church bazaar or something, and tell him you think he'd enjoy them more than you becuz you don't smoke 'em."

I got the message loud and clear.

I rolled *Two To Tango* out on the apron in the wan sunlight of the hazy sky of Long Island Sound. The old girl was filthy. After the trip, there were cheese cracker crumbs, a couple of old paper cups, and two empty soft drink cans in the cabin. I got her cleaned out. Then I borrowed some Stoddard solvent from Wimpy, scrubbed the engine down, and got the accumulated grime off it. The leading edges of the wings and horizontal stabilator were coated with a fine black scum where they had met the crud-filled air over Pennsylvania and New York. So I washed her down, too.

Although NEMECO had its own fuel storage and pumping facility for its aircraft, I felt it would be too much to ask for some sort of arrangement for fuel with Wimpy. So I went to the nearby FBO, plopped down my gasoline credit card, and arranged for an account for 100-octane.

Tammy Dudley was waiting for me when I got back to the NEMECO hangar.

"Flight review for the Mile-High Club?" I asked her.

She smiled. "You promised to check me out in this bird."

"That I did. You current?"

Whereupon Tammy Dudley pulled out her wallet and displayed her FAA commercial pilot's license with instrument rating, current second class medical certificate, FCC third class radiotelephone operator's permit, and Connecticut pilot's license. She also handed me her log book.

Damn if she didn't have more than 1,500 hours, some of it in heavy multiengine stuff like the Douglas DC-3. That didn't surprise me; there are still thousands of old Gooney Birds flapping their wings along the airways of the world.

She also had a camera bag and two flight bags with her.

"Going somewhere?" I asked her.

"Martha's Vineyard," she told me. "We can shoot the ILS approach up there. I need to get some instrument time. So I packed an overnight kit for you, too."

"You figure on staying overnight?"

"We've been working pretty hard. We need the change. Ever been to Martha's Vineyard?"

"Nope. How are the grapes?"

"It's a pretty place. You'll like it."

"If you let me see any of it . . ." I told her.

It was only about an hour's flight. I got her checked out in the Cherokee, but she checked me out on flying in the East Coast environment with its low visibility and high humidity. I was used to flying high in the West. Tammy taught me to cruise about a thousand feet above the water in order to stay away from the jet traffic between New York and Boston.

We spent Saturday night in a little old colonial type inn. It had a genuine feather bed. Feather beds do indeed have a great deal to recommend them.

The fog had rolled in overnight. We filed IFR for return to Bridgeport, and I took off under zero–zero visibility conditions. I had filed for a more-or-less direct flight, but Center had their own ideas of where I ought to go. So I canceled IFR, and cruised above the fog bank to Bridgeport, where the gunk had burned off by the time we arrived.

I found that the trip, short as it had been, left me completely relaxed and feeling six feet broad across the shoulders. Turned out that Tammy was a good pilot. "You can fly the right seat with me any time you want," I told her after she had shot a perfect ILS Runway 6 approach, not letting the instrument needles drift a fraction off center during the approach.

As we got out of *Two To Tango* in front of the NE-MECO hangar, we met Bob Destry and Phil Sanatella about to go aboard the Aero Commander with Pete Kukowski.

"Hi!" Destry called out. "Your plane, Mike?"

"Yeah. Where you headed?"

"Pittsburgh. Mill Controls Division joint marketing conference with Mill Equipment Division tomorrow morning," Sanatella remarked. "Where'd you fly to?"

"Oh, we just went up to the Vineyard on a sight-seeing flight," Tammy put in. Well, she was right, even though it sounded like we'd been out for a couple of hours or so.

I pushed *Two To Tango* over to the corner of the

apron and left it there. "Let's not unload quite yet," I remarked to Tammy. "Wait until they've gone. Let's go to Mama's and have some lunch."

The Aero Commander was gone by the time we got back.

Carl and I got well along on the sky hook on Monday until Vic dropped by to see what was going on. "That doesn't look right," he said as he checked the equipment. He went over and looked in Carl's lab notebook. "What are you two building here?"

"The load compensator circuit," Carl told him. I kept my mouth shut.

"This isn't the system I designed!" Vic complained.

"I don't know anything about that, Vic. It's the one Len said for us to put together."

"What about this, Mike? Who changed my design?"

"It isn't your design," I told him flatly.

"What?"

"Like Carl told you, Bill and Len told us to build this one . . ."

Vic growled several phrases in Arabic that I did not understand. He started to storm out of the dynamics lab, then stopped short and turned to me. "Mike, did you and Tammy enjoy Saturday night at Martha's Vineyard?" And without another word, he left.

Carl looked at me. There was a certain amount of admiration as well as envy in his expression.

"Now, how do these rumors get started?" I asked nobody in particular.

"I don't know," Carl remarked, "but it's a good one, Mike! If it's true, I want to find out what you've got that I ain't got!"

I decided to joke my way out of it. "Sex appeal! She likes them six feet tall and built accordingly!"

Carl laughed, and I hoped that it would be the end of that.

How did Vic know?

Osbourne checked in later in the day. "Going to make Thursday?"

"Should have it cooking tomorrow, boss," Carl remarked.

"No troubles foreseen unless it doesn't pass the smoke test," I added.

"Good! Mike, let's go up to Tammy's office. I want to check something with you."

Once in Tammy's office with the two of us, Bill closed the door, turned to me, and asked, "Did you two go to Martha's Vineyard over the weekend?"

Tammy almost came unglued. But I looked Osbourne straight in the eye and softly told him, "Doctor, what we do with our private lives is none of your business."

"I thought so." He sat down on a corner of Tammy's desk and told us, "Look, I really don't care who does what to whom outside this lab. But, for God's sake, don't make the mistake of being obvious in front of corporate headquarters types. I don't mean to intrude in your private affairs, but sometimes they might have implications that affect all of us in Corporate Research. End of lecture."

"Bill, who told you this? I want to find out where such a rumor could get started," I snapped. If I sounded a little angry, I was. But not for the reason I hoped Osbourne would expect.

"Never mind."

"Dr. Osbourne," Tammy put in, vexed. "I want to know who's spreading ugly rumors involving *me*."

The research director sighed. "Here's the way I got it. Sanatella and Destry were on the NEMECO ramp when the two of you landed yesterday . . ."

"Yeah, I remember them when we landed. Tammy asked me to check her out in my Cherokee. So we went up the Sound to Martha's Vineyard," I explained.

"Sanatella went over to look inside your ship while you two went for lunch. Claims he saw overnight bags in the back seat. He called Vic this morning from Pittsburgh to have Vic check some marketing numbers for him, and he told Vic. Vic—out of no malice on his part, mind you, but recognizing the possibilities—told me, as he should have."

Tammy put her face in her hands. I just sighed.

"As I told you, I don't care," Osbourne went on.

"Purely circumstantial evidence insofar as I'm concerned. Ugly rumor passed along by a man who's going up the ladder by running over people with his track shoes on. But Destry's a prude and Sanatella's a sneak. Both of them are on the make. Sanatella now has a juicy tidbit on you, Mike, and he'll use it if he can at the most inappropriate time for you and with the best timing for him. I don't know when and where such an occasion will take place. Now, I don't care if you two are sleeping with each other or not. And you don't have to tell me. Frankly, however, I would be *very* surprised if you were not. You're both young, and neither of you are unattractive. You've got plenty of opportunities. I would worry if either of you didn't have a private sex life of some sort because nearly all creative people have exceedingly strong sex drives . . . myself included, by the way."

Osbourne got up. "Look, you are both adults. But I want to point out something to you. This is a paternalistic company. It has a long history of being run by straight-laced New England Puritan types. We may have a romantic as president right now, but it won't always be that way. There are still a lot of Puritans in corporate headquarters. Some of them are out to get Halden. Some of them are out to get whatever they can get. Some of them are out to hoist themselves up the ladder, using whatever means they've got at hand to do it. And some of them do not like Corporate Research. If we get in a crunch, if we get into a cash flow bind, or if the country goes into a major recession, Corporate Research will be the first to go. But, being a paternalistic company, NEMECO will find jobs in other divisions for most of the people here . . . except those whose moral integrity is suspect . . . in spite of the fact that hardly anybody at corporate headquarters is lily white in that regard. They've managed to cover it up. But, please. Be as discreet as you can . . ."

I didn't say anything. Neither did Tammy.

"That's all," Bill added.

"Fine. Now, let me ask you something else," I put in. "Do you want Carl and I to continue building our version of the load compensator circuits, or do we build Vic's?"

"What were my instructions to you?"

"Build the Tammy-and-Mike version."

"So? Carry on! Vic is my problem."

"That's what you think!" I told him.

Chapter Twelve

We decided on a twenty-kilogram load for the sky hook to push, this being the same weight as the unit. We also had to select the dimensions, so we made it one meter long. Mac hogged a bar of three-inch-diameter steel down to a diameter of about two and a quarter inches on the lathe and mounted two supports fore and aft. This permitted us to hang it as a ballistic pendulum directly in front of the sky hook.

We also had him build a load consisting of a twenty-kilo steel load two meters long, and it was a willowy rod a little over an inch in diameter. And he made a forty-kilo rod load one meter long. The purpose of the three loads of differing weights and dimensions was to give us some handle on the validity of the equations we had used.

Insofar as the sky hook was concerned, the characteristics of the load that should theoretically affect it were a combination of mass and dimensions.

By Wednesday afternoon, we had the twenty-kilo meter rod hung in front of the sky hook with its rear face just touching the front face of the drive. The following morning, with Wendell Stone's help, we set up a very simple position-measuring system consisting of a photocell on the load looking at a light source along the thrust axis of the pendulum system. As the position of the pendulum changed, the output of the photocell changed because of the inverse-square law relating to the amount of light it saw from the fixed-position light. As a measurement system, it didn't have any direct mechanical connection to the experiment and it was extremely accurate, the output of the photocell being proportional to the position of the unit. We could swing the pendulum system by hand and watch the electric output of the photocell write a sine wave on a recording oscillograph.

Even Vic had to admit that it was elegant.

I met Dr. Ted Mayan in a most unusual way. I was flat on my back underneath the sky hook making a final adjustment of the photocell when I heard somebody say, "You're right, Bill! If it doesn't work, you can probably sell it to Hollywood for their next science-fantasy epic!"

I looked up to see a heavy-set man in his fifties sporting a short crew cut—a rarity in those days—and brandishing with great arrogance a cigarette holder that was even longer than Bill Osbourne's. I rolled out from under the sky hook and was about to throw this outsider out when I saw Bill standing behind him.

Carl called out, "Hi, Dr. Mayan!"

That was my formal introduction to one of the most amazing men I have ever met. I shook hands tentatively with him and found my hand in a powerful grip.

"Does Mike stand for Michael or Micro?" Mayan asked me. "If it's Michael, it means 'you are like God.' "

"Doctor, I'll let you figure that one out for yourself if I don't set fire to a bush first," I shot back with a grin, not really knowing how to handle this obviously ego-powerful man about whom Len had warned me.

Len's warning had been simple: "Never get into an argument with Mayan and grant him his initial assumption; he'll end up leading you down the garden path until you must logically agree with something that is totally ridiculous!"

Bill gave Mayan a quick briefing, adding, "I'll give you the full treatment when Serge gets here."

"Whatever you wish. I'm on your time now." The big man turned back to me. "Since you're an astronomer, how do you think this work will eventually affect your discipline?"

"I'm not really sure, Doctor," I told him. "If there

really is GI radiation and the fourth or inertial field, it'll create problems for the relativists."

"That's putting it mildly! See here, have you worked through the equations as applied to the instabilities of satellite orbits?"

"That's more in Vic's line," I admitted. "I was strictly an observational planetary astronomer."

We adjourned to the conference room. Within a few minutes, we were joined by Professor Serge Korsinski who turned out to be a very impressive looking man, partly bald, with a definite Slavic accent and a very proud bearing. But his noble looks betrayed a very personable and cultured manner. "Well! A distinct pleasure to meet you, Dr. Call. Bill has told me a great deal about you!"

"Just plain Mister Call, Professor," I corrected him.

"In view of what Bill says you have managed to accomplish with the sky hook in the past few weeks, I rather suspect that either Dr. Mayan or I can correct that situation in due course of time. Tell me: How did you happen to come up with this wholistic approach to load impedance matching?"

"I didn't. It was Wendell Stone, the engineer from the Mill Equipment Division who's working over here getting the shot-alloying process ready to go on-line," I confessed. "I'm just an experimentalist, gentlemen. Vic handles the theory and the math."

"From what I've heard, you're belittling yourself," Mayan broke in. "Didn't you stop Aboud cold on the load matching matter?"

"Not really. It's pretty hard to stop Vic. He just bulldozes ahead and gets his way no matter what you do."

Mayan roared. Even Bill Osbourne laughed at this. Korsinski smiled knowingly.

At that point, Vic showed up in the figurative cloud of dust. "Sorry! I forgot that we had this meeting this morning!" he said, trying to be apologetic.

"That's all right," Korsinski told him. "We'll manage to get it out of your hide in some fashion today, Vic."

Len also showed up with Vic. The conference room door was closed. And I found myself in an intellectually exhausting activity. Bill and Vic got up and gave a general briefing of what had happened in the last thirty days. But these two academicians were not from the typical mold. They were real thinkers, teachers, and searchers, each in his own individualistic way.

Mayan was an incredibly intelligent physicist with a broad spectrum of knowledge outside his own field of expertise. He was one of the best generalists I've ever run into.

Korsinski, on the other hand, had a very thorough and in-depth knowledge of modern physics. He'd made the original attack on Bill's first NYAS paper, pointing out some serious discrepancies in the rationale, logic, and mathematics. Korsinski didn't attack now; he commented. He behaved simply as a classically educated scientist would be expected to behave, searching for inconsistencies and demanding complete derivations and logical rationales for every step. "I am convinced that you are correct," he mentioned in his mannered voice at one point, "but we must approach this properly according to the well-established and long-used scientific method. It will not withstand peer review otherwise." He exhibited no advocacy at any point, but he did display an astounding depth of understanding of the internal politics of the scientific community.

"We must be *very* careful," Korsinski pointed out during an argument over a minor point in the construction and interpretation of one of Vic's field equations, "that we *do not* directly negate any of the current beliefs of the relativists or the particle physicists because they are firmly in control of the publications and of the peer review process. While it is entirely possible that your hypothesis will probably reveal many new aspects to subnuclear physics, the data must be presented in such a manner that these specialists can easily adjust their own beliefs and findings to live more comfortably with your hypotheses than with the ones they are presently enmeshed in."

"Serge, if Bill and his people have a working experimental demonstration in the laboratory, the scientific community's going to have to sit up and take notice,"

Mayan objected. "They'll have one hell of a time wishing away Bill's theories when anybody can buy an operating sky hook!"

"No, they will ignore it and think it will eventually go away . . . which is precisely the reverse of what will actually happen," the Stevens professor pointed out. "In ten years, we will see the next generation coming along and presenting their scientific papers on it because the Old Guard will have retired by then. Right now, the Guard is sitting there with tenure . . ."

"Baloney!" Mayan exploded. "I've got tenure, and I'll put up one hell of a fight over this. Serge, I'll be teaching this at the freshman level during the next academic year because I'll *have* to . . . just as my noble predecessors had to drop teaching vacuum-tube electronics because the students were walking around between classes with transistor radios held to their ears."

"I hadn't expected to get to this subject this early in the game," Bill Osbourne remarked. "Our first job is to make a working product; then we can afford the luxury of scientific acceptance."

"Ah, but, Bill," Korsinski pointed out, "a trip to Stockholm would undoubtedly be viewed by your marketing people as outstanding publicity that is otherwise unobtainable at any price!"

"If the Stockholm trip happens at all," Mayan observed, "I believe it'll be the first time that the Nobel Prize has gone to investigators from an industrial research organization since Bardeen, Brattain, and Shockley won it in 1956 . . ."

"I had in mind," Osbourne mused, "that we'd make our work known by means of a *tour de force* that nobody could ignore and that would result in the total inability of the government to classify our work. That's why I brought Mike aboard. In addition to being a good astronomer and an even better experimentalist, he's a pilot. When Mike lands on Mars in a space vehicle driven by a sky hook, it'll be very hard to ignore or classify our work."

"Have you discussed this with your management yet?" Mayan wanted to know.

"Of course not."

"Good! I like the idea! It has shock value! It'll unstuff a lot of stuffed shirts and unscrew the inscrutable," Mayan said with a grandiose gesture. "I'll enjoy watching some of my esteemed colleagues getting their noses rubbed in it!"

"I believe you are being a bit harsh on our esteemed colleagues," Korsinski pointed out quietly.

"I don't doubt for a second that Bill and his crew here can manage to pick up enough surplus NASA and Air Force equipment to build the basic vehicle. I have a graduate student, George Rockledge, who wanders around the surplus yards between Boston and Washington buying and swapping bits of space hardware. And there's a surprising amount of it available! George once managed to collect enough parts to assemble a complete Titan-I ICBM . . . except for the nuclear materials for the warhead . . ."

"Do you have his address?" Bill wanted to know.

"Not with me. I'll call you and give it to you. But he may not be available; I'm never certain when he's going to be in class. He disappeared for about three weeks a short time ago. The CIA brought him back. Seems he was dickering with a Middle Eastern nation for that Titan-I missile before the CIA stepped in."

"I won't trust my life to a piece of surplus gear," I interjected. "We can probably get by with standard general aviation equipment in most cases. After all, it's not going to be a very long flight . . . about twenty days if we boost at one-tenth gee."

"And how do you propose to provide energy for your space vehicle?" Korsinski asked, directing his question mainly at Bill Osbourne.

But I answered. "Probably the superbattery we've got under development here."

"Oh, that! Do you really believe it will be adequate?" the professor went on.

Mayan was working with a pocket calculator. "I figure about thirty-two million kilowatts, assuming a thousand kilogram vehicle mass and an eighty percent efficiency."

Osbourne and Vic immediately brought out pocket calculators. "You're close," Bill told him.

"Check your numbers again!" Mayan fired back. "You always had a tendency to get sloppy with your numbers as a graduate student!"

"That's thirty-two gigawatts," I pointed out. "Think we can steal a nuclear reactor from somebody?"

Len looked confused. "What are you talking about? We've got a space drive. Once it's working, there are plenty of energy sources for it."

Korsinski went to the chalkboard and began to write the ballistic and acceleration formulas and the basic energy equations. "Mike assumed a constant-boost flight at an acceleration of one-tenth of a gee or zero point nine eight meters per second squared. Let's figure that the distance is roughly a hundred million kilometers— although the distance to Mars is about fifty million kilometers at opposition, you might not want to wait around as long as twenty-six months. Work out the energy change required. Any of my undergraduates could do it."

"Oh, cripes, yes! Of course!" Len smacked his forehead.

"It will therefore require that you supply about three point two times ten to the ninth watts of energy to go to Mars . . . and the same to get back," Korsinski said, nodding at the equations on the board.

Mayan squinted through his rimless glasses. "Going to Mars with a space drive is a noble goal . . . and the pun was intended. Len, how's it coming in the superbattery department? Have you achieved three million joules per kilogram of battery weight yet?"

"Not anywhere near it, Doctor. We've got to solve the electrode disintegration problem at the high temperatures generated by the discharge rates. We might be able to get about two megajoules per kilogram."

"Okay, then how about low-earth orbit instead? That's less energy," I remarked. I saw the Mars trip going down the drain because every one of us had been so engrossed in the sky hook itself that we forgot that it would need a very long extension cord.

Vic looked up from his calculator. "Three megajoules per kilogram of mass placed in a two hundred kilometer orbit," he announced.

Osbourne was shocked. "We can't even make a unit that will lift itself plus its energy source . . . much less any payload!"

"That's why rockets are used," Mayan pointed out.

"I don't see what you mean, Ted? A rocket has to throw away mass," Osbourne said.

"True, but in order to get the energy density required," Mayan explained, "you must work at very high temperatures. Batteries that work at, say, two seventy-three degrees Kelvin have a lot less energy per kilogram because that energy comes from the breaking of chemical bonds. At higher temperatures, there is more energy available because you break more bonds quicker. This is why chemical combustion is used in rocket engines, *and* at the highest possible pressures and temperatures. Nuclear rocket engines would have been better because of the higher temperatures possible."

"Do you mean we're going to have to go nuclear in order to get the energy densities required?" Len wondered. "Mike, do you have any lead underwear?"

"Forget nuclear!" I snapped. "Even if we wanted to go that route, I don't think anybody in this room could pull enough strings to get the materials."

Osbourne looked whipped. "It sounded like such a great idea!"

"It is!" Mayan said.

"Why did I let you two in the door this morning?" the research director asked. It was strictly a rhetorical question.

"Because you hired us to keep you honest, Bill," Korsinski told him smoothly.

"All right! We're paying top dollar here! Anybody got any bright ideas where we might get the energy, even for a limited mission of low-earth orbit?" Osbourne suddenly asked.

"Magic," Mayan suggested.

"I'm paying for brilliance, not humor," Osbourne said.

"I mean what I said," Dr. Ted Mayan retorted.

"How is magic going to give us enough energy density to get enough lift out of the sky hook?" Vic remarked.

Lift! Wings! *Flying!*

I stood up. "Gentlemen, we may have an answer. We're thinking in rocket terms: lifting something straight up against gravity. We don't need to take that approach."

"What are you suggesting, Mike?" Osbourne wanted to know.

"That we don't try to *lift* something into space. Let's try *flying* into space!"

There was dead silence in the conference room. I could almost hear the thinking going on.

"Look," I added, "the service ceiling on my little Cherokee is nineteen thousand feet. I can't fly it any higher than that for one simple reason: the internal combustion engine that turns the prop that provides the thrust has lost so much power at that altitude there is no excess power available to continue making the airplane climb. If I had an engine that could put out a constant hundred horsepower regardless of altitude or air density, there are only two things that would limit how high I could go: one, the speed of sound, and two, myself. Unless I could get a full pressure suit, I'm limited to about forty-five thousand feet with a full pressure oxygen system; above that altitude, I need a pressure suit. My aircraft probably has a limiting Mach number of about seventy-five percent of the speed of sound, and just above stall which is sixty-five indicated airspeed, I would probably get to . . . Vic, gimme your calculator!"

"Never mind! I figured it. Your bird would reach about ninety-five thousand feet before it ran into its limiting Mach number."

"See what I mean? I just happened to choose my plane because I'm familiar with the numbers. But, if you were to take, say, a high performance sailplane with a low wing loading and low stalling speed and give it about a hundred horsepower thrust *all the way to space,* you could fly it into orbit, neglecting heating effects. If we built one with a very low wing loading, we could probably even keep the temperatures down below two hundred Celsius . . . which means aluminum construction." I looked around. There were a couple of doubting faces—Len Marshall and Serge Korsinski. Neither flew. But Mayan probably didn't fly either, yet he seemed ecstatic, but that could probably be due to his sheer enthusiasm for this project in the first place.

"Hundred horsepower, huh?" Osbourne was musing, pulling at his moustache. "Len, that could be done with two hundred kilograms of superbattery, couldn't it?"

"Depends on how long you need the energy."

"Gentlemen," Mayan intoned as though he were delivering a lecture in his class on the philosophy of science, "new propulsion systems usually require a new approach to their use. One must take a fresh look at methods of application. That's what we have just done. We cannot possibly apply the concepts of rocket flight into orbit with the sky hook. The sky hook requires a source of electrical energy. The only such source with adequate energy density to permit the vertical takeoff rocket approach is magnetohydrodynamic power generation, which is a complex and heavy technology at the moment. The obvious answer is Mike Call's: Fly into space at constant indicated airspeed, using the atmosphere instead of fighting it as drag force or neglecting it entirely."

"What we're looking for is a sailplane powered by the sky hook," Bill Osbourne mused. "When I was in the Air Force, Kelly Johnson at Lockheed solved a similar problem that way: He designed and built a very high-performance jet-powered sailplane. We called it the U-2. Okay, we may not have the energy sources to go directly to Mars, Mike, but we can sure get you into orbit!"

Vic was squirming. "I want to go run some numbers on this. It's a whole new ball game. Not that I distrust your ballpark figures, Mike. You're damned good at that sort of thing. But I want to add the decimal points." Coming from Vic Aboud, that was extremely high praise indeed.

We adjourned to the dynamics lab while Vic disappeared in the direction of Tammy's office and the computer terminal.

Carl was ready. I made a couple of excuses. "Dr. Mayan, Dr. Korsinski, last week . . ."

"I detest such formality between colleagues," Mayan broke in. "It's a lot easier if you just call me Ted. Time we were on a first name basis, Mike. And you're brighter than most of the Ph.D.s being turned out these days. I'm certainly going to do something . . ."

"Uh, thank you, Ted." I felt very uncomfortable being on a first name basis. I had been too thoroughly indoctrinated by years in academia. "Anyway, as I was about to say, don't expect success here today. We ran something like this last week and it didn't pass the smoke test. Now I think we've got it solved. At any rate, this is a pure and simple experiment . . ."

"We are well aware of experimental success ratios, Mike," Korsinski said. "It would indeed make my life easier if all experiments succeeded. Tell me what you're doing here . . ."

Between Bill and myself, we explained the sky hook set-up to the two consultants. We told them of the serendipitous mistake that Carl had made in building the phasing coil. And I explained the load compensating circuit and why it was needed. "First thing we'll try this morning is just to show you that we did achieve a rather significant breakthrough last week. We'll run the sky hook without a load. Ready, Carl?"

"Ready, Mike."

Carl had pulled the first load rod away from the sky hook and fastened it up against the wall where the sky hook would not push on it.

"Okay, let's repeat our twenty-watt experiment."

This time, it was done with Wendell Stone's photocell light intensity measurement system working into a recording oscillograph. Carl and I had the settings well under control now. We went through our check list, got powered-up and stood back while the sky hook displaced its entire length from the vertical rest position . . . and stayed there.

I thought that Dr. Ted Mayan was going to suffer a seizure, he got so excited. He was down on his hands and knees, passing his hands around and under the unit, checking for air jets. Professor Serge Korsinski just walked around and around it, looking carefully.

It was Korsinski who finally spoke. "I believe that this is one of the significant experiments in physics of this century. There is no doubt about it. The device is producing a constant force of some sort that is holding it displaced from the vertical. I see no trace of magnets, air jets, or anything that might lead anyone to claim fraud. However, Bill, I would suggest that you install some magnetometer sensors at critical places around the unit to prove that there is no displacement caused by electromagnetic forces. I will run an analysis on where you should place them so that it will be most convincing."

Then we tried the twenty-kilogram load. "This is the untried experiment, gentlemen," I remarked. "If it works, it means that the sky hook will do useful work."

We went through the check-out on this one very carefully. We knew more or less what the phasing should be and what sort of power settings we should have. Again, because I was slightly unsure of precisely what we were working with, I started out at very low power . . . about five watts.

"Gently, gently!" I admonished Carl as we brought the power up. "How's the compensator doing?"

"Beautifully! But something's skewing the drive wave shape!"

"That's the compensator adjusting for the reaction forces," Osbourne observed.

"Four watts should just about move it . . ." I said. "Okay, we're adjusting into resonance here . . . coming in fast . . . Hold it! Cut her back to two watts!"

The sky hook plus load was now hanging out almost as far as it had all by itself with twenty-five watts on the drive.

"Son of a gun!" I erupted as I looked at it. "It works *better* when it's pushing a load!"

"Sure you want to go only as far as orbit?" Ted Mayan asked.

Chapter Thirteen

The sky hook turned out to be weird. It had a "resonance point" when it was pushing a load. Up to a point, the heavier the load became—about fourteen times the weight of the sky hook unit itself—the more efficient the unit became, approaching an unbelievable 95.6 percent efficiency pushing a 282-kilogram load. Above that load level, its efficiency fell off slowly.

But that wasn't the whole story.

The dimensions of the load were critical. The longer we made the load up to a certain point, the more efficient the sky hook became!

We thought we were going to end up with a two-dimensional matrix array that would tell us how to handle loads with various weights and dimensions, but a third variable suddenly surfaced: The point of attachment of the load to the skyhook was also critical! When we coupled the load to the mid-point of the sky hook unit, a completely different set of operating characteristics manifested themselves! And when we coupled to the rear phasing coil, it was different still!

Osbourne and I were baffled. Vic became annoyed and even more irritable than normal. Tammy was purely mystified.

This took a couple of weeks. We couldn't run a whole series of tests of this sort in an afternoon. Mac had to make new loads for us, and that took time. In addition, Tammy and I had to wrestle with the numbers to figure out what was going on. I don't think Tammy ever did get a grip on it. Vic claimed he did, but at that point he was so deep in mathematical theory and field equations that he existed almost in another world.

Most industrial research and development work is downright boring, just as any R&D work is. To paraphrase an old aviation saying, it's hours of sheer boredom punctuated by moments of brilliant inspiration. Edison said it was 10 percent inspiration and 90 percent perspiration. But I think he was being overly optimistic on the 10 percent. It's more like 1.

In the meantime, my relationship with Tammy Dudley continued to grow. We did not make the mistake of being seen together at the NEMECO hangar again. And we were careful about going places where we might be seen under less than platonic conditions.

Actually, our relationship had ceased to be platonic and had become increasingly plutonic.

I detected that Tammy was slowly getting a sense of humor back, as if she had had to suppress it for years. Not only was she a very bright and intelligent woman whose appearance totally belied the everyday image of a female technical type, but she was beginning to blossom in the most amazing ways. She still maintained her reserve around others, but with me and those at Morse Manor, she began to effervesce and to exhibit a growing joy of living.

Ruth remarked on this to me privately one day in my office when she picked up my time card. "You'll think me an old snoop, Mike," she said, "but I can't help but notice a growing closeness between you and Tammy . . . Not that I object, mind you! I think it's about time, because Tammy was so withdrawn. Anyway, I wanted you to know that I think you're doing wonders for that girl, because I was very concerned about her and I like her very much."

"Ruth," I said, looking up from my papers, "I do, too."

"I know it. And I don't think it will surprise you to learn that most of the rest of the lab gang knows it, too. There's a certain amount of envy, Mike, because Tammy is really a very beautiful person. There isn't a young bachelor here who wouldn't want to date her. However, if I may say so, you are handling the affair with a great deal of tact and gentleness."

"Ruth," I told her with a smile, "there is no other way to handle Tammy . . . or any woman, for that matter. Remember the movie *Camelot* where King Arthur sings about his concern, 'How to Handle a Woman?' Well, that's what I'm trying to do. There's still a lot I don't know about Tammy, but that doesn't matter . . ."

"There's a lot most of us don't know, Mike. She still has far too many closed doors in the hallways of her mind." Ruth started to leave, then stopped in the doorway, looked back, and added, "And don't think I don't appreciate the most careful way both of you have handled the affair." She didn't say another word, but left.

That made my day, but it still didn't explain the crazy results we were getting with the load-pushing characteristics of the sky hook.

The practical Vermont engineer, Wendell Stone, contemplated the situation for a period of time before he finally told Carl and me, "I think you're running up against a phenomenon of the nature of matter itself. What have you been using for load material?"

"Cold-rolled steel," Carl replied.

"I think you may have fun when you try to push material with various crystalline structures," Wendell suggested.

"What happens when we start working with directionally oriented materials such as fiberglass?" I wondered.

"Or wood," Wendell added.

"Or a colloid?" I said.

So we tried. On top of the three-dimensional matrix, we had to add a fourth dimension that was dependent upon the material and its stress-strain characteristics in different directions.

"This is getting out of hand!" Vic Aboud complained loudly in one of our meetings in Len's office where most of the meetings seemed to take place in spite of the conference room, which appeared to be used only for VIP's.

"Not at all," Bill Osbourne observed calmly. "It's just the sort of thing you expect to run into in basic research. After all, if we knew all the answers, we wouldn't have to do basic research. Well, we know enough answers now to call in the Front Office again and ask them in which direction they want us to take this development."

"You're not going to let Sanatella into the act, are you?" I wanted to know. If anything, I did not want that little jerk involved at all. I was not jealous of him for being small like I was; but I detested the fact that he tried to cover it up.

"We've got to," the research director pointed out. "We now have an operating unit. It can push a load, just as Sanatella asked for. I want to put the monkey on Sanatella's back, gentlemen, because we'll give him a totally new product for NEMECO, and *he* must come up with the market that will be best suited for it." Bill Osbourne sensed the anxiety in the faces of those of us present in Len's office—Len, Vic, and myself. "I believe that it's time for another dog-and-pony show, gang. We've reached the point where we could go off into a protracted research program determining just how to push various kinds of loads. Since the number and variety of loads are legion, we cannot possibly investigate them all. And I couldn't justify doing it anyway. Since we now have a device that works, it's up to our vaunted marketing department to tell us how to aim our efforts. Except I want Ted Mayan and Serge Korsinski here as the heavy artillery . . . which is not necessary for Halden and Newcomb, but we may well need with Destry and Sanatella."

"Does this mean that our little flying project is off?" I wanted to know.

"Not at all. As a matter of fact, Mike, now that you've completed most of the experimental work on the sky hook, get on the flight project to the full extent your time will allow," Osbourne ordered. "Figure out what you're going to fly into orbit, what kind of sky hook is going to be required, how much power it's going to take, and what it's going to cost. Len, will you back him up with all of the data we have on the superbattery? Vic, although Mike's going to be riding the beast, I want you to double-check his numbers just in case because the flight program *cannot* be permitted to fail."

"You're damned right it can't!" I put in.

"I'll check Mike . . . but I'm going to be pretty busy on the systems design work of whatever Sanatella comes up with," Vic remarked.

"My numbers will be simple, Vic. Aerodynamics isn't that complex," I told the mathematician.

"We need a good cover name for the project," Len pointed out. "Something that won't give it away, since it's a covert lab activity until you decide to pop it on the company and the world."

"Well, how about the Model Twenty-Two Thruster?" I suggested. "That sounds obscure enough that we ought to be able to dream up all sorts of reasons for calling it that."

"I like that," Vic said. "Sometimes, your English language swings."

It was becoming autumn in New England, and I could feel the nip in the air every morning when we drove to the lab. The big oak trees in front of Morse Manor began to turn. Ruth suggested that it would be a good time to go up to Vermont to see the colors. I asked Tammy on Friday if she wanted to fly up to Montpelier over the weekend.

I was a little dismayed when she replied, "Oh, Mike, I have something else planned this weekend. You don't know how much I'd like to, but I have to go over to New Jersey. It's an . . . invitation that I accepted months ago, and there's no way that I can get out of it."

It was going to be a lonely weekend. Len had house repair work to do, putting up the storm windows against the coming winter. Carl wanted to finish up his kilowatt ham rig. Vic had other plans with a Rockette in New York. I asked Wendell Stone and got a very surprising answer: "I never go up in those things!" So I asked Ruth, "How long has it been since a young man has propositioned you?"

Ruth blushed, then shot back, "Just what did you have in mind, sir?"

"You suggested that I fly up to Vermont this weekend and see the colors. Would you like to go with me?"

Ruth's eyes sparkled and she replied with a sense of humor that I didn't suspect she possessed, "Shall I call ahead and get reservations for twin beds or a double?"

"Suit yourself!"

I have no Oedipus complex. It was like taking my mother on an airplane ride. We even had separate rooms in the Holiday Inn up there. It was a beautiful flight, the colors were magnificent, but the "mountains" of Vermont were sand piles compared to the giants I had flown over in the West. Coming back, it was a perfectly clear autumn day with the best visibility I'd encountered since leaving Arizona. So I took *Two To Tango* right down on the deck as low as I could manage to go, and we flew down the valleys back to Bridgeport, sometimes *slightly* below the FAA minimum altitudes.

It was beautiful, and it relaxed me completely for the week that was to follow. Ruth was a fine companion. I would have preferred Tammy, but at least I got a good night's sleep for a change.

I also had the chance to think about what I was doing. As we tooled down the beautiful valleys of Vermont and western Massachusetts—the states back here are *so small!*—I marveled at the landscape slipping under the wings of *Two To Tango*. This was a beautiful planet. Perhaps I had not seen enough of it. Did I really want to go to the stars?

Yes, as long as I could come back occasionally!

And I had the chance to talk to Ruth.

"Things are going very well," I told her. "I'm very happy with my life right now."

"That's certainly a change from when you arrived here in August," she pointed out. "Mike, your ears were dragging the ground like a bassett hound's, as my husband was fond of saying."

"I have work that is interesting and challenging," I told her as *Two To Tango* sped down a gorgeous valley where the tall white steeples of New England churches poked up through the trees as beacons warning me of little towns that I should not flat-hat at low altitudes. "I've found some very wonderful people . . . and a

very wonderful girl that I'm becoming very fond of. I
would like to do this kind of work for the rest of my life
as long as I had someone like Bill Osbourne to keep the
corporate politicians off my back. You don't know how
much that disturbs a creative person, Ruth! Some of us
are interested in power over the universe; others want
power over people. The two types don't mix. It's unfor-
tunate that 'universe' people have to work for 'power'
people. Some of this internal politics is such a waste of
time when we have a whole universe out there to dig
into and use . . ."

"We *do* have a unique place," Ruth admitted.

"Do you ever get the feeling that it's too good to
last?" I wanted to know.

"I've been around a long time and I watched my husband go through similar experiences. We could pull
some incredible blunders at the lab, and it probably
wouldn't change things very much. On the other hand,
we could end up doing a fantastic job for NEMECO
only to have something change in the corporate headquarters that would close the lab in less than a week
. . . and all on the word of one person. We should
enjoy it while we can, Mike, and hope it will last. The
chances are against it."

"Maybe we can manage to hold something together
in NEMECO, come what may. It's a pretty paternalistic
company, and I don't think they'd just turn us out on the
street on a moment's notice . . . Sorry, got to get back
to work now. Springfield up ahead, and there's West-
over Air Force Base traffic area that I don't want to
fly through without talking to Approach Control on the
radio."

"You're a very fine pilot, Mike. Of course, I don't
know too much about it, since this is my first flight in a
small plane."

"I figured you were an old hand because of the way
you acted!"

"No, I was scared to death," Ruth admitted. "But I
was going to do it because I've never done it before. I
will admit that it was a very beautiful way to see the fall
colors in Vermont." She smiled. "The fact that the two

of us spent the night in Montpelier should cause some
interesting lab rumors, don't you think?"

Ruth Morse was one hell of a woman . . .

Tammy didn't come back to Morse Manor that Sunday night. This was strange since she had planned to.
Both Ruth and I became concerned when Tammy
hadn't arrived by ten o'clock, so Ruth called the number Tammy had left. I heard only one side of the conversation:

"Is Tammy Dudley there? . . . This is Ruth Morse,
her landlady in Bridgeport . . . I see. Well, if she
can't come to the phone, can you tell me when she
might be back? She had planned to be home this evening, and I grew concerned when she hadn't arrived
. . . Oh, then she'll be coming up on an early train?
Well, just tell her I was concerned and that I'll see her
at work tomorrow morning." Ruth hung up looking
strangely at the receiver.

"It was a man's voice," Ruth said quietly. "And he
didn't introduce himself. I didn't think Tammy had any
family over in New Jersey . . ."

I bit my lip. Well, I certainly had no exclusive with
Tammy. But I decided I would ask about this when the
time was ripe to do so.

Bill Osbourne called a staff meeting almost immediately the following morning. Tammy was not there, and
Bill inquired about her. Ruth told him Tammy had
gone to New Jersey over the weekend and was due in
on the morning train from New York.

"Damned thing's probably late again if it didn't break
down in Stamford as usual," the research director
growled, then got down to business. "We've got a big
dog-and-pony show coming up here on Wednesday," he
told all of us there in the machine shop, which was the
only area large enough for the whole crew of twenty.
"We're going to demonstrate the sky hook pushing
loads. Halden, Newcomb, Sanatella, and probably Destry will be here from Corporate. I've asked Mayan and
Korsinski to come in as well. Len, they may also ask for
a review of the superbattery program as well."

"We'll be ready for anything," Len Marshall replied confidently.

"Okay, then the big push this week will be on those projects in addition to staying on schedule with the shot-alloying program. By the way, Wendell, how's that coming?"

"We're slipping," Stone admitted.

"Why? What's the problem?"

"It just isn't working right. I can't control the impact velocities closely enough to obtain a uniform penetration of the secondary alloying material, and . . ."

"Never mind the details right now," Osbourne cut in. "Vic and I will get with you and Tom after this meeting. Destry is going to want to see results or be told why the process is behind schedule. Okay, figure Wednesday about ten in the morning. Mac, *please* put on a clean shop coat just before ten o'clock! And, Mike, if you've got a tie, please wear it this time even though I know it's apparently against your religion or something . . ."

Bill Osbourne walked into my office about an hour later, asking, "How's it going, Mike?"

I looked up from where I was doing some basic calculations. "I'm beginning to get a handle on the numbers for orbit. Critical factors seem to be the wing loading, the wing aspect ratio, and the stall speed. Beyond that, we've got to have enough useful load to carry the sky hook and its power supply, plus life support equipment for me." I tossed my pen down on the pad of paper that was rapidly becoming filled up with numbers. "We have to keep the wing loading low because that not only determines the minimum speed required to climb and maintain less than Mach-One, but also how much heating we're going to get when I have to bring that mother back through the atmosphere."

"Which means keeping it very light on the same principle as the Lockheed U-2 and the General Dynamics WB-57F high-altitude weather reconnaissance plane," Osbourne mused. "How about a modified sailplane?"

"Not enough useful load, although the wing loading is low," I told him. "Usually wood or fiberglass wing structure, which won't stand up to what we want to do."

"The Czechs make a good all-metal sailplane, the Blanik . . ."

"Bill, how much trouble do you think you're going to have buying an airplane for Corporate Research, much less one from Czechoslovakia?" I asked.

"Yeah, and Czechoslovakia doesn't even have 'most favored nation' status," Osbourne mused. "You are right. Some of the all-American types in the Front Office would get up-tight about that. Well, do you have any other ideas?"

"Yeah. A Pilatus Porter PC-6 would do it. So would a Helio Stallion. Or a DeHaviland DHC-2 Beaver. Or, if all else fails, we can ask Wimpy Winfield to let us use the Aero Commander for about two weeks . . ."

"What?"

"Strip that Aero Commander of all the plush interior, and it will haul the mail for us," I pointed out.

"Um-m-m. Well, let me investigate that possibility . . ."

"If that doesn't work, Bill, let me go out to Arizona and see what I can find in the old airplane yards at Tucson and Falcon Field . . . Incidentally, can you give me some idea of my budget on this? I would love to have a pressurized airplane, but that may be too rich for our blood."

"Everything's going to be too rich for our blood," Bill replied quietly. "I have no budget for it at all. I'm going to have to sneak it out of various other budget cubbyholes, and we're going to have to become very creative when we write up the purchase requests . . . But, please let me worry about that. Work with some ballpark numbers with the aircraft you've mentioned, plus the NEMECO Aero Commander. Try to get us some costs, too."

"By Wednesday?"

"No time limit. Wednesday, I'll want you on deck for that lab demo because you're the guy who really understands what's going on with the sky hook."

"But Vic . . ." I began.

"Vic has a theoretical grasp, but you combine both

theoretical and experimental aspects, Mike. I think at this point you probably know more about this whole thing than anybody because you've been thinking about applications all along."

High compliments do not come my way every day, and I relished that one for quite some time.

Tammy walked into my office shortly before lunch. "Hi!"

She looked gorgeous, but also somewhat distressed. "Hi! Train late?"

"Yes. Let's go to lunch, and then you can take me over to Morse Manor so I can drop off my bag," she suggested.

We went to Mama's because I knew nobody from NEMECO except the pilots would be there . . . and they didn't care about corporate politics.

Tammy was very quiet, almost subdued. It was as though part of her inhibitions had returned over the weekend. We ordered lunch, and she toyed with her napkin.

"Did you have a good weekend, Tam?" I finally asked in an attempt to break the ice.

"No."

"I'm sorry."

"I felt I needed to talk to you about it. I'm afraid I disappointed you."

"You had a previous engagement. Family?" I asked. She nodded. "An uncle, you might say."

"Don't let the weekend worry you. There will be others . . . I hope."

"So do I."

It was just small talk the rest of the lunch. She wanted to know how the colors were up around Montpelier, and I told her. We discussed the sky hook, the forthcoming corporate dog-and-pony show, and the work I was doing on Model Twenty-Two Thruster.

"That number sounds familiar," she remarked. "Did you suggest it?"

"Seems I have a soft spot in my heart for a number ending in two two T."

"*Two To Tango*. Yes, it always does require two."

"I guess you might call it wishful thinking on my part."

"Are you sure it's still wishful?" she asked.

We drove back to Morse Manor, and Tammy got her bag out of the front of the Bug. "Come in a minute. I want to show you something."

She let herself in with her key, and I followed. In the middle of the day nobody was there, of course. The living room was strangely dark.

"Stay here. I'll bring it down," she told me.

I picked up a copy of *National Geographic*, turned on a light, and started to leaf through the magazine. A few minutes went by, then I heard a soft, whispery voice ask, "Forgive me?"

She was in the doorway, and she was wearing one of the sexiest black lace baby-doll nighties I had ever seen. It was one advertised by those Hollywood lingerie outfits, a design that shaped without covering. And Tammy didn't need shaping at all.

She walked over to me. "I stopped in one of those shops on Forty-second Street on the way back this morning," she said as she sat in my lap. "I thought you would like this. Forgive me for the weekend?"

I didn't get the chance to answer because her mouth covered mine.

"Tammy . . . The lab . . . It's the middle of the afternoon . . ." I managed finally to say.

"Haven't we got some compensatory time coming? Let's find out if it's better in the afternoon . . ."

We did.

It was.

Chapter Fourteen

The Big Day arrived. Mayan and Korsinski showed up at nine o'clock.

I wore a tie. It felt like a noose.

Mac put on a clean shop coat.

Len and I entertained Mayan and Korsinski while we waited for the contingent from corporate headquarters to arrive.

"I suspected as much," Mayan observed when I told him about the problems we had matching various types of loads to the sky hook. "Every object in the universe is essentially unique. I doubt if there are even two photons alike. Even two supposedly identical automobiles made at the same time on the same production line will be different in small ways . . ."

"That is just the result of variations in tolerances of parts," Korsinski pointed out. "But I think we can say, to some extent, that your observation holds true down to the subatomic level, at any rate. The proper statement of that is perhaps inherent in the Heisenberg Principle."

"Just because you can hang a name on it, Serge, doesn't mean that you can explain or even understand it," Mayan fired back.

I could see that Mayan was playing his usual role of "hair shirt." If it bothered Korsinski, who seemed to be considerably more straight-laced and proper as a scientist, the Stevens professor didn't let it show. He appeared to be unflappable. I knew he wasn't, because I had watched him become flapped when he first saw the sky hook work. But Korsinski was a man very much in control of himself and very conscious of the fact that, in

the presence of his peers, he had to maintain image—
even though beneath that image lay a mind and an im-
agination at least the equal of Mayan's.

Mayan would make a fantastic undergraduate physics prof, the kind who would be able to inspire and excite his students, the sort of teacher who made science
and technology out as something fascinating and full of
wonder.

On the other hand, Korsinski would be the perfect
thesis advisor, capable of leading the now-jaded graduate student through the maze of erudition and buzz-
worded jargon of an acceptable oral and thesis.

They made a perfect pair to advise us on the sky
hook. I had grown to respect and to listen carefully to
both of them.

Korsinski, true to form, wanted to know how the
Model Twenty-Two Thruster project was coming.

"For a three-ton gross weight aircraft with a reasonable wing-loading, we'll need only about two hundred
horsepower," I reported. "I'll fly the bird always at the
maximum lift-over-drag configuration, right at the bottom of the power curve, which means I'll be almost at
full stall all the way."

"But why are you worried about Mach-One?" Mayan
wanted to know. "You'll be flying up at a constant subsonic indicated airspeed."

"True," I explained, "but you must remember that
the air density falls off with altitude and temperature.
Thus although indicated airspeed remains the same,
true airspeed increases. No matter which subsonic airframe I use, I'll be pushing the limiting Mach number
of the airframe *shape* somewhere between seventy-five
and a hundred thousand feet . . ."

"I see! Which means you're going to get some rather
nasty changes in the flow field around the plane. Have
you calculated what it will take to ram the airframe past
Mach-One?"

"A lot of extra horsepower," I remarked, "if the
plane doesn't come apart around me . . . if I don't get
all sorts of control reversals . . . if I don't run into a

whole series of other problems that face any subsonic airframe trying to get through Mach-One."

"Why not buy a supersonic airframe to begin with?"

"Occasionally, I see an F-86 Sabrejet advertised in *Trade-A-Plane*, but I've never seen a supersonic aircraft available," I told him. "We can forget supersonic, although that may be the way to go eventually."

The corporate delegation showed up with Osbourne and Vic shortly after ten. We took them into the dynamics lab, where Carl and I put the sky hook through its paces pushing loads of various masses, sizes, and materials. We explained that we could now design a sky hook to push or *to lift* any load provided we knew what the load was. Grant Halden, Hayward Newcomb, and Bob Destry appeared impressed with the progress made in a few short weeks. I couldn't tell from Sanatella's face what he was thinking, but I was *very* careful not to make any remark that harked of smugness on my part for getting the sky hook to produce useful work in accordance with Sanatella's previous demands. That was *not* the way to handle that twerp.

Professor Serge Korsinski added after we concluded our demonstration, "Gentlemen, I am speaking from the purely scientific standpoint, and I realize that you have economic factors in mind. Nevertheless, what we have seen this morning amounts to one of the most significant technical breakthroughs of this century. This could well lead to a Nobel Prize for those who participated in its development. I am not an experienced industrialist, and I therefore hesitate to express an opinion outside my field of expertise. But I would venture to say that this device and its developments will have *profound* effects upon the industrial world."

Bill Osbourne added to that, "According to John Whiteside, NEMECO is in a good situation to hold the basic patents."

Mayan was hunkered down near the front end of the sky hook. "Mike, there's one experiment that I want to try. It won't give you much data, but it will convince me *and nearly everyone else who tries it* that there's no trickery involved here . . . and that's one of the first things that will enter the minds of any scientific review panel. Mike, will you set this up so that it will give about a five kilogram push on my bare palm?"

I swallowed. Here was another unanticipated experiment. "We'll try," I gulped. After all, we now had the load compensator in the circuit. It should be able to handle the phasing involved with a five kilo push on a colloidal mass resting on the ground.

Bill was apprehensive. "Ted, we're not sure what the GI radiation might do to your hand."

"Well, let's find out. You certainly haven't detected any gravitational radiation coming from this thing yet! And I'm perfectly willing to act as the human guinea pig."

"If you get hurt . . ." Hayward Newcomb began.

"If I get hurt, I'll waive damages. Get me the required papers to sign."

"Go ahead, Dr. Mayan," Grant Halden put in. "If something goes wrong, NEMECO will take care of things. But please use your left hand!"

"No, I'll use my right. I'm left-handed!" Mayan replied.

This was the first time the sky hook had pushed against a human subject. Mayan was just the sort of wild card who would want to do something like this, and I should have anticipated it.

We set things up, but I insisted that Mayan wear an insulating vinyl glove because of the possibility of some high-voltage leakage that we had not anticipated. I pointed out the high-frequency electromagnetic radiation leakage that might cause some heating effects, but Vic made a rapid calculation and determined that it would not exceed the accepted industrial maximums for a single exposure.

Everything was ready. "Okay, Dr. Mayan, put your palm against the front of the sky hook. We're coming up with the drive frequency . . ."

Mayan's face lit up in a broad smile. "It's pushing! I can feel it pushing my hand! That's the most convincing instrumentation in the world! Serge, come try it!"

In the next few minutes, all of us tried it. There were

no apparent ill effects and no strange sensations, just the feeling that the sky hook was pushing hard. It was there. It was real. It was a force that could be felt.

"Very convincing!" was Halden's accolade.

Even Bob Destry had to admit that this was not some far-out Buck Rogers gadget and that it could really do something.

We retired to the conference room.

Bill did not stand up as he began the presentation. He had taken the seat at the far end of the conference table from Grant Halden. The rest of us were scattered down both sides of the table, seated in no particular order. I did make a point not to sit near Phil Sanatella.

"We've reached the stage where basic research on the sky hook is nearly concluded," Osbourne began. "Our scientific consultants, Dr. Mayan and Professor Korsinski, have carefully monitored the scientific aspect of our work and have done an excellent job of guiding us in the proper theoretical directions. We've instituted all the necessary patent filing actions through John Whiteside. We have a unit that can perform in a predictable fashion within the limitations of its size, design, and power handling capabilities. It will push a load, as we've all witnessed in a very dramatic fashion this morning. It's now a matter of design to make a sky hook that will not only lift itself straight up, but also do it with a load. We can design a unit to meet nearly any requirement . . . *but we cannot design a universal unit that will do everything!* It must be designed for a job, for a specific load or a specific range of loads." The research director paused and looked at both Grant Halden and Hayward Newcomb. "Gentlemen, we are now ready to develop to a market. Where do we go from here? What do you want the sky hook to do? This is a marketing function outside our responsibility although we've thought about it and are prepared to make some concrete recommendations about markets."

It was obvious that the president of NEMECO was enthusiastic and excited. The vice-president, Dr. Hayward Newcomb, managed, as usual, to keep his emo-

tions under control as he had learned to do so well in the
Air Force.

"We have here," Newcomb began in terse, clipped
tones, "a force-generating device that does not produce
a reaction force. It appears that we have two options
open to us vis-a-vis products that will have some sort of
fit with our existing lines . . ."

I noticed that Sanatella was making notes frantically.

Newcomb went on in his terse yet quiet tone, "We
have a potential propulsion device. One first thinks of it
as a replacement for the rocket propulsion system, but I
would like to voice a strong opinion that we do *not* attempt to market it in this fashion until *after* we have
received issued patents that cannot be classified under
a secrecy order from the Department of Defense."

"This leaves out the possibility of a potential product
for the Marine Engineering Division in New London,"
Halden put in.

"Correct. This would also eliminate any involvement
by the Airborne Controls Division in Tempe for an aircraft or spacecraft propulsion system."

"That leaves my division," Destry added, "and Max
Keller's Heavy Construction Equipment Division. Why
not give pushers to one of us and lifters to the other?"

"I'm not sure at this stage that we can make that sort
of an arbitrary division between functions," Osbourne
pointed out.

"Well, we've certainly got a pusher," Destry went on.
"Why not give me a crack at turning it into a product?
If we spin off some other products with different appli-
cations, we can certainly bring Max into the act."

Destry moved quickly and smoothly! I could see how
he figured that this would help him consolidate his bid
for Halden's job.

"You've certainly developed a workable arrangement
with Corporate Research on the shot-alloying process,"
Halden mused, thinking about the implications of what
Destry had suggested. But Halden was no fool. "I'd like
to see Max brought in at this point, however. He may
have some inputs from his people that could be very

important. As a matter of fact, I want to bring this before the Board at our meeting in a few weeks."

"Do you think that it's wise at this point, Grant?" Newcomb asked. "It could present a conflict of interest to some of the Board members . . . and we may want to license some of this to, say, Consolidated Industries' Great Western Aero down the line. The Federal Trade Commission might get upset if there were any record of revealing the sky hook to Hettinger or Mather ahead of a public announcement. Technically, from the patent point of view, it's unwise to reveal this at all until we are certain of the patent position."

"But that could be years!" Bill Osbourne pointed out.

"True," the NEMECO president said, nodding. "I don't want to wait that long before getting a return on our investment. The Board will certainly ask questions long before that."

"Gentlemen!" Dr. Ted Mayan boomed. "Excuse me, but you don't have any time to spare! You may not even have a year!"

"What do you mean?" Halden asked.

"The history of science and technology is rife with examples of parallel developments," the generalist explained, waving his arms. One thing for certain: When Ted Mayan wanted the attention of everyone in the room, he certainly knew the histrionics required. "Both Newton and Liebnitz worked out the calculus independently. People think that Darwin was responsible for the Theory of Evolution, but Wallace actually preceded Darwin into publication! In more recent times, Shockley, Brattain, and Bardeen were not the only persons working on solid-state electronic devices, which were actually invented and patented years previously . . . but they were the first to announce. Give me a few minutes and I can present you with a list of several dozen developments in the past decade that have been carried out in complete isolation independent of one another, and yet were nearly identical in scope and content.

"Mark my words: Somewhere, at this very moment,

there is a high probability that someone else is working
on this! I don't know who it is. I don't know the approach they're taking. But if the basic anomalies of the
universe were there for Bill Osbourne, Vic Aboud, Len
Marshall, and Mike Call to see and work with, they are
there for others to see and work with too!"

"Dr. Mayan is quite correct in his assessment," Professor Korsinski broke in with his quiet, measured,
slightly accented tones. "Once the basic patent applications have been *submitted*, you must move at once to
make a public disclosure."

Hayward Newcomb suddenly began to nod in agreement. "Grant, I believe that our consultants are right."

"Do you have any suggestions, gentlemen?" Halden
asked.

"Both Dr. Mayan and I can arrange for suitable
early publication, if not in *Physical Review Letters,*
then at one of the New York Academy's many symposia. This would be coordinated, of course, with the
submittal of the significant patent applications."

"This still wouldn't prevent the Department of Defense from coming in and slapping a secrecy order on
our work . . . and from stopping the publication of
any articles," Newcomb observed with some agitation.
"If there is anything that I would not want to see, it's
government security classification of this work!"

"But that wouldn't necessarily mean that NEMECO
couldn't make any money from sky hook work," Robert
Destry pointed out. "There will undoubtedly be contracts available to do further work on the principle if
the government classifies it."

"Bob, listen to me and believe me," Newcomb told
him. "I used to work for those people. I know them
well. NEMECO might get some government contract
money, but more as a sop to keep us quiet and under
control. The big money would go to their bosom bud-
dies in the aerospace industry whom they've supported
for a couple of decades now."

Bill Osbourne added, "I can second that and add
something as well. If it happens, the sky hook work will
take back seat to other propulsion work because the

aerospace firms involved in propulsion activities—
turbojets, ramjets, and rockets, for example—will be
given time to write off their capital investments in those
areas and to retire their engineers who are specialists in
those fields. In twenty years we might see the sky hook
mature into something more than we've got now. There
would be more than a hundred and twenty tons of very
expensive research reports to show for it, if you could
get access to them, much less read all of them."

"But, gentlemen, if the security of this nation is at
stake . . ." Destry began.

"That statement has been used to cover a multitude
of sins, Bob," Newcomb said, interrupting him.

"Naturally, there will be some aspects of the sky
hook work that will be of interest to the Department of
Defense," Grant Halden remarked, "and NEMECO is
certainly not unpatriotic in that regard. Applications
that might be useful in weapons technology would certainly be discussed thoroughly with the government and
if necessary, turned over to them for their use in national security."

"Mr. Halden!" Mayan thundered. "I don't wish to
seem impertinent. I know that NEMECO holds no government contracts whatsoever and acts only as an OEM
supplier to firms working on government contracts. But,
sir, if you believe that the federal government will simply come in and calmly discuss with you those aspects
of this work it feels will affect national security, you'll
find that they'll appropriate it *all* just to be on the safe
side! I've been down this road. I've seen some of my
colleagues fall prey to the same rationale, and I've seen
it destroy them. Fortunately, I have the inclination to
run like hell shouting loudly when such things happen
to me."

"I would tend to agree with my colleague," Professor Korsinski added quietly.

"Do you have any suggestions regarding what we
might be able to do?" Halden asked.

"Yes!" Mayan stated flatly. "The thing that they will
not want is publicity! They will not be able to classify it
once it becomes public knowledge . . . and I don't

mean publication in some obscure journal of a scientific society where it can be conveniently hidden and forgotten for a quarter of a century or more. Therefore, if I were in your shoes, President Halden, I would get Bill Osbourne and his crew of inventive geniuses working at once on some manner of airborne or space vehicle in which someone like Mike would orbit the world in the blinding light of publicity. And I would do it immediately after your attorneys file the patent applications . . . *immediately* afterward! Professor Korsinski and I will follow up at once with a special symposium on the sky hook at NYU, Stevens, or the New York Academy of Sciences."

Serge Korsinski was nodding in agreement.

I sat there dumbly. Mayan was getting away with it! If Osbourne or I had approached Newcomb or Halden with the proposal, it might have been our necks. But Mayan could get away with it, and he was doing it! And with the full support of Korsinski!

Halden turned to Osbourne. "Bill, how about it?"

"We can do it."

"How quickly? What will it cost?"

"Can I give you an answer Friday? And, Grant, I think it may cost considerably less than we think."

"Give me a verbal report on Friday morning," Halden told him. I could see that the proposal had struck home with the NEMECO president. It was just the sort of romantic activity that he would enjoy . . . and Mayan had given him the full rationale for doing it and justifying it to the Board of Directors and the stockholders.

"If we're going to lock this up for ourselves and also gain all this fine publicity," Bob Destry put in carefully, "I think we should also be prepared to move on the product end as quickly as possible and firm up as many of the industrial applications as we can."

"Quite true," Newcomb remarked. "But this may set us up for a raid, Grant. And it will certainly send our stock value sky-high . . ."

"Especially since there is so little of it available on the market," Destry added.

"We'll be ready for that," Halden said quietly. "Hay, once this meeting is over, we'll get together with the other officers and staff at headquarters. In the meantime: products. Phil, how about it?"

It was the first time Phil Sanatella had spoken. He had been watching and listening carefully. I could almost feel the man's mind working, trying to determine the best way that he could profit from this. "Sir?"

"Bill and his people have had some thoughts on applications," Halden told him. "Please get with him. Also get with Bob Destry and his people. If you want to call in Max Keller, check with me first. I want an analysis of the potential markets for the various industrial applications of the sky hook as both a pusher/puller and as a lifter."

"No defense applications?" the little man asked.

"No, we'll get those for free as soon as this breaks," Newcomb reminded him.

"How soon do you want it, Grant?" the marketing man asked.

"As quickly as you can get the numbers together."

"I could give you some market analysis on a superficial level in a couple of weeks after I get the chance to come up to speed on the implications of this, but I can't give you any analysis in depth quickly."

"Phil, I brought you in on this early so that you could get up to speed on it," Halden pointed out, looking directly at the marketing man. "I want some preliminary market estimates of the various immediately obvious applications by next week. By the time of the next Board meeting, I want in-depth analyses."

Sanatella may have been slightly cowed by that attack, but he didn't show it, and he bounced right back. "You'll have it, Grant! Bill, can I get with you and your people starting right after this meeting? And, Bob, will you have some of your people available in a few days . . . say, by Friday?"

"We'll talk to you any time, Phil," Osbourne told him. "We're right here, and you know how to find us."

"Give me a call," Destry told Sanatella.

"Very well!" Halden looked around the table. "Do we have our ducks set up on this? Bill?"

"Plan and cost estimate for a dramatic public operation to you by Friday!"

We had most of it already!

"Dr. Mayan? Professor Korsinski?"

"We will be in touch with Bill regarding suitable forums and publications, but we will want to coordinate thoroughly with Bill regarding the timing. It is most important!" Korsinski pointed out.

"Phil?"

"Yes, sir! Preliminary marketing plan to you by a week from Friday. In-depth marketing studies before the next Board meeting!"

"Good. Hay, I want you to monitor the patent aspect of this thing with John Whiteside."

"I think I should also evaluate some options in case we happen to be stymied by DOD. I know that game fairly well."

The president of NEMECO looked around the conference room. "I want to thank you, Bill, and the rest of you here at Corporate Research. You have done an outstanding job on what I consider to be one of the most significant pieces of pure industrial research of our time. I have always had faith that Hay Newcomb and Bill Osbourne would produce, given the people and the facilities to do so. The results have far exceeded my most sanguine expectations. And, Dr. Mayan and Professor Korsinski, I'm encouraged to know that there are two academicians who are real scientists." He paused and looked around. "You all have my full support and that of NEMECO. But I cannot emphasize the extreme importance of moving rapidly with the tightest possible security. Bill, you always were a space cadet. Now you've got your chance!"

"Not me," Osbourne said. "Mike Call . . . star gazer and airplane driver. This is exactly what I brought him aboard to do! Fortunately, he has turned out to be more than I bargained for!"

Chapter Fifteen

"Wimpy, we need the Aero Commander."

Wimpy Winfield pulled his head and shoulders out of an inspection hatch in the lower wing of the DC-4, looked at Bill Osbourne and me, and said, "Did you get it scheduled with Jake?"

"Nope," I told the old pilot. "We'll need it for a couple of months and we want to strip most of the interior out of it temporarily . . . starting right away."

Wimpy almost fell off the ladder. Regaining his composure, he clambered down and peered at the two of us. "I've been flying that DC-4 too high without oxygen! Would you tell me that again, please?"

"Corporate Research needs the use of the Aero Commander for about a month, maybe two," Bill Osbourne told him. "We've got approval from Halden for this."

"Waalll, now!" Wimpy drawled. "If you guys just wanted to go for a jaunt for a few hours, I could arrange it. But if you want that airplane for a couple of months, you'll have to clear that with Jake, approval or not."

"Where is he?" Osbourne wanted to know.

"Beyond the blue horizon somewhere, as usual. Let's go look at the dispatch board."

Inside the flight lounge of the NEMECO hangar, the board said that Jake Stock and George Pound were in Denver with the DC-6B. "Guess he's at the Ceramics Division. Said something about having to deliver twenty thousand little ceramic potties to Airborne Controls in Tempe."

Thirty minutes later, Bill and I came to the conclusion that Jake Stock and his co-pilot were airborne

163

somewhere over the Great Divide. Nobody at either Denver or Tempe seemed to know. They had been in Denver; they were not there now. They were not in Tempe. Bill thought about calling the FAA, but Wimpy said, "If Jake is in the air, he's working Denver Center or Albuquerque Center on IFR. If he is not on instruments, he isn't listening to the Flight Service Station broadcasts; he's got the Automatic Direction Finder tuned to a broadcast station listening to a ball game."

"Okay, we need the Aero Commander. We have to start working on it immediately. What do I need to get you to release it to me?" Osbourne asked.

"An act of God."

"Will a letter from Grant Halden do?"

"If it's countersigned by Jake Stock," Wimpy replied. "Look, Bill, Jake is my boss, and I have no authority to turn the Aero Commander over to you, even if you were to fly it to the Moon and bring it back full of diamonds for everybody." He put money in the Coke machine. "What are you drinking? I'm buying."

We sat down with cans of soft drink, and Wimpy said, "Tell me what the problem is. Maybe I can do something until we get Jake Stock back long enough to make a decision."

"Wimpy," Osbourne told him, "this is a project of the highest secrecy. Destroy Before Reading stuff . . ."

"So you finally got the gadget working and you're on the Mars trip kick again, eh?"

"How did you know that?" I wanted to know.

"Heard Sanatella talking to Destry yesterday on the ramp here when they didn't think anybody could hear them. Jake took them as far as Detroit to get together with Max Keller. Supposed to pick them up coming back, I guess."

"Wimpy, you'd damned well better not let that information go any further than this!" Bill Osbourne snapped.

"You think I'm nuts? I like it here, Bill!" He sat down, drained the last of the orange pop, and expertly tossed the empty can into the wastebasket. "Tell me what the problem is, and I will do my damndest to help you out . . ."

Bill filled him in on the Model Twenty-Two Thruster project enough to give him the picture insofar as the Aviation Department was concerned.

Wimpy thought about this for a minute. He got up and got himself another can of orange pop by opening the machine, taking thirty cents out, closing the machine, putting thirty cents back into the coin slot, and extracting the aluminum can. Then he said, "Look, that Commander's in constant use because it doesn't require a co-pilot and has a deluxe executive interior. Along with the Bonanza, it's flying most of the time. *But* that DC-4 out there—November one three seven eleven, and she's really a damned good old ex-Air Force C-54E, not a DC-4—she's already stripped for cargo. She's not pressurized. But there're less than four hundred hours on all four of those engines. She's stand-by for the DC-6B. We've got four pilots in the department—five with me on stand-by. That means that we can fly the DC-6B, the Commander, and the Bonanza. But even with me as stand-by pilot, we cannot get all four aircraft airborne at once. Not enough pilots because the DC-4 requires a co-pilot. So Jake will not scream about Seven-Eleven. I can turn her over to you today."

Bill glanced at me. "How about it, Mike?"

I looked out across the ramp at that big monster sitting out there, big three-bladed props on all four Pratt & Whitney 1400-horse Twin Wasps. Not what I had counted on. My license says "airplane single—and multi-engined land," but the biggest plane I had ever wrestled was an old twin-engined Convair 240. "I'll have to go back and refigure, Bill. And I've never flown a DC-4. I'd have to get type qualified."

"That's no problem," Wimpy muttered. "Come on, let's see if you can fly it and if it'll do the job for you. Mike, we'll get you some heavy time while we're at it."

It was like flying a bus! It clanked, it banged, it groaned, it roared. But that old reliable Four flew.

Wimpy filed a flight plan for Buffalo at 14,500 feet. After landing for a Coke in Buffalo, Wimpy put me in the left seat and Bill in the right coming back. I had to grab a cushion from the bunk in order to see over the instrument panel, but I could fly it. Wimpy put us through our paces—engines out, feathering the props, turns away from two dead engines on one side, and stalls with various combinations of engine power settings and flaps. Both Bill and I were sweating profusely by the time we began our letdown over Pawling. I had never handled twenty tons of airplane before. I bounced it twice after a ragged descent into Bridgeport.

Wimpy remarked, "Bill, give me about eight hours with this squirt, and he'll be flying this like he drives that Cherokee."

I still had to see what we could do in the way of putting a sky hook in that flying subway car, so I took the flight manuals with me. I made the mistake of taking them back to Morse Manor with me because it was too late to drop them by the lab. And, like any pilot learning a new machine, I couldn't put the manuals down. I found myself reading through them in the living room after Carl and I finished washing the supper dishes.

"Poker?" Peter Wilding asked as he bustled into the room. "Whatcha reading?" He came over, the DC-4 manuals being something new.

"We're short of pilots in the Aviation Division," I told him. It wasn't a lie; we were. "I'm getting checked out in the DC-4 we keep out at Sikorski. I may be spending some nights away from home."

"Flying the corporate brass around, huh?"

"Not exactly, Peter. This is a cargo plane used to haul NEMECO equipment around to customers."

Tammy was sitting there, but she just listened. She tossed me a look that said, "So you didn't get the Aero Commander, eh?"

"Well, how about some poker?" Wilding persisted.

"I'm game!" Carl called as he walked out of the kitchen.

I put down the flight operations manual. "Okay, I've had it with this anyway. How about it, Tammy?"

Tammy looked up. "Are you sure you want me in your game?"

There was a bit too much sarcasm in her tone, and I detected the fact that she was trying to pull my leg. "Know how to play?"

"A little. But you may have to answer a couple of questions now and then."

"Aw, we'll teach you, Tammy!" Wilding told her with bravado.

Tammy Dudley was indeed coming out of her shell. And she didn't need lessons from any of us. She cleaned us out of more than a hundred dollars that night. I caught on to her sweetness-and-innocence ploy, played to it, and together we took Peter Wilding for quite a pile. Wilding finally huffed off to bed. When he had gone up the stairs, Tammy giggled, turned to Carl, and said, "Sorry you had to be the fall guy."

"Where did you learn to play poker? The Marines?" Carl wanted to know.

"Never mind! Here!" She expertly peeled back a sheaf of bills and handed them to Carl.

"What's this? I lost fair and square!" Carl complained.

"Well, let's just say that it's for last night," Tammy told him sweetly, got up, and walked upstairs leaving Carl gaping at the money in his hand.

I was learning more and more about the woman that I frankly was beginning to care a great deal for. Tammy Dudley had more sides to her than a cut crystal bowl. And every side that kept revealing itself to me told me that she was one terrific woman.

"Look, gang," I told Ruth, Carl and Tammy the next morning, "I may have to go out to the airport this afternoon, and there's no telling where Wimpy Winfield's going to have me drive that DC-4 . . . maybe to Greenland, for all I know. Anyway, I'd better take my own car down so I don't get stranded at Sikorski."

"I'll ride with you," Tammy volunteered. "Bring me up to date."

So I did during the drive down to the lab.

"That's a pretty big airplane!" Tammy remarked.

"Yeah, but we can get it, and we can't get the Commander. So we recrunch the numbers this morning."

The numbers looked bigger than anything we had worked with on the sky hook project.

Fully loaded, the DC-4 in her cargo configuration had a gross weight of 94,300 pounds. Empty, she weighed 40,000 pounds. She could cruise at full power at 36,000 feet with superchargers blowing all four 1400-horsepower engines.

"It's going to take a damned big sky hook," I decided, leaning back in the chair and tossing the pencil at the computer terminal. "About five thousand horsepower . . . which is almost thirty-eight hundred kilowatts of electrical power."

"Yes, but that's at ninety-four thousand pounds, Mike. How much can we strip it down?" Tammy suggested.

"Well, at full power, one gallon per minute per engine, that's two hundred forty gallons per hour or fourteen-forty pounds of gas. Let's say we put two thousand pounds of fuel aboard, plus my one-twenty-five pounds as pilot . . . What does that leave us in the way of margins within which we've got to build a sky hook plus its power supply?"

"How about the co-pilot?"

"Huh?"

"A C-54E or DC-4—whatever you want to call it—requires a co-pilot," she reminded me.

"Well, I guess we'll have to add in about one-eighty-five pounds for Bill Osbourne."

"How about me?"

"What?"

"I weigh one-oh-four. That's a saving of eighty-one pounds that we can use for something else."

"Tammy, you can't fly a DC-4!"

"Why not? I've got more than four hundred hours of heavy time in a DC-3!"

"Okay, okay! Incidentally, how did you manage all that heavy time?"

"I once worked for an outfit that had DC-3's for hauling things around."

I sighed. I hadn't exactly figured on going into orbit in this lash-up with Tammy. It made me feel rather queasy. I don't mind taking a lot of chances in the air when I'm alone. But I've always felt extra cautious when I've had someone important to me along.

We got the numbers, and I presented them to Vic about lunch time.

"Are you sure?" he asked.

"No. That's why I'd like you to double-check. Here's the operational manual with the basic numbers. I hope to God I haven't made a mistake!"

"The numbers look pretty big," Vic noted. "Why couldn't you get the Commander?"

"We just couldn't, and we'll have to leave it at that."

He quickly glanced down the pages of figures, then came to a stop. "Tammy? As co-pilot?"

"She's qualified, and she weighs a lot less than anybody else around here who is, such as Bill Osbourne."

Bill Osbourne didn't bat an eyelash when I told him later in the day. "I'd hoped to be able to go, but Tammy weighs less. Every pound is going to count. My God, this sky hook unit for the DC-4 is *big*!"

"Yeah, I don't even know if we can provide the energy to run it or not," I admitted.

"Vic and Len will work on that end of it. They'll get you a sky hook and an energy source. You and Tammy let Wimpy get you both type-rated in the DC-4." He looked down again at the photocopy of my calculations. "By the beard of my sacred aunt, fifteen hundred horsepower just to keep that thing in the air!"

The next two weeks were probably the most halcyon days of my life. I was flying most of the time. Furthermore, I was flying with Tammy. True, Seven-Eleven was an ancient clunker, but it flew. It was sound, solid, and secure. Wimpy did an excellent job of checking Tammy and me out in the bird. When he signed us off, he called the FAA office and told them we were ready for the check ride. We took a boring flight up over the hills of Connecticut with a bored FAA check pilot riding in the flight engineer's seat between us. He pulled a couple of engine-out emergencies on us, had us shoot a landing at Westchester County Airport, and said, "Wimpy, you always do a good job. And these two have enough time that I don't have to worry." He signed-off our type-rating.

I wouldn't say that Jake Stock was exactly pleased that Corporate Research was taking over one of his airplanes, and he insisted on being absolutely certain that Tammy and I were type-rated by giving us a check ride himself, much to the visible disgust of Wimpy Winfield who knew more about that old DC-4 than the Chief Corporate Pilot. Jake Stock was indeed an ancient pelican, lean and grizzled, radiating competence and self-assurance, chewing on his ever-present cigar. He had his own way to fly a DC-4 and claimed to have had several thousand hours in the type during World War II when he flew as an airline contract pilot for the Air Corps on the African run. After a couple of hours of a *real* check ride, Jake Stock pronounced us qualified to fly Seven-Eleven, but added, "I want you to take good care of this bird. She's my spare. I know that Bill Osbourne got a letter from Halden authorizing the temporary loan of an aircraft to Corporate Research, but I fully expect to get this airplane back from you in the same excellent condition as when we signed it over. Any reconditioning to bring it up to *our* standards is not going to come out of our budget in the Aviation Division!"

Tammy and I then proceeded to "explore the performance envelope" of the old bird. We had to know what the ship would do. For many pilots, this is just an excuse to log some time. In our case, we needed the data *and* the experience of hours in the air with Seven-Eleven.

Seven-Eleven was equipped with a demand regulator oxygen system, so Tammy and I flew the ship to its maximum altitude—full throttles, maximum manifold pressures on all engines, and as light as we could arrange it. The book was wrong; this DC-4 would sail along at 38,500 feet. True, she was mushing through the sky right on the edge of a stall. But she would do it.

We kept feeding this data back to Vic and Len. I also

told them, "Look, this is not a pressurized airplane. Somewhere you've got to come up with full pressure suits for Tammy and me."

"Where are we going to get space suits?" Vic wanted to know.

"Easy!" Len Marshall said with a smile. "We get in touch with Ted Mayan, and he gets that surplus-scrounging graduate student of his to find two of them!"

That was a slim chance. I was therefore surprised when Ted Mayan showed up in his Lincoln Continental at Sikorski one morning with big boxes sealed in the usual imperishable, impenetrable government shipping and storage materials. They were surplus U.S. Navy MK IV full pressure suits capable of working in a vacuum. And he had the necessary auxiliary equipment to pressurize them. They didn't fit perfectly. They were not fireproof nomex built to the latest NASA specifications. They wouldn't keep us alive more than about six hours in orbit. But they would work. We tested them on the ground and put them away.

Tammy and I took some long cross-country flights in Seven-Eleven. We practiced single-engine landings on short landing strips, simulating emergencies. We flew single-engine at the maximum altitudes we could manage with that amount of power. We even performed the most dangerous and deadly of all maneuvers in a large, heavy, multi-engine airplane: complete dead-stick landing with all four motors stopped, their propellers feathered, and *no chance* of making a go-around if you didn't hit it dead-nuts on the first try. Now I know what the Space Shuttle pilots go through!

Tammy was a no-nonsense, capable, cool, and quite competent co-pilot. The controls in the DC-4 are not hydraulically boosted, yet she exhibited strength that belied her minute size by wrestling those controls successfully.

Naturally, we had to perform a critical test on the autopilot, and the DC-4 was built with a forward cabin in which a relief crew could sack out during long trans-oceanic flights. Both of us requalified our memberships in the Mile-High Club, statute and nautical, several times at several altitudes, just to make sure that we did qualify.

Back at the lab, a new sky hook was taking shape. Vic had managed to find the original design manuals for the DC-4 in the National Air and Space Museum and the MacDonnell-Douglas library archives in Santa Monica. To get copies of those old documents gave us an excuse to take some very long cross-country flights in Seven-Eleven. Carrying no cargo and only fuel, Tammy, Vic, and myself, we made it to California non-stop.

It was an experience for Vic. He had ridden airplanes only as a passenger in the cabin of jet airliners. In spite of the fact that he didn't really know what was going on, he spent most of the time in the flight engineer's jump seat behind the center throttle console, watching with obvious enjoyment.

He also told me something that took some rough edges off our relationship. "Mike, I had lots of trouble understanding you when you joined the lab. I'll never understand Tammy here; she's a woman." Tammy thumbed her nose at Vic, but the mathematician went on, "You try to be good at whatever you do, but I could never understand what turned you on about flying. Now I know. This is probably the closest thing to sex I've ever experienced. The view, the smoothness, the feeling that we are surrounded and secure and warm because of technology . . ." He grinned. "It's an aerial orgasm!"

The new sky hook unit was designed around the specific structural characteristics of the DC-4—its resonances, bending moments, mass distribution, and interfaces between various components and subassemblies. It wasn't an easy job for Vic. There were many days when Tammy and I didn't fly; we worked with the microcomputer tied in on a time-sharing net with Serge Korsinski's big general-purpose computer.

Things were just going beautifully!

Then we had the marketing meeting.

It was another dog-and-pony show, this time orchestrated by Phil Sanatella up at corporate headquarters. Bill Osbourne insisted that Len, Vic and myself be present.

The conference room was the one used for meetings of the NEMECO Board of Directors. It was plush in comparison to our lab conference facilities. Sanatella passed around a bound document about an inch thick, took a position on the right of Grant Halden at the head of the huge table, and began with, "Gentlemen, I believe we are going to have trouble finding a market for the Corporate Research sky hook!"

Bill exploded. "What?"

Sanatella held up his hand pontifically. "Please let me finish my opening remarks. Then I'll be more than pleased to answer any detailed questions regarding my methodology, approach, or data. I've spent all my time since the last conference working on the marketing for this device. In short, I've concluded that there are no apparent industrial applications for a lifting or pushing device that are not currently being satisfactorily handled by other devices and systems which, in the long run, may be less expensive. My study has also concluded that it will require a large capital outlay to move this device into production status, to establish suitable marketing strategies and sales teams, and to come head-to-head with firms making other devices that are now on the market and doing satisfactory jobs."

Bill Osbourne was doing a magnificent job restraining himself. Vic and Len looked dumbfounded. It was the executive vice-president, Dr. Hayward Newcomb, who quietly asked, "Can you tell us what markets and applications you surveyed?"

"They're listed in detail in my report. All of you have copies."

Osbourne finally could no longer withhold comment. "Phil, why didn't you work with Corporate Research on this?"

"I did."

"You talked with me for one hour, most of that over lunch. Vic, how long did Phil talk with you?"

"About ten minutes," the mathematician replied. "I tried to explain the theory to him, but he . . ."

"I'm not interested in the theory of how or why the device operates. From a marketing point of view, my main concerns must be applications, the value of the device in doing those jobs, and how many devices we can anticipate selling before we reach market saturation," Sanatella explained rapidly.

Bill ignored him. "Len, how long did Phil talk with you?"

"About a half-hour. I gave him a photocopy of all the memos we'd generated on applications, plus copies of my special applications laboratory notebook," the lab director remarked, obviously disturbed and disgusted.

"Those applications notes were far-out dreaming with little relationship to the realities of . . ." Sanatella tried to put in.

Osbourne turned to me. "Mike, how much time did Phil spend with you? You've probably come up with some of the most prosaic applications in the agricultural industry because of your background as an ag pilot."

I looked Grant Halden straight in the eye and said, "Mr. Sanatella didn't talk with me at all."

Osbourne lifted the inch-thick report. "Grant, how can this be worth the paper it's printed on? We have had applications in mind since Day One of this project! Hay, you know how often you and I have talked about it!"

"I suggest you read the report," Sanatella told him. "I have to deal with the realities of the marketplace. I can't put credence in projections of inventors who have always historically overestimated the value of their inventions. I spent a great deal of time with Bob Destry at the Mill Equipment Division and with Max Keller here up at the Heavy Construction Equipment Division in Roseville, Michigan." Sanatella indicated the man sitting next to Destry, a sandy-haired, heavy-set, solid "construction engineer" type who, obviously, must be Max Keller. "I worked for weeks with the marketing people from Mill Equipment and Heavy Construction Equipment. We thoroughly surveyed the marketplace and the various pieces of equipment currently performing lifting and pushing jobs—everything from fork lifts to heavy extension cranes to . . ."

"How about our tech reps?" I broke in.

"Pardon me?"

"Did you spend any time out in the field with our technical representatives where NEMECO equipment is being used?" I asked. "Did you find out what the problems of our customers were? Did you . . ."

"There was no time for that," Sanatella put in. "I had to depend upon the inputs I received from the marketing people at Mill Equipment and Heavy Construction Equipment . . ."

Bill Osbourne had calmed down a little bit. "Grant and Hay, we haven't discussed this before because I didn't want to make enemies among the people Corporate Research is designed to serve. But, as you know, one of the reasons we have Corporate Research is because of the very factors that Phil has run up against in the various divisions."

Hayward Newcomb knew that he was also in trouble at the moment. He answered with his customary calmness, coolness, and rationality, "What Bill refers to, gentlemen, are two factors that exist in every sales and marketing group and, as a matter of fact, even in the Department of Defense as well. One of these is the so-called 'NIH factor' which stands for 'not invented here.' It means that one has such blind and implicit faith in one's abilities and the abilities of one's subordinates that if it wasn't invented in your shop, it isn't worth a damn . . . to put it bluntly. Now, Bob, let me finish before you attempt rebuttal! The second factor is the ordinary 'sales force hype.' A sales force without sales force hype isn't a good sales force and cannot sell. It's a philosophy that says, in essence, that our competitors are a nice but incompetent bunch of guys who have a good product, but it isn't as good as ours. And . . . Hold on, Bob! You'll get your innings! And on top of that is the fact that such organizations are so overconfident that there is a better than a ninety-five percent chance that they haven't even seen the competition's

product, *much less even tested it against their own!* I have
not read this report, Grant, but I feel that this is what
Bill has in mind."

"Grant, I *know* what's in this report because my people and I worked with Phil in getting the data together."
Bob Destry quickly stepped into the breach. "We tried
to do an honest job. I cannot agree with Hay's position."

"Nor can I!" Max Keller growled. "I haven't seen
this scientific miracle from Corporate Research, but I
find it difficult to accept that it's an actual working em-
bodiment of that old fraud, the so-called 'reactionless
drive.' I have to assume it's real because I'm told that it
is. But I can't foresee any applications for it in the
heavy construction equipment marketplace where there
are perfectly adequate devices for lifting and pushing
and pulling already. What I would like to see from Corporate Research is a development that would greatly
improve the efficiency of what we have or new processes that would permit us to make existing products
better or with less cost in terms of labor and material
. . . Labor costs are eating me up, and I don't need a
brand new invention! I need significant improvements
on what we've got . . . improvements, I might add,
that are coming out of my own development teams regularly . . ."

Halden looked pained. Open warfare had erupted between his operating, money-making division chiefs and
his ace-in-the-hole hedge against the future in Corporate Research. "Gentlemen," he said quietly, looking
around the room, "this is obviously a highly emotional
issue. We don't run NEMECO on emotions or gut feel.
A business must be run rationally with just the right
amount of gambling in certain areas where costs are
low, probability of success is reasonable, and potential payoff can be high. I'm rather surprised at the
brief conclusions of this marketing survey; I had fully
anticipated *some* market, and I'm still prepared to back
this as a gamble worth taking. *However,*" the
NEMECO president emphasized, "a rational decision
cannot be made in this environment. Perhaps some of

you have read Phil's report." He looked at Destry and Keller. "I haven't. Nor has Hay Newcomb who has primary responsibility to me for Corporate Research. Nor, obviously, has Dr. Osbourne. I require the time to read and digest the contents of this voluminous report which appears to be exceedingly thorough. I will make no decision on this today. I suggest that all of you read it carefully. I'll call another meeting on this matter when I've had the opportunity to study this report." He took off his glasses, carefully folded them, and placed them in the inner pocket of his suit coat. Halden was upset. I could tell that in the testy way he snapped, "Meeting is adjourned. Thank you for coming, Max. Let's get back to work." And he strode out.

Bill, Vic, Len, and I did not go back to the lab. Bill felt we should not because our expressions and tones would decimate the morale on this project since nearly everyone in the lab knew that a marketing meeting of great importance was going on. I suggested we go to Mama's for the usual reasons.

We sat down and all ordered coffee.

"Vic, you haven't said much," Len observed.

"Phil Sanatella has a point," Vic mused. "We tend to forget it in our cerebral work at the lab. If the sky hook can't be sold, it's nothing more than a nifty technical trick . . . and we'd better get on with something useful to NEMECO!"

"It *is* useful to NEMECO!" I blurted out. "That was a fantastic hatchet job by Phil Sanatella for the benefit of Robert Destry and with the full support of Max Keller!"

"You're both right in a way," Osbourne said. "Before the automobile existed, the horse and buggy did fine, and nobody wanted an automobile. Now, nobody seems to be able to do without one. The same holds true of the telephone. We did our marketing with Halden and Newcomb, but we didn't do it with Destry and Keller. We have to figure out how to sell our work to them."

"What's our plan of action?" Len Marshall wanted to know in his pragmatic manner. "Where do we go from here?"

"Damn the torpedoes! We have not yet begun to fight! You may fire when ready, Gridley!" Osbourne snapped suddenly. "We get that DC-4 in orbit, and we do it as fast as we can . . . And if we can't get it into orbit, we get it as high as we can, higher than any DC-4 was ever designed to go! Finish your coffee, gang! There's more coffee at the lab, and we have one hell of a lot of work to do in one hell of a hurry if we are going to save our asses!"

Chapter Sixteen

It was a lash-up if I ever saw one!

The DC-4 sky hook was about ten feet long and was bolted through the floor directly to the fuselage structure over the aircraft's center of gravity in the cavernous cabin.

Carl had done a magnificent job of miniaturizing the electronics. The hundreds of pounds of electrical equipment that had accompanied the original sky hook had been reduced to about forty pounds of solid-state electronics whose major weight was in the aluminum framework that held it all together.

The superbatteries were Len's department. I wanted to know more about them, but Len just told me, "Look, we're working around the clock to put each one together by hand. Someday, I'll have the time to go into the most minute detail with you. But not now!"

I persisted. I like to know what's in the airplanes I fly.

"Briefly, they use high energy density chemical couples with a solid ionic conductor as an electrolyte. They're good for a little over a megajoule per kilo, which is many times what's available from any other low-temperature primary battery. Now, please let me out. I have to get back to the lab and build another one!"

The fuselage of Seven-Eleven was getting crowded with wiring, plastic tubs that contained superbatteries, and the liquid oxygen system that Wimpy was installing for the pressure suits. I was weighing everything as it was installed, and Tammy kept up with the weight and balance calculations.

There were nights when we didn't go back to Morse Manor. We worked until we got tired, then tried to find someplace to sleep. "Look," I told everyone, "Tammy has first call on the crew bunk up forward. She has to help me fly this thing."

I didn't get the chance to read Sanatella's marketing report. I might get that chance later if the Twenty-Two Thruster project was successful. Otherwise, it would make little difference. Osbourne was spending his time up at corporate headquarters running interference. He showed up from time to time to report progress or lack of it.

On one such visit, Tammy and I confronted him. "Bill, we *must* test fly this plane before we commit to the all-out operation," I told him.

"We've got enough superbatteries aboard now to cruise with aerodynamic lift," Tammy pointed out.

"Will it set back the schedule?" Osbourne wanted to know.

"It may set it forward," I said. "We need to tune, and we can't do that on the ramp . . . only in the air."

Osbourne thought a moment. "If it fails . . ."

"Then we'll just have more time to either correct it or start looking for new jobs," I said.

"I was thinking of what might happen if you dropped her into Long Island Sound on takeoff."

"Don't worry," Tammy told him. "We could climb out with only two engines. We're not switching to sky hook power until we have lots of altitude."

"When do you want to go?" Osbourne wanted to know.

"As soon as Len gets that next cell in place. That'll be tonight. Let's make it dramatic: Dawn tomorrow morning, if the weather's okay."

Bill grinned. "Okay, dawn it is, right out of the old test-pilot movies!"

I didn't go home that night. Neither did Tammy. We were too busy. We decided we wouldn't exceed 36,000 feet during the test flight, and therefore wouldn't wear the pressure suits. But we'd wear seat pack parachutes not only for safety but because they eliminated the need for both of us to use seat cushions to see over the instrument panel.

The nights were cold and clammy on the ramp at Sikorski with the damp air from the Sound forming little pockets of fog on the ground where it was wetter than elsewhere. I checked the outside of the aircraft. About eleven o'clock, Wimpy lumbered over to me. "Mike, are you an Authorized Inspector?" He was referring to the special authorization on my airframe and powerplant mechanic's license which permitted me to certify the airworthiness of an aircraft.

"Sure am, Wimpy."

"Well, I didn't want to take any chances. I noted you don't think that the sky hook installation is a 'major alteration' according to Federal Air Regulation Forty-three."

"We made no changes to the airframe, powerplants, controls, weight-and-balance, or performance. I went over those regulations pretty carefully." I looked at him. "You've been at this longer than I have. What do you think?"

"Waall," Wimpy drawled, "some pass-gauge FAA inspectors might feel we were stretching those regs if they claim the sky hook's an auxiliary powerplant."

"We bolted something to the basic fuselage structure that doesn't affect the basic performance of the ship. She'll still fly according to the book," I pointed out. "I'm willing to sign it off on the logs. I've made more serious modifications than this to ag planes. Most of the time, the alterations were overlooked in any accident investigation because the engine quit and caused the crash . . . so the FAA and National Transportation Safety Board never bothered to look any further."

"Tell you, Mike, I'll sign off the log book as A&P for NEMECO . . . and because I've got something you don't have. I'm an FAA Designated Engineering Representative, and I don't think you've made any changes requiring a Form Three-thirty-seven to be filed and approved. How about that!"

"Thank you, Wimpy. You don't need to take the responsibility for this pile of junk. I'll do it."

"Well, let me . . . because if anybody asks, I'll tell them I knew what you were doing . . . because you do. Chances are that the FAA will never question it anyway unless you prang the airplane . . . in which case, you'll have other things to worry about."

"Wimpy, thanks."

"Just bring it back. Jake Stock'll have my hide for a door mat if you don't."

Carl clambered down the temporary boarding stairs rigged against the rear cargo door and stumbled up to me. He was nearly exhausted. "Mike, she's tuned the best I can do it on the ramp. It'll be different in the air. You may have to make some adjustments to the load compensating circuit."

"Go home and get some sleep, Carl."

"No, Wilding will have questions if I do. He's been bugging me to find out what's going on out here. I'll just sack out in the hangar. I want to be around tomorrow morning." He stumbled off across the ramp.

It was cold. I finished the external inspection, climbed up the stairs, and threaded my way down the littered cabin toward the flight deck.

I tried to sneak quietly through the crew compartment where Tammy was stretched out on the lower bunk, clad in the dirty coveralls we now all sported because we had been working too hard to do more than take a shower in the hangar from time to time. But a little voice came to me. "Mike?" She rolled over to face me.

"Sorry, I was trying to get through without waking you."

"I wasn't sleeping, just resting."

"I thought I'd try to get some shut-eye up in the left seat."

"Everything okay outside?"

"Best I can tell, it ought to fly."

"Come here," she told me. "It's too cold in here tonight for you to sleep in that seat. Keep me warm, hon."

We kept each other warm. The bunk in a DC-4 isn't very big, but we weren't big people.

After much exchanged warmth, she said in her whispery voice, "Mike, suppose it doesn't work?"

"It'll work okay," I tried to reassure her. "This your first real flight as a test pilot?"

"Yes. I'm a little scared."

"Don't be. Or don't be too much scared. If anything goes wrong, you go out that cockpit side window as fast as you can just the way I showed you. And don't wait for me because I'll be holding things together long enough for you to clear before I go out my own window."

"I've never jumped before."

"You've done something comparable to it."

"Huh?"

"That first night you came into my room in the dark. I think that was probably harder for you to do than make a parachute jump."

"I'm ready to make that kind of a jump again any time . . ."

"Tammy, my dear, I know that." The conversation was not proceeding as quickly as this; it was interrupted for long periods at random moments when our lips were doing other things that prevented talking. "When this is over, I want to take a bigger jump. I don't want to lose you . . . ever."

"The same, Mike. But there will be some things that I have to do first so that you don't become upset . . ."

"Why, Tammy? Nothing in your past makes the slightest difference to me now."

"Oh, Mike, just hold me! Dawn is coming too soon. And we'll work all this out when this is over. I'm glad I'll be with you, because if you didn't come back . . ."

"But we're coming back!"

"Shush! And keep me warm!"

Light broke through the cockpit windows. I realized it was dawn. I got to my feet. Tammy was asleep. I crawled through the cabin and clambered down the steep temporary stairs to see Bill Osbourne driving up in his TR-7. He got out with a picnic basket, grinning as he said, "Hot pilots ain't worth a damn without a hot breakfast!"

Both Tammy and I felt better after orange juice, a couple of sweet rolls, ham and scrambled eggs, and lots of hot coffee. We ate in the crew compartment just aft of the flight deck.

"Thank your wife for this," I told Bill.

"I will. She wants us all to get together soon. We haven't gotten to know one another socially."

"We've been busy," Tammy remarked.

"That we have. Maybe there will be some time . . ."

"There's never enough time," I said.

The wan disk of the sun was well above the horizon when we closed the cargo door, buckled ourselves into our parachute harnesses, fastened our safety harnesses, and went through the prestart check list. I pushed back my cockpit window. Wimpy was standing on the ramp next to the fire cart, giving us the "all clear." He then pointed to an engine and rotated his hand.

"Starting Number Three!" I called. Tammy engaged the starter.

"Four blades . . . six . . . seven . . . nine . . . twelve! Ignition both! Boost pump low!" she called back. I flipped the magneto switch and hit the primer. "Auto rich!" she called and I moved the mixture control accordingly. Engine Number 3 coughed, shuddered, blew a cloud of white smoke, and settled down to run. Fuel, oil, hydraulic pressures . . . all normal. We got the other three engines started without trouble.

"External power?"

"Removed!"

"Radios?"

"On!"

"Vacuum?"

"Within limits!"

"Gyros?"

"Set and uncaged!"

"Flaps?"

"Down!"

"Bridgeport Ground Control, Douglas November one

three seven eleven at NEMECO ramp, taxi for take-off!"

"November Seven-Eleven, Ground. Good morning, Mike! Taxi to runway Two Four. Wind two three zero at five. Altimeter two niner seven seven. Where you and Tammy going today?"

It may sound coolly professional and technical, but there are times on the radio when there is some warmth. And this morning we needed it.

"We'd like a right turn out after takeoff. Going up over Pawling, Albany, and Hartford to check some new equipment," I told the voice from the control tower.

"Worked kind of late last night, didn't you?"

"Airlines have schedules, and we've got deadlines."

We did our pre-takeoff engine run-up at the approach end of runway 24, and Number 4 engine was rough as hell. Tammy looked worried. "Forget it," I told her. "Wimpy said we fouled the plugs on that last low-power approach. It's got new plugs in it. Valve may be sticking. It'll burn the lead out under takeoff power."

"Well, we're light enough to climb out on three engines," she observed.

We got takeoff clearance from a female voice from the tower, wheeled out onto runway 24, and lined up with the center line. Those four throttles are a handful, and I inched them forward as Tammy steadied the control yoke.

"Vee-One!" Tammy called over the roar of four engines. We were past the critical engine failure speed. We could now continue the takeoff on three engines if necessary.

"Vee-Two!" I eased back on the big wheel, and Seven-Eleven broke with the Earth.

"Gear up!"

"Gear coming up! Three lights!"

"Climb power!" I felt Tammy reduce power to 2300 rpm and 33 inches of manifold pressure. I reached over and hit the flap switch. "Flaps coming up, five degrees at a time!"

"November Seven-Eleven, Bridgeport Tower. Right turn on course approved! Contact Westchester Approach on one two zero point five five. Have a nice flight!"

"See ya later!" I replied and settled down to making the ship fly. "Tammy, switch to Approach and then turn on the multicom frequency so we can talk with Wimpy and Bill."

I took up a heading toward Pawling, contacted Westchester Approach, told them we were VFR out of two going to 10,500 and would be maneuvering at that altitude on a test flight. A definite New Yorker told us to "maintain VFR on your own navigation!" In other words, he saw our radar transponder blip on his screen, but he didn't want to be bothered with us.

We levelled off at 10,500 feet and set up cruise power—1600 rpm and 24 inches. "NEMECO Bridgeport, this is NEMECO Seven-Eleven on multicom frequency one two two point nine. How do you read?"

Osbourne's voice crackled back, "Loud and clear, Seven-Eleven!"

"We're level at ten-five, pulling sixteen hundred and twenty-four, one ninety one indicated," I told him. "Warming up the unit now!"

We had a separate check list for the sky hook, and we'd changed the terminology so that nobody would suspect that we were trying a new propulsion system. Carl had rigged up a "kilowatt-hours remaining" digital count-down indicator on the drive control panel so we could keep track of the superbattery power. It wasn't critical on this flight because we also had the capability of recharging the superbatteries from the aircraft electrical system.

We powered-up the drive. Plasma voltage on . . . and I could see the flickering glow in the cabin through the aft doorway. Phasing on. Drive voltage on. Load compensator on. Slowly, I turned the knob that advanced power to the unit.

There was a slight bucking of the airplane that I detected through the parachute pack and the seat. "Out of phase slightly!" I said. "Tammy, take it! I'm going back to make an adjustment!"

It was perhaps the strangest sight I'd ever seen in an airplane: those banks of plastic bucket shapes, a maze of heavy cables, and that glowing drive unit bolted to the floor. I got rid of the bucking by a slight adjustment to the load compensating circuit and a readjustment of the driving wave shape. I went back to the cockpit and strapped in.

"Next time, wear your parachute!" Tammy snapped. "I don't want to lose you!"

"Next time," I told her, "don't make personal comments over an open microphone! You're so up-tight you've got your thumb clamped down on the push-to-talk switch!"

"Oops!"

"Never mind, Seven-Eleven!" Bill's voice came back. "You're just adding a little spice . . ."

"Easy, hon! She's running smooth now. Let's see if it'll push this bird!" I gently advanced the sky hook power controls.

I got an immediate increasing indication on airspeed, rate of climb, and altimeter. "Unit's on and adjusted," I reported over the multicom radio to Bridgeport. "Reducing as planned." I turned to Tammy. "Kill the outboard engines and feather the props!" She pulled the mixture controls to "Idle Cut Off" and killed the ignition on engines One and Four.

The nose dropped slightly and airspeed reduced to 190 miles per hour. But the altitude held.

"NEMECO Bridgeport, Seven-Eleven! One and Four are shut down. We're holding airspeed and altitude as anticipated with the calculated power settings on the unit!"

"Roger, Seven-Eleven! Sounds good! Will it steer?"

"Stand by!" I did a gentle fifteen-degree bank to the left, then to the right, and then turned to a due-north heading. "Bridgeport, Seven-Eleven. Flies like a dream. We're going to Procedure Number Two!"

I increased the sky hook power again. The glow from

the drive unit was bright now. I watched altitude, airspeed, and rate of climb increase. "Cut Two and Three and feather them, Tam!"

N13711 continued to fly, the props on all four engines stationary and feathered. Airspeed settled in at 195. Altitude held at 10,500 feet. I called, "Bill, are you recording this?"

"Roger!"

"We should make another profound historical statement. We've got four shut down and a DC-4 flying normally!" I released the mike button, leaned across the center throttle pedestal, and kissed Tammy.

The ship was just as maneuverable as ever. I reached down, picked up the flight manual, thumbed through it, and found that at this weight I could safely pull about three gee's acceleration. "Hang on, Tam," I told her, "and don't get shook up. This isn't in the flight plan."

I slow-rolled the DC-4 with four dead engines.

It was kind of sloppy, and I let the nose fall off a little bit as we came around. But, since I had never rolled a DC-4 before, I thought it was passable performance.

Tammy had gone dead white. "Don't *ever* do that again with a ship this big!"

"No problem! Tex Johnson rolled the Boeing 707 prototype at five hundred feet in front of a crowd of airline presidents!"

"This is no 707! Just don't do that again!"

I didn't report it to Bridgeport. I called New York Center and requested an IFR clearance to 30,000 feet direct to Albany, then via Victor 2 airway to Gardner, Victor 229 to Hartford, and Victor 99 to Bridgeport. New York Center came back with the approval.

"Roger, Center, Douglas Seven-Eleven leaving ten five for Flight Level three zero zero!" To Tammy I said, "Let's start 'em up!"

I shut down the sky hook once we had all four engines set for climb power. At 12,000 feet, Tammy and I donned oxygen masks. New York Center handed us off to Boston Center, transferring control and surveillance to the other Air Traffic Control Center. We were outbound on Victor 2 airway from Albany before we got altitude, and I called Bridgeport again on multicom. "Bill, we're level at thirty indicating two fifty. Proceeding with Procedure Three."

Again, I turned on the drive, brought it on line, had a slight tuning problem because we had burned off several hundred pounds of fuel during our climb, then shut down all four engines.

High in the cloudless blue sky of the stratosphere, we sailed along with all four engines dead and no sound in the cabin except the boundary layer whispering past the windshield at more than two hundred miles per hour.

"Boston Center, Douglas Seven-Eleven requesting Flight Level three six zero for test purposes."

"Douglas Seven-Eleven, Center. Climb and maintain Flight Level three six zero. Report reaching. That's close to your absolute altitude, isn't it?"

"Roger, Center. We won't be up there long."

"Okay, let me know when you want to come back down."

"Appreciate your cooperation, Center."

On drive power alone, we climbed Seven-Eleven to 36,000 feet. I kept an eye on the remaining battery power. It was dropping rapidly, but we still had plenty to get us back to Bridgeport. We stayed up there where no DC-4 with dead engines should rightfully be until we approached Hartford on the southbound leg. I requested a lower altitude, got permission to descend "at pilot's discretion," and left 36,000 feet for 17,000 feet.

Over Hartford, we ran into trouble, and I should have anticipated it.

We couldn't get engines One, Three, and Four to start. They'd gotten too cold at minus 70 degrees Fahrenheit up in the stratosphere, and the oil had congealed. Number Two started reluctantly.

Tammy was a cool number. "Knock off trying to start them, Mike! We're so light we can make it back on one with the drive helping! Cancel IFR clearance and get us down where we've got some lift and some warmth!"

I didn't report the trouble to Center or to Bill. I

didn't want the fire trucks waiting along the runway at Sikorski. I got us below controlled airspace, cancelled our IFR clearance, and let Seven-Eleven drift down. We stabilized at 4,000 feet with full power on Number Two and the drive unit pulling the rest of the load. "No sweat, Tammy! There's Bridgeport!"

"Roger! No emergency, Mike!"

"It'll look strange making a landing with only one engine," I remarked, "but we won't declare an emergency."

"Better let them know," she advised.

"Bridgeport Tower, NEMECO Seven-Eleven with you, ten miles northeast on Victor Ninety-nine! Request straight-in approach to runway Two Four. We have an engine problem, but no emergency."

"NEMECO Seven-Eleven, Bridgeport Tower. You're cleared for straight-in approach to runway Two Four. Wind calm, altimeter two niner seven five. Need the fire trucks?"

"Ah, negative! Couple dead engines, but we're runnin' light!" I replied in my best professional, calm, and bored airline captain's voice with just the slight drawl they all affected.

. "Seven-Eleven, advise when you have the airport in sight. Show us a landing light, please."

Tammy flipped the two landing light switches on the overhead panel.

I picked up the localizer back course radio signal. Then I saw the bright strobe lights of the runway end identifiers. "Bridgeport Tower, Seven-Eleven has runway in sight."

"Roger, Seven-Eleven. Cleared to land!"

We kept the wheels and flaps up until the last possible moment to reduce drag and power requirements. As soon as the tires touched the concrete, I turned off the sky hook so we could stop Seven-Eleven.

"NEMECO Seven-Eleven, Bridgeport Tower! Need any help getting back to NEMECO ramp?"

"Thanks, Tower. We can taxi okay on one engine."

"Roger. Contact Ground point nine leaving the runway!"

There was concern and worry on everyone's faces as we calmly taxied up to the NEMECO ramp and shut down the one operating engine.

Tammy grinned at me. "Nice work!"

"Easy, with your help. Think we'd make a good team?"

"I think we already have it made!" she grinned back at me. "Except you've got to learn not to sweat those engine-out approaches!"

I discovered that I was wringing wet with perspiration. "Well, you ain't no antiperspirant ad yourself!" I slid my cockpit window open and yelled down to Wimpy, "No sweat, Wimpy! The oil congealed and we couldn't get 'em started again! Everything else is copasetic!"

We started back through the cabin. In the privacy of the crew compartment, Tammy turned around, grabbed me by the ears, and kissed me soundly. "And *that* is for aerobatics in a DC-4 at ten thousand feet without any engines!"

"Would you like to review inverted flying procedures tonight?" I asked her.

Once on the ground, my first thought was to get that airplane into the hangar and locked away as quickly as possible. The tower people had seen us working last night. Who else had been watching? Bill agreed. But he wanted a full debriefing.

"We'll give you a full report at Mama's. I'm hungry! Then I want to sleep for about a week," I told Bill.

"I used to feel that way after a mission over Hanoi. But we need your verbal reports while it's fresh in your minds . . . particularly what happened after you started to descend."

It wasn't as historic as that day in 1903 when the first powered airplane flew, but we'd flown an airplane with a totally new form of propulsion system that might take that old DC-4 into orbit around the Earth.

The sky hook was more than a laboratory experiment now.

Chapter Seventeen

"How can Sanatella possibly say there's no market for the sky hook now?" I chortled in the lab the next morning. "Even if we don't do anything else, we've done something nobody's done before!"

Len and I were having coffee together in his office. I was still high. Len wasn't.

"Well, Mike, we did something in the lab here that nobody else had done, either . . . and Sanatella didn't even bat an eye. In fact, he's trying to shoot us down."

"Why? *Why?*" I couldn't understand this. Why would this one little man try to screw up the technical breakthrough of the century?

"I'm not sure it's Sanatella alone," Len remarked, pulling his copy of the marketing report out of his desk drawer. "Have you read it?"

"Haven't had time!"

"Before you go flying that DC-4 into orbit, you'd better. I'm not up on all the latest in-fighting, but you and I both know what Destry's up to." Len held up his hand as I started to say something. "Now, don't worry! It will be done in the most gentlemanly way possible! There will be no public recriminations or name calling. Just a smooth and gentle transition of power. I don't know how Destry's working it, but he's got Max Keller on his side. And he probably has an arrangement with Sanatella . . ."

"Len, does Vic figure into this in any way that you can determine?"

"No, and it bothers me. Vic's an enigma, even though I manage to get along with him. You're doing a much better job of that than I am," Len grinned.

"I've always respected Vic for his prowess with mathematics and women, although the latter may be sheer bravado on Vic's part," I admitted. "At any rate, I think Vic now respects me for possessing some expertise in his field, mathematics, as well as my aviation activities."

"I think he also respects you for what you've done for Tammy."

"*For* Tammy?"

"Do you remember the way she was when you came?"

"Yeah. But, Len, I didn't change Tammy. She did it herself."

"Have it your own way. When are you getting married?"

"Tammy still has a hang-up somewhere. I'm patient. She'll work it out. I'll be there when she does."

"I hope you're not disappointed," Len warned me.

"Why?"

"You may not be around when she works it out. She may be somewhere else."

"Wherever she is, I'll be there."

"My dad was right: Never comment on a person's religion or love life. Okay, you'd better get busy and read Sanatella's report," Len indicated the bound document, "because it's important to the sky hook's future."

"Not any more!" It was Bill Osbourne standing in the door. His small, dark, deep-set eyes were angry, and he almost bristled. "Len, where's Vic?"

"He hasn't come in yet. What's the matter, Bill? You look like you've been in an accident! Are you all right?"

"I'm not all right, but I haven't been in an accident. Mike, sit down! This concerns you!" The research director closed the door to Len's office, strode over to the desk, punched the intercom button, and said to Ruth, "This is Dr. Osbourne. When Vic comes in, send him down to Len's office immediately. Otherwise, hold all calls and don't disturb us!"

"Yes, sir!" Ruth's voice came back. "Shall I bring in coffee?"

"We won't need it!" He turned the intercom off,

then whirled to us. "We're in deep trouble! John Whiteside filed our patent applications on the sky hook. He informed me late yesterday afternoon that the Patent Office has declared an interference. Somebody was there ahead of us! I was called over to Halden's house last night at seven o'clock, and I didn't get home until three this morning! And I've been on the carpet up at corporate headquarters this morning!"

"You've gotta be kidding!" Len exploded.

"I can't believe it!" I shook my head.

"Why not? There's even been an interference on the load compensator invention!" Osbourne was more than angry. I'd never seen him in that state before. "And the interfering applications were not filed until *after* I hired you, Mike! What have you got to say for yourself?"

"Only that I didn't break your confidence and didn't peddle NEMECO lab data or information to *anybody* else!" I said vehemently, still on my feet.

"Then, *who*? We know who's penetrated us and who they're working for. We've eliminated them from consideration because *their* clients were not the ones who filed!"

"It sure as hell wasn't me!" I had to look up at Bill Osbourne standing in front of me. "I work for NEMECO . . . period! If you're accusing me of stealing NEMECO secrets and selling them to somebody else, you know something I don't know!"

"Bill, it couldn't be Mike," Len put in. "I checked him out personally because, believe it or not, *I* was worried that *you* were being taken by an industrial spy! Mike is *not* your spy. If he is, I'd better go out that door with him because I'll not be worth a damn to you or NEMECO after this! Let's get back to the basics. Who are we in interference with?"

Bill sighed, then the anger seemed to drain out of him. He plopped into a chair, took out one of his dark cigarettes, and lit it without bothering to use his holder. "Sorry. It's been a long night, and there's a lot of pressure . . . Universal American AeroSpace filed before we did."

"You-Ass?" I blurted out, using the unflattering

nickname the company had earned in the aviation field.

"That rules out Peter Wilding," Len observed.

"And Mac Roston, who's reporting to his father in Greenwich."

"Mac Roston?" This sounded incredible to me. Good old Mac?

"We knew it two weeks after he joined us," Len pointed out to me. "There was a lot of stuff going out the back door with Mac's Formula Vee race cars. He was down here when nobody else was. But he didn't know that we knew what he was taking."

"How about Vic?" I asked. "He knows more about the theory of the sky hook than anybody, including you, Bill."

"What about Vic? He isn't here yet," Bill said.

"We don't know *where* he is half the time. He comes in late. He doesn't show up at all some days . . ." Len pointed out.

"Vic has other responsibilities up at corporate headquarters."

"Bill, Vic Aboud obviously has lots of Middle-East oil money. He has a new Mercedes every year . . . and a Mercedes is the kind of a car that if you have to worry about what it costs to operate it, you can't afford it." Len drummed his fingers on his desk. "Who owns Universal American AeroSpace?"

"I don't know."

"Did anybody in the Front Office think to check it out? They've got the contacts on Wall Street through the NEMECO Board. Winthrop Dykmann has a seat on the New York Exchange," Len Marshall pointed out to his boss. "How much of Universal American AeroSpace is owned by Mid-East oil money?"

Bill Osbourne didn't say anything for a long minute. Then he did say, "Mike, I apologize. I haven't had much sleep, and I'm under pressure to find the leak. Sorry. I'd figured out that it was you. My profound and abject apologies. I should never have suspected you at all . . ." Bill Osbourne looked very tired.

"Your apology accepted, Bill. You couldn't be any more shook up or dismayed than I am."

"You don't know the whole story yet," Osbourne went on. "Halden has elected not to fight the interference. He's falling back on Sanatella's report to hold the support of Destry and Keller. It's Hay Newcomb whose neck's *really* on the line at the moment! I was given two orders by Halden and Newcomb just minutes ago. I was first told to find the industrial spy in my operation. My second order was even worse: We are to cease all work on the sky hook and everything to do with it because: a, we will have no patent position; b, we are in no condition to fight Universal American AeroSpace; c, we are told there is no market for the sky hook among our classical NEMECO product lines."

"Bill! You can't! NEMECO can't!" I was on my feet again. "We've got a working device that propelled a twenty-ton airplane through the air at more than two hundred miles per hour . . . and it's just a lash-up *prototype*! That airplane with the sky hook in it can go higher than it should be able to by all the rules of flight! It can go into orbit! Give us a week, and we *will* be in orbit with it!"

"And we'll be facing potential litigation from Universal American AeroSpace for patent infringement when their patents issue," Osbourne pointed out.

"To hell with patent rights and infringements and interferences! We can prove we did it first! We've got the data right here! NEMECO can have the Moon, it can have Mars, it can have the whole Solar System! We're giving up the stars to one of the classical government-supported aerospace companies *without a fight?* We're going to let them diddle around, get it classified, keep researching it, and maybe utilize it twenty-five years from now?"

I leaned over Len's conference table toward Bill Osbourne. "Bill, an airplane with NEMECO painted on its side can be in Earth orbit next week. Let me do it, and then the lawyers can fight about it later. *But let's do it!*"

"I wish it were that simple," Osbourne said dejectedly. "But I've been given a direct order by my boss and by the president of this company. If I disobey or ignore it, I'll lose my job, we'll lose this lab, and all of you will lose your jobs, too. Then everything is down the tubes."

Len sighed. "Well, Bill, we could always go to work for Universal American AeroSpace after we did it . . ."

"Not if we disobeyed management orders at NE-MECO," Bill warned. "No corporation will take the risk of hiring a person who's done that once, because if he did it once, he's capable of doing it again."

"Me work for *that* outfit?" I put in. "Not on a bet, whether they'd have me or not! I flew one of their ag planes once . . . for twenty minutes until it started to fall apart when I pulled up at the end of the field! Bill knows what they'll do with the sky hook. Len, you know what they'll do with the sky hook! And I know what they'll do with the sky hook. I won't sit around on my ass for twenty years collecting their paychecks and letting the sky hook molder in their so-called development group!"

"You're right, Mike. That's exactly what would happen," Len Marshall said.

At that point, Victor Aboud walked in.

When Bill told him, Vic just shrugged his shoulders. I had expected an explosion.

"Vic, tell me something, and tell me the truth," Bill Osbourne asked him. "Did you sell out to Universal American AeroSpace? Or to anybody who might have given the data to Universal American AeroSpace?"

"Why should I?" Aboud said with another shrug. "What would I have gained? You know that I can quit right now, walk out of here, and still have enough money every month to spend a hundred bucks a night on a fancy Park Avenue call girl with a couple of thou left over to play with. I was doing this because it was *fun*!"

"Then why are you shrugging your shoulders and writing the whole thing off?" Len wanted to know.

"Because what else can I do? This isn't the end of the world. In my country, if you manage to hold on to what you've got for more than one generation without somebody taking it away from you, you're rich and respected! For centuries, we've had armies come through every few years, looting everything in sight and leaving us to build it all up again so that we could enjoy it for a little while before another army came through or some dictator took over in a coup. This sort of thing has happened to my ancestors so many times that what can I do but shrug my shoulders, pick up what I can, and go on from here?" He got up and started for the door. "You aren't going to get any work done around here today. And neither am I. I'll be in New York at Jan's place. Ruth has the number." And he left.

"Maybe he's got the right idea after all," Bill Osbourne observed.

"The hell he has!" I exploded. "His people may own half the oil in the world, but it just lay there beneath them for centuries until somebody risked everything and started pumping it out of the ground!"

"So what are you going to do?" Len Marshall wanted to know.

"I may go out and get a little time in a DC-4."

"You're not going anywhere in a DC-4," Osbourne told me. "Jake Stock has been told already. Wimpy has the airplane locked up. Their instructions are to let Tom, Carl, and Mac in to remove the equipment. Sorry, but it wasn't my decision, and I didn't give those orders. Halden is simply protecting this company against the very real possibility of a future patent infringement suit for what we've already managed to do!" Osbourne looked completely defeated, his confidence gone, his enthusiasm sapped, and his effectiveness as a leader of a research team completely destroyed for some time to come. "Let me repeat the orders I was given: NEMECO is no longer interested in pursuing the dynamics systems program or the sky hook development. We are to cancel the program immediately. The sky hook equipment is to be disposed of as surplus equipment. No further funds are authorized or will be spent on the dynamics systems or sky hook program. The technicians' time removing the equipment from Seven-Eleven is to be charged off against G&A. Understand, Len?"

"Yes, sir."

"Understand, Mike?"

I sighed and nodded.

"Len, call Tammy in and tell her. It would probably help if you were here, too, Mike."

"Len," I broke in, "let me tell her. This is likely to cause her to come all unglued just when she's beginning to put herself back together again. But you'd better figure that we're going to take the rest of the day off. I'm still beat from yesterday."

I wasn't as beat as I looked. But I knew it would do no more good to sit around Len's office and commiserate.

I had roughly formulated two plans of action in my mind, Plan A and Plan B, because of what Bill Osbourne had just said. If the first one wouldn't work, the second one would. I was damned if I was going to stand idly by and let the stars get away from me for the second time in less than a year! I needed some help on Plan A. If Plan A didn't work, I'd fall back on Plan B. But I couldn't discuss either plan with Osbourne or Len. If I failed, it had to be my ass in the sling, not theirs. In the meantime, I had to hold off the jackals.

I didn't go see Tammy first. I found Carl and explained to him what had happened. He didn't believe it at first, either. I told him, "Carl, when you take those electronics out of Seven-Eleven, for God's sake don't sell them to the junk yard down the street or bust them up! Bust something else up instead, and stick that good stuff quietly away up in the storage space above the offices. Don't tell anybody about it. We're going to need that gear again. It's now officially surplus, unwanted, unneeded, and unaccounted for. Do you get my drift?"

Carl didn't really understand what or why, but he said, "Hell, Mike, whatever you want, you've got!"

"I can count on you?"

"You bet! I think we've been screwed!"

"Right to the wall, buddy! What have you done with the experimental sky hook that was in the dynamics lab?"

"I took it down and stole some parts off it for the DC-4 unit."

"Okay, we haven't been told to destroy it. Put it back in working shape, then hide it. We're going to need it, too."

Then I went to see Tammy. "Come on, hon. We've got to get out to the airport."

"Mike, what's wrong?" Tammy had spotted something in the way I looked or my tone of voice.

"Grab your coat. It's cold out today."

I didn't stop at the turnoff for the NEMECO hangar but kept on driving out to Lordship Point.

"Why are we going this way?" Tammy wanted to know. "We passed the NEMECO hangar."

"I know. But we've got to talk." I pulled the Bug up next to the breakwater overlooking the Sound.

"About what?"

"About us."

"What's happened, Mike? You look like the world just caved in on you."

"It did. I told Bill Osbourne and Len Marshall that I'd like to tell you, but you've got to promise me something . . ."

"Anything, Mike."

"Promise me that you're not going to come apart, because what happened had absolutely nothing to do with what we did."

"What happened in Len's office this morning, Mike?"

"You knew about the meeting?"

"Everybody in the lab did. What was it about?"

"Halden and Newcomb told Bill to cancel all work on the sky hook project immediately."

She just looked at me without saying a word.

"Aren't you going to ask why?"

She tried to say something but couldn't.

"I'll tell you, then. Universal American AeroSpace filed patent applications on a sky hook before we did. NEMECO's in interference and facing a possible infringement suit if and when the patents issue to Universal American AeroSpace."

I can't describe Tammy's expression. It seemed to be a combination of extreme distress, disbelief, physical shock, and grief. "No!" she moaned. "Oh, no!"

"The reason I came out here today was to get my Cherokee out of the NEMECO hangar . . ."

"Mike, did they fire you? Did anybody lose their jobs?"

"Not yet. But Halden has ordered Jake Stock and Wimpy to lock up Seven-Eleven and only let Carl, Tom, and Mac inside to remove the sky hook equipment. I want to get my Cherokee out of there . . . right now!"

"What's going to happen at the lab?"

"I don't know. We still have other projects. But Osbourne looks and acts like a defeated man. Newcomb's suffered a serious set-back over this. So has Halden. We've lost a very important round. I think we're all right unless and until something changes in corporate headquarters . . . although I don't know how effective Bill Osbourne will be from now on."

She huddled into the fur collar of her cloth coat and stared out at the gray waters of the Sound. Suddenly, she looked small and vulnerable and frightened. I didn't like to see her that way. I liked her the way she was yesterday, clad in a dirty orange coverall that was much too big for her and rolled up at the sleeves and ankles, confident, professional, cool even when scared, and absolutely unflappable during the single-engine let-down and landing.

"Len was going to tell you, but I persuaded him to let me do it," I went on. "NEMECO doesn't feel they can afford to fight Universal American AeroSpace over the patent thing, and they fell back on the Sanatella marketing report. Halden had no choice. So You-Ass—as Universal American AeroSpace is unaffectionately known in the aviation field—is probably going to sit on the sky hook for at least seventeen years until the patent rights expire." I reached over and took her hand in both of mine. It was cold.

In a very small and vulnerable voice, Tammy asked, "How did Universal American AeroSpace do it? Was it a duplicate research effort as Dr. Mayan suspected might happen?"

"No, You-Ass stole it from us. Bill was told to find the industrial spy who leaked the data. It wasn't Peter Wilding, and it wasn't Mac Roston, because Len knows what Mac took . . ."

"Mac was an agent?" she asked in disbelief.

"That's what I'm told. Osbourne thought it might have been me because the dates on the You-Ass applications coincided with my employment at NEMECO. But Len checked me out independently because he thought I was an industrial spy. And Vic just doesn't fit the bill at all. So Osbourne is still looking for the leak . . ."

Tammy looked over at me. Tears were streaming down her cheeks and her beautiful face was screwed into an expression of extreme grief. "Mike! Oh, Mike! I kept telling you there were . . . things you didn't know! But I had to do it! I had no alternative . . . and I didn't know where the data were going . . ."

"Tammy, what are you saying?"

"Mike, I'm your spy! My uncle in New Jersey isn't my uncle. He's the head of a large industrial espionage group . . ."

It was a long and tearful confession, and I had trouble believing most of it. I knew there were international espionage organizations, but this wasn't one of them. Its business was sometimes international, but most of its clients were within the United States. Tammy admitted it all to me between sobs that racked her small body bundled in her bulky cloth coat.

She had fed them all the sky hook data on her trips to New Jersey. But she was certain that the information had gone to Universal American AeroSpace because of remarks that had slipped into the conversations with her "uncle."

"I didn't believe . . . I *can't* believe . . . that this is the outcome!" she sobbed. "The people at the lab are the best friends . . . the only real friends . . . I've ever had . . . I didn't mean to hurt them . . . And I didn't mean for them to hurt you, Mike . . ."

"Those two goons in the parking lot?"

"I found out later after . . . after I had learned to care a great deal for you . . . which I was not supposed to do! They wanted you because you knew more about it than I could tell them."

"They would have had one hell of a time making me talk . . ."

"Oh, no, Mike! Within minutes, you would have been so full of psychodrugs that you wouldn't know where you were or what you were doing. They would've drained you dry! I've seen them do it to others . . . If you were lucky and if they'd gotten what they wanted quickly and easily, you would have probably come to in some back alley somewhere with little knowledge of what had happened to you . . . if you were lucky. They destroy people . . . I hated them . . . *I hated them!*"

"Then why did you do this, Tammy?"

"Because I had to . . ."

"Did they pay you well?"

"No. I didn't get paid."

"What have they got hanging over your head, Tam?"

"I'm an illegal alien, Mike."

"You're *what*?"

"I was an English translator with a trade mission . . . and I just walked away in New York City one day. But somehow, the espionage organization found where I was. They track defectors like me and use us. I think the trade delegation passed the word to them to watch for me . . . and they eventually found me . . ."

"But you could have requested political asylum!" I pointed out.

"You don't understand. How could you understand? My father, my mother, my brothers . . . They're still over there. If I asked for asylum, they would become unpersons. They would never starve, but they would never be able to lead even the normal lives of people over there. If I just disappeared into the crowds here in America, it could be considered that I'd been mugged, raped, and murdered. The police here aren't as thor-

ough as they are there, and America is considered a
very dangerous place full of criminals. At least, it is a
convenient excuse to use when someone like me disap-
pears. They don't have to make retribution back home,
and they've got a piece of good propaganda for domes-
tic use. So here I am. Every paper I have is forged,
obtained for me by my 'uncle,' who has the option of
informing your immigration authorities about me or reporting back that I secretly sought political asylum here
to protect my family."

This was the side of Tammy Dudley that I had neither known nor suspected. How could she have told
me? How could she have broken through the wall of
guilt and fear that surrounded her life?

Strangely, even though she was the person who was
responsible for losing my chance at the stars, it did not
change my feelings toward her. Now I knew. So what?
The important thing was to figure out where the two of
us could go from here.

Gently, I told her, "Tammy, all of those documents
cannot be forged. You couldn't have flown that DC-4
the way you did yesterday. You couldn't have handled
my Cherokee like a real pro if that FAA license had
been forged . . ."

"It's forged," she admitted. "The DC-3 heavy time
was logged in an exact copy of it the Soviets call the
Li-2. I learned English because it's required for both air
force and state airline pilots. I was transferred to the
trade commission because I was a better pilot than most
of the men . . . so don't believe all they tell you about
female equality over there." She didn't say anything for
a time, and we both watched the dull gray rollers wash
up the sides of the breakwater at Lordship Point. Finally, she broke the silence with, "Well, Mike, shall we
get back to the lab so you can report me, or do you
intend to drive right over to the Federal Office Building?"

At that moment, I discovered for the first time in my
life what "love" really was. The happiness, the well-
being, and the security of Tammy Dudley was absolutely essential to me over everything else. It was not

that I *couldn't* go on without her; it was that I *would not*! My whole life changed.

"Neither!" I said without hesitation. "It doesn't make any difference anyway! We're going to get *our* Cherokee out of the NEMECO hangar and put it in our hangar, probably up at Waterbury, Meriden, or some other airport that is out of the way. We've got some things to do with that bird . . . and I have already taken care of most of the necessary arrangements. Tammy, my dearest, I am basically mean and nasty, and I fight dirty. I'm not going to roll over and play dead for a bunch of corporate politicians. I'm going to do the one thing they dread most. Correction: *We're* going to do it!"

I reached down through the fur of her collar that she had turned up and took that beautiful face in my hands. "In the meantime, I also have a solution to your problem, and we'll do that right away. It will not only make it difficult for the federal immigration service to do anything to you, but it may also get your spy organization off your back."

"What do you mean, Mike?"

I kissed her tear-stained face. "Tammy, my love, you are about to marry an American citizen, and by the time the lawyers and the bureaucrats and the politicians get it all figured out, it will be too late . . . if they can figure it out at all! The Cherokee will get us to Providence in less than an hour. Under the circumstances, ' 'twere well it were done quickly,' as Shakespeare said. We're going to act faster than they can move to stop us!"

Tammy managed a wan smile. "Mike! Dear Mike! Why Providence? Why not just go to the Bridgeport City Hall?"

"Because in Rhode Island, there's no waiting period! Don't you think I have been checking these things out, Tammy?"

"I . . . I didn't think that this could ever happen to me . . ."

"What's that, hon?"

"I shouldn't tell you, but I must. I have to. I can't keep it bottled up. You *did* turn me on that first night after you beat off those goons of my 'uncle.' But afterwards, I was operating under instructions . . . including the afternoon in Morse Manor when I wore that sexy little piece of lace . . . But, Mike, my dearest, you started to do more than just turn me on, and you started to become something more than another job I had to do for my 'uncle' . . . I love you, Mike! We were instructed to never let it happen . . . but it happened to me. Mike, I'll marry you forever and ever with all the love I've got, but you *must* forgive me for what I did . . ."

"For what you did? Tammy, do you know how it makes me feel to be treated as a cold business deal at the start and be able to change that into real affection? Dearest, you don't know what a compliment that is to me! And what difference does it make *now*? You have absolutely *nothing* to be ashamed of, and I'm going to fix things up so that you will never be afraid of anybody for anything again!"

"Mike, how did I ever manage to find you?"

"Maybe someday we'll have time enough to find the answer."

I never really liked a VW Bug: the front seats are bucket seats with a brake lever and a gear shift between. I made up my mind that after I had arranged for a wife here, I would also arrange for a good old Ford or Chevy with a bench seat in front and the gear shift on the steering column where it belongs. That sort of thing makes for easier closeness . . .

Chapter Eighteen

We signed our names in a full round hand in the book in the Township of Warwick, County of Kent, State of Rhode Island. I wanted it to be as public as possible. I wanted to be sure that numerous skeptical clerks and the judge who performed the civil ceremony had seen all the documents—driver's licenses, Social Security cards, pilot's licenses, and all the assorted ID's—and had acted on the basis of their authenticity. I wanted to leave a trail as broad and conspicuous as the Connecticut Turnpike. We checked in for our honeymoon night in the Sheraton Motor Inn in Warwick where I paid for everything with American Express so that there would be record of our stay.

We called Bill Osbourne from the motel room, told him where we were and that we had been married that afternoon. He managed to convey his congratulations and wishes for future happiness. I told him we would be in the lab late tomorrow. "No, take a couple days, if you want. You deserve it."

We took a whole week. I knew that Tammy required it. I didn't think I did, but I discovered otherwise. It had been months of very hard work.

The colors were long gone, and the barren shades of gray that characterize the New England countryside with the coming of winter did not provide the most spectacular of sights. But we took a little aerial jaunt around New England anyway. Everywhere we landed and refueled, I paid with a gasoline credit card so there would be a record.

And I found that the name of my Cherokee was very apropos. It does take two.

I didn't give Tammy time to crawl back into her shell of suspicion, fear, guilt, and anxiety. I don't know whether her former husband was an American pilot or not, but he had mistreated her. I gave her no reason to fear our relationship, and she responded with a growing eagerness and aggression that had only briefly and haltingly surfaced on a few occasions before.

Knowing what I did, I realized why she always seemed to dress in severe clothing without color or style. Well, any bride should have a proper trousseau, and we'd left Bridgeport in *Two To Tango* with nothing but the clothes on our backs. So I bought her clothes that began to bring out the bright, intelligent, happy person that she had become.

In a little colonial inn near Lebanon, New Hampshire, I explained to Tammy what we were going to do.

"We have to do it! We can't stand by and do nothing!" She had some excellent suggestions to add.

What would a couple of scientist-types do on their honeymoon? Buy a new programmable calculator and spend hours working over complex equations! Actually, we did more than that, but that is nobody's business but our own.

There was a big celebration when we got back. They needed something to celebrate.

"Damn it, Mike, you didn't give me the chance to give you a proper bachelor's party!" Vic bubbled, slapping me on the shoulder. "We went ahead anyway with the dancing girls and all the rest . . ."

"Initiate any new carpets in the process?"

Ruth was lovely. "Now, Mike, I see no reason for you and Tammy to look for an apartment somewhere else. I have room at the house to give you plenty of privacy. And I'm not a prude."

"You never were," I reminded her.

The gaiety did not last. We had to face the NE-MECO Corporate Research Center Laboratories without the sky hook and with a badly demoralized Bill Osbourne. I went to work on the superbattery development project, to which Carl was also reassigned. Tom, the little technician who had been working on it with

Len, was moved over to the shot-alloying process full-time.

The superbattery program didn't excite me but it kept me at NEMECO Corporate Research Center Laboratories with facilities that I could use, a paycheck coming in regularly, and everyday contact with my colleagues. Plan A required co-conspirators, and I recruited them using the best covert techniques. They included Tammy, Carl, Wendell, Wimpy, Mayan, and Korsinski.

It was a big risk, and some of us could lose our jobs because of it. But all of us felt very strongly about the sky hook.

It didn't bother Carl. "A good electronic technician can always find a job."

Wendell approached it with his usual dry rationality: "Damned shame that the company won't fight for the inventive rights of its employees. I'm an engineer; there's always work for an engineer to do in this world."

In Mayan's case, it was a political disaster of the highest sort that he wouldn't let anyone get away with. And Korsinski was disturbed over the possibility that the sky hook work would never be published. "I was once told by a colleague that he hoped Bill's Academy paper was never published. I do not like people who do not play by the rules."

Wimpy Winfield's approach was different. "Mike, you gotta have a good A&P besides yourself. I know Cherokees. I want to tag along so you don't kill yourself. What I do in my spare time is my business; I didn't have to sign that yellow-dog disclosure agreement because I'm just a mechanic in this outfit."

Carl and Wendell got the equipment out of the lab in dribs and drabs. Len never knew that Carl had squirreled it away anyway. Bill Osbourne didn't know, and Vic never noticed. That was good because I didn't want to implicate them.

There were two tough problems. One of them was checking the calculations for *Two To Tango*. The other was getting the superbatteries out without leaving evidence that they were gone. So we used the old trick of putting something in place of each superbattery as we removed it. If Len had asked for an inventory audit, it would have shown up immediately. But Len never asked for such things.

We didn't need many superbatteries to power the old laboratory sky hook that we installed in *Two To Tango* at Waterbury.

We had to move as fast as possible, but we could work only on weekends and an occasional night when the weather wasn't too bad. When it snowed, we didn't want to be stranded in Waterbury and have to call in from there to the lab.

It gets *cold* inland away from the water of the Sound! We rigged infrared lamps in the Tee-hangar, but that uninsulated steel building wouldn't hold the heat. It was the longest, coldest winter of my life. I may have been frustrated by the cancellation of the sky hook project, but we were well along with Plan A.

"Honey, don't you think you'd better make contact with your 'uncle' pretty quick?" I happened to mention one day as we were driving up to Waterbury. "Won't they think something's wrong if you're silent this long?"

"No," she said quietly. Then she turned to me and smiled. "They got what they wanted. An agent can't be used constantly because they burn out or lose their cover . . ."

"You've certainly lost yours!"

"Yes, dear, but only with you!"

"So what do you think we should do if you get another call?"

"I won't," she said with a smile that radiated her aura throughout the Chevy El Camino.

By mid-February, Plan A was almost ready to go. Thank God for Wendell Stone! He came to understand aircraft technology very well and worked out so many shortcuts that I lost track of all his contributions. With Wimpy's help, Wendell became a passable A&P. Wimpy tried to talk him into going for an A&P rating, but Wendell declined, saying he was an engineer and didn't need to become a mechanic.

"And you'll never get me up in one of those things," he added.

"That's what the caterpillar said when he saw the butterfly fly over," Wimpy told him.

Together, we managed to strip everything out of the Cherokee that wasn't required. We left the cabin insulation in place; it didn't weigh very much, and we'd need some insulation. The back seats came out, as did the platform on which they were normally bolted. The baggage compartment floor came out. We removed the aft cabin bulkhead; that made it easier to install equipment. I took the oil cooler off the engine; it was too cold to require it, and the engine would be frozen solid halfway into the flight anyway. We even ditched the ash tray and the cigarette lighter, causing Wendell to exclaim, "Why, that's downright un-American!"

We scheduled a go-date, and I called Ted Mayan.

We planned the flight for a Sunday morning so that we wouldn't be absent from work. The weather was perfect: sky overcast, ceiling 2,000 feet, three middle-level cloud decks above that, thin cirrus at 30,000 feet. The runway temperature was a chilly 12 degrees Fahrenheit, and it was damp. The wind was light and variable.

The briefer on the phone at Windsor Locks Flight Service Station was rather surprised when I asked for the winds at 24,000, 30,000, and 36,000 feet. The jet stream was north of us that day, and winds at those altitudes were less than 70 knots. I filed an instrument flight plan for a "PA-28 Cherokee"—a designation that covers more than a dozen models of the basic airplane—at Flight Level two two zero, test flight at extreme altitudes. I got an IFR clearance, but not my requested routing. That didn't make any difference. I expected that. It was Sunday, and the airspace was busy.

That meant everything we did in the air was going to be on the FAA voice tapes and the computer records of their radar scans. And we had an academic observer on hand whose reputation was unblemished and unassailable.

Tammy and I bundled up. We couldn't afford the energy for heated flying suits. We needed every kilowatt-
hour for the sky hook. We finally crawled into the cabin
of *Two To Tango* and squeezed in next to the sky hook
bolted lengthwise through the cabin and attached firmly
to the main wing spar that went right behind both front
seats. We closed the door and latched it. Wendell and
Carl rolled back the Tee-hangar doors and pushed
Two To Tango clear of the hangar.

Wimpy had preheated the engine in the hangar so
that we would not have to waste a moment of time from
start-up to takeoff. "Clear prop!" I yelled, quickly shut
the storm window, and cranked up the Lycoming.

"You've got vacuum! You've got alternator!"
Tammy called out.

"And I've got fuel pressure and oil pressure. Radios
on!"

We taxied immediately to Runway 36 through the
slush. I tried to go slowly to keep from splashing slush
up under the wings where it would freeze and create
additional drag. We made a quick engine check at the
end of the runway, ran through the instrument panel,
gave a takeoff call on the unicom frequency—one reason we had chosen Waterbury-Oxford was the absence
of a control tower—and taxied out on the runway.

I was glad it was cold because it made the air denser.
We must have used nearly 4,000 feet of that runway,
and *Two To Tango* literally crawled into the air.

"Off at three five past the hour!" Tammy sang out.

"What did you figure this plane weighs?"

"Twenty-five hundred and ten pounds."

"A little over maximum permissible gross, wouldn't
you say?" I asked as I struggled to maintain a climb at
85 miles per hour.

"It's flying, isn't it, dear?" Tammy replied.

"Barely! Westchester Approach, Cherokee one four
two two tango with you out of fifteen hundred feet, off
Waterbury at three five!"

"Cherokee two two Tango, Westchester. You're still
too low for my radar. Climb on course. Report Pawling."

We went into the overcast at 2,000 feet, and I flew the gauges while Tammy set radios. "Plan A Base, Plan A Bird with you!" she called to Carl and Wendell on the aeronautical multicom frequency.

"Plan A Bird, where are you?"

"Somewhere over Planet Earth!" Tammy shot back. "We're climbing in the clouds. Stand by the frequency for reports."

Westchester Approach handed us off to Boston Center, who got us in radar contact, asked us to verify altitude, and requested better rate of climb. "Negative on climb rate," I told them. "We're loaded, and this is a test flight to maximum altitude."

They were peeved, but we were the ones with our tails in the clouds.

Tammy made regular reports to the ground crew at Waterbury.

The climb rate improved slowly as *Two To Tango* burned off fuel. At 12,500 feet, both Tammy and I donned the oxygen masks that I had bought, a standard full-flow system with a 50-cubic-foot cylinder that would give us both about five and a half hours of oxygen.

At 17,250 feet, I couldn't get another foot of altitude out of the overloaded *Two To Tango*.

"Let's get the drive on, Tam. We've been cleared to twenty-two thousand, so we've got to have some push. You take it. I'll get things cranking."

We were about 2,000 feet below the altitude that had been calculated for starting drive operation. And I had some brief problems, as usual, phasing the unit. But they weren't as bad as with Seven-Eleven.

We leveled at 22,000 feet, and the Lycoming was gasping. Had it not been for the thrust of the sky hook unit maintaining about 90 miles per hour indicated airspeed and creating some breeze past the prop, I am sure the engine would have stopped from sheer lack of oxygen. I reported level at Flight Level two two zero, and Tammy reported conditions to the crew at Waterbury. Then I requested Flight Level three two zero from Center.

"Uh, what model Cherokee are you?" Center wanted to know.

"One-eighty with special power mod," I told them. "We're going for maximum altitude test."

"Okay, Cherokee two two Tango is cleared to Flight Level three two zero. Report reaching . . . if you do."

"Two two Tango out of Flight Level two two zero for three two zero."

I reached down and turned off the Lycoming's ignition. There would be little chance of getting it started again on this flight. The outside air temperature was already minus-40 degrees Fahrenheit.

"Plan A Base, this is Plan A Bird. Main shutdown at twenty-two on schedule. Running on stand-by unit now," Tammy reported to Waterbury.

Without the engine, we lost our cabin heater and the vacuum pump that drove the attitude indicator and the directional gyro. "Sweetie," I told Tammy, "you're going to have to operate the drive unit. I've got my hands full flying partial panel." It's possible to fly an airplane under instrument conditions with nothing but the turn-and-bank indicator which is electrically driven, the magnetic compass, and the airspeed indicator—"partial panel."

We made 32,000 feet, but the windows were so fogged and frozen up with the condensed moisture exhaled from our oxygen masks that I couldn't see anything. It was strictly full gut-tearing instrument work on a partial panel.

There we were, higher than any Cherokee had ever been before, and we couldn't see anything! It must have been beautiful out there.

"Plan A Base, this is Plan A Bird, level at thirty-two, getting ready to go up to thirty-six," Tammy reported. "We have seventy percent power left, but the windows are frosted up and we can't see. We're operating partial panel under full instrument conditions."

"Okay, Plan A Bird. I'm glad we stayed on the ground!"

"Center, Cherokee two two Tango requests Flight Level three six zero."

Boston Center came back at me with, "Please say again. Did you request Flight Level three six zero?"

"Affirmative!"

"And you're a Cherokee One-eighty?"

"Affirmative."

"Can you estimate time to climb to Flight Level three six zero? We have considerable jet traffic at that flight level. We've got to fit you in."

"We can make four hundred feet per minute, Center."

"What have you got in that thing?"

"Special power mod."

"Center clears Cherokee two two Tango to Flight Level three six zero. Report reaching!"

"Two two Tango leaving Flight Level three zero zero for Flight Level three six zero. Will report reaching."

I remarked through my oxygen mask to Tammy, "I'll bet half the supervisors at Center are hanging over the controller's shoulder not believing their own equipment!" As required, *Two To Tango* had a unit capable of responding to a radar pulse from the ground with a coded reply giving our identification as well as our altitude.

I could see the twinkle in her eyes over the top edge of the oxygen mask. She just nodded. It was difficult to talk with the oxygen masks on.

"How's power?"

"Sixty-two percent."

So we went up another 6,000 feet into the tropopause, a place where Bill Piper and Fred Weick had never guessed that one of their Cherokees would ever fly. But we *were* flying . . . right on the edge of a stall, but with sky hook power to spare.

Two To Tango could have gone higher, but we wouldn't be able to avoid hypoxia, even breathing 100 percent oxygen. We needed a system that would *force* oxygen into our lungs under pressure at any higher altitude.

"Center, Cherokee two two Tango, reporting Flight Level three six zero!"

"Jet traffic six o'clock, ten miles, will overtake you on the right, an American 727."

"Roger. He's in our blind spot."

"American Flight Six Nineteen, traffic twelve o'clock, now nine miles, same direction, Cherokee at Flight Level three six zero."

"Center, American Six Nineteen." Another drawl came from the cabin loudspeaker. "Say again please. A *Cherokee* at this flight level?"

"Affirmative! Now twelve o'clock, five miles."

"Center, tally-ho! American Six Nineteen has the traffic. All three of us on the flight deck see it! To be honest, I don't believe it! We're right under him now, and his prop is stopped dead!"

"American Six Nineteen, Center. Say again!"

"American Six Nineteen just went past that Cherokee. His prop is stopped dead and he's maintaining altitude."

"Affirmative, we show him maintaining altitude, Six Nineteen. Thank you for the information. Cherokee two two Tango, Center. Confirm your engine is inoperative."

"Center, two two Tango. Our normal engine is shut down, but our auxiliary test propulsion unit is functioning normally. We're maintaining assigned altitude and eighty knots I-A-S!" I told them, glancing at the airspeed indicator.

"Are you in any trouble?"

"Center, two two Tango, negative! We're proceeding according to flight plan."

"Uh . . . Ah, roger, two two Tango." It was a confused tone from the air traffic controller sitting in his warm and comfortable darkened room in Boston.

We were getting very cold.

"Forty percent on power reserves," Tammy informed me.

I made my south turn over the Albany VOR. "Okay, let's go down."

"Yes, please! I'm beginning to freeze to death!"

"Center, two two Tango has completed flight test at altitude, request descent to eighteen thousand."

"Two two Tango, descend at pilot's discretion, maintain one eight thousand. Contact New York Center on frequency one three one point five."

That was a special Center frequency, and I knew I was going to be talking to some high brass there.

"Plan A Base, Plan A Bird descending blind out of thirty-six, and New York Center wants to talk to us on their special frequency. We're cold and the windows are getting worse. We can't see a thing!"

"New York Center, Cherokee two two Tango with you on one three one point five!"

"Two two Tango, this is New York Center. Please confirm you're on IFR flight plan for a test!"

"Affirmative, sir, flight plan filed through Windsor Locks, clearance received and acknowledged two hours ago."

"Two two Tango, just curious, but you were a little high for a Cherokee! Care to tell us what's running that airplane?"

"Negative! Proprietary information. Sorry, Center!"

"Roger, two two Tango. We had a telephone call from an upstate newspaper who was monitoring the frequency, plus a report from an American Airlines jet westbound out of Boston. Couple of reporters are here now wanting to know what kind of UFO you're flying."

I took a deep breath of 100 percent oxygen, then replied, "Center, this flight crew is not authorized to make statements to the press. Contact Grant Halden, president of New England Mill Equipment Company in Bridgeport."

"Roger, thanks much. Safe flight, two two Tango. Looks like you've got some sort of altitude record there. Contact Westchester Approach frequency one two zero point seven."

"Two two Tango to one two zero point seven."

"Plan A Base, this is Plan A Bird descending through twenty thousand. We made thirty-six."

Westchester cleared us down to 4,000 feet and the ILS Runway Three Six approach to Waterbury, crossing the outer marker radio beacon southbound at 4,000 feet.

"We gonna make it?" I asked Tammy as I shucked off my mask at 12,000 feet. It was frozen to my face, and it hurt when I pulled it off.

"We've got slightly more than twenty percent. Can we get the engine started?"

"I'll try."

It was frozen solid.

"Mike, can you land if we don't clear the windows?"

"I doubt it."

"Let me try something I learned flying in a *very* cold part of the world," Tammy said. She took off her heavy gloves and began to scratch away the frost with her fingernails.

Scratch and fly. Both of us kept at it until, at 5,000 feet, the temperature had warmed up to zero, and there was a clear patch about a foot square that I could see through.

"I'll make it now. Thanks, hon."

Tammy was sucking on a finger. "Broke a nail."

"I'll buy you a new one," I promised her. A light flashed on the instrument panel and a series of long beeps came over the cabin loudspeaker. "Almost home! There's the outer marker!"

I really didn't need the hole in the frost of the windshield until we were coming down the ILS glide slope and I saw the runway at 1,500 feet. It was a lousy landing. I had to open the storm window to see to turn off on the taxiway and head for the Tee-hangar. There was enough power left in the batteries—about 7 percent—to use the sky hook to taxi to the Tee-hangar. That had been cutting it just a little bit close!

It seemed so much warmer here!

Wendell, Wimpy, Mayan, and Carl were waiting for us. We were extremely cold. And *Two To Tango* was frozen solid. "Let's get it started and moved out of here!" I told them. "Then we can go somewhere and celebrate!"

"And get warm," Tammy added.

"I'll get you as warm as you want," I told her softly.

"I'll have this engine ready in less than five minutes," Wimpy said, moving quickly. "Wendell, hand me those infrared lamps! Now put one here, and the other one there! I'll work on the other side. Carl, get those propane heater hoses jammed into the cowl openings up front!" Wimpy knew what he was doing. True to his boast, he knew a lot about Cherokees!

"Did it go right?" Mayan wanted to know.

"Perfect. We got to thirty-six thousand feet and a Boeing 727 went past us, reporting to the FAA that our prop was stopped!"

"Good! We couldn't ask for better confirmation!" Mayan said, overjoyed.

"It'll be on the FAA tapes, too!" Tammy added.

"Fine, but let's get moving!" I put in quickly. "We haven't got much time! The cops and reporters and God knows who else will be here any moment. And Plan A doesn't call for us to be here when they get here!"

We did it. Carl and Wendell had already cleaned up the hangar. We poured two five-gallon cans of 100-octane av-gas into *Two To Tango*'s tanks. It took about five minutes for Wimpy to get the Lycoming thawed out. A little deicer fluid from the windshield washers on Wendell's van got the cabin windows clear. And a battery jump from the van got the Lycoming started.

There was nothing to show we had been at Waterbury an hour after we landed. By that time we were all over at the Meriden Airport seventeen miles to the east where we rolled *Two To Tango* into the hangar rented in Mayan's name. Only when we knew that *Two To Tango* was locked away in an obscure Tee-hangar on an airfield smaller than Waterbury did we feel secure enough to head on down the Wilbur Cross Parkway for a quiet celebration.

Plan A was well under way.

Chapter Nineteen

The next morning down at the lab, we waited for the other shoe to drop.

And nothing happened.

Tammy began to fret. She didn't like waiting for the other shoe to drop.

Wendell was stoic and went about his work on the shot-alloying process as though nothing had happened.

Ruth knew that something was going on, but she kept quiet about it.

Len sensed it, too, and it bothered him. "I can't reach Bill on the phone. He's in a meeting and is unavailable. Ruth just got a call from Helen in the Front Office instructing Ruth to *accept no telephone calls* except those that came in on the tie-line from corporate headquarters. But I can't get through to corporate headquarters to talk with Vic because all six lines have been jammed all morning and the tie-line is busy or not working! What's going on?"

The other shoe was getting ready to drop! "Why don't we wait to see what happens? As Vic said," and I shrugged as the mathematician had done months ago, "what else can we do?"

One of the most important aspects of Plan A was to let the pot come to a boil while we waited.

The very last thing that would help Destry, Keller, Sanatella, and those involved in the Corporate Research Hatchet Job was public disclosure, exposure, or attention. But I hated having Halden, Newcomb, and Osbourne involved.

It was tough to wait. I wanted to run out and shout

to the world that we had a new device that opened the universe to mankind. But I couldn't.

The whole day went by. Nothing happened.

After work at Morse Manor, I sat down with the Bridgeport *Post* and looked at the New York Stock Exchange closings. NEMECO had risen 7 points to 34, but only 2,000 shares had been traded. There was no comment about this stupendous rise in the closely held stock of a medium-sized corporation. But a 26 percent rise in a stock's price in one day was certainly indicative that something was going on. I knew what it was. I had NEMECO stock accumulating in my retirement plan, *plus* a stock option to purchase at twenty-five!

We played poker at Morse Manor that night. Wilding saw that I was edgy and that Tammy was upset. Carl, on the other hand, seemed to be taking it in stride. As a result, Wilding managed to take us for a wad. So *he* knew that something was going on. He tried to probe it out of us, but we wouldn't talk.

With the way NEMECO stock was behaving, I didn't mind dropping a few quid at poker. All of us were going to be even better off than Vic was.

If Plan A worked . . .

As for Plan B, I hoped that I'd never have to use it. I was in a fighting mood. Plan B was rough. But Tammy would manage to come out all right. *That* I'd made certain of!

Later that night, Tammy became almost hysterical with fear which she had kept under control all day long. I held her tight while I tried to explain, "Tammy, it's going to be all right."

"Oh, Mike, they'll find us! They'll come after us!"

"There will be no midnight knock on the door. We don't do that here."

"I wish I could believe that, darling!"

"Look, everything we did on the flight was properly carried out according to the Federal Air Regulations. We don't have to worry about the government. It's strictly between us and our employer."

"But that can be just as bad . . ."

"No, because NEMECO is working very hard to try

to keep what we've done out of the public eye. They want it to be completely internal. If you become involved, you know there's a plan to protect you . . ."

"Oh, I know about it. We've been over it time after time. But, Mike, I'm still afraid of what 'uncle' might do! You don't know those people! You have no idea how utterly *evil* they are! Or how violent! They don't care a thing for a human life! They must also know what we did . . . and that makes you and me *very* valuable to them! I know what they would do to me, but I can't bear to think of what they'd do to you!"

"They're not going to get the chance to do *anything* to either of us because I'm not going to let it happen. They're vulnerable just like everyone and everything. Even the biggest person or organization in the world has one or more vulnerable spots . . . and that's where to hit them. As for size, if they're big, it just means that they move slower; they've got a longer reaction time. Sociological analogy of the sky hook theory, Tammy."

"Mike, someday I may understand you . . . Why are you willing to stand and fight when the odds are stacked so high against you?"

"Well, I can't just shrug my shoulders like Vic does. I wasn't brought up that way. But I've got a suggestion that may make you feel better . . ."

"What's that?"

"Sometimes I don't understand you any better! How do you feel about some mutual understanding right about now?"

One thing about Tammy: I never had to wait at all for *her* to drop the other shoe!

But when the other shoe was not dropped by corporate headquarters the following morning, I began to get a bit worried.

It came to a head as Tammy and I were walking back from getting a sandwich at the deli. The classical long black car pulled up to the curb alongside us and two very big men jumped out.

Tammy screamed, "Mike! It's *uncle*!"

I was suddenly very busy. After I put the closest

goon through the windshield, the fellow behind the wheel tried to get out. I saw out of the corner of my eye as Tammy slammed the heavy door on both his hands. The scream of agony told me Tammy had scored. I must have broken ten ribs in the second goon when I kicked in his chest with both feet.

The whole thing lasted less than five seconds.

I picked myself up off the sidewalk, scuffed but unhurt.

There was considerable blood . . . theirs. The guy who had gone through the windshield was badly cut; I did something to ease the pain and to put him out for at least an hour. I performed the same Tae Kwan Do procedure on the man whose hands Tammy had ruined. I didn't know whether or not I'd killed the gorilla whose chest I'd kicked in; I didn't check to see whether or not he was breathing. I didn't care.

Tammy looked like a cat who'd just fought and won. No frightened, cowering, fearful little girl she. Something had happened. "Mike, help me get his gun! He always carries one! I'll kill him! So help me, I'll kill him right here and now while I've got the chance!"

I had to restrain the tigress my wife had become. "Tammy! No! There are other ways!"

Wendell, Len, Mac, and Carl were running toward us from the lab. "We're all right!" I told them quickly. "Get the cops. Have them hold these three. I'm preferring charges! Tammy and I will be up at corporate headquarters."

"But they haven't called us yet!" Tammy pointed out.

"That part of Plan A is changed. *We're* going to drop the other shoe *on them*!"

We burst into the NEMECO lobby. The very efficient receptionist was still there, the same one who had greeted me when I first walked through that door. "Hi, we're the Calls from Corporate Research. Mr. Halden and Dr. Newcomb want to see us right away!"

The receptionist looked surprised. "They're both in a meeting of the Board of Directors in the conference room, and they didn't leave any message with me to . . ."

"Tell me," I asked her, "have they put all their messages through you since yesterday morning?" She was just as confused as all the other employees about all the things that I knew had to be going on around the Front Office. "We know where the board room is. Don't bother." And before she could collect her wits, we were past her, into the hallway, and into the board room.

I closed the door behind me. There was a meeting of the full Board of Directors of NEMECO in session. I didn't know most of them personally, but I'd studied the annual reports, where their photographs had appeared. I thought I could recognize most of them. I'd tried to do my homework.

The white-shocked man in the dark suit at the head of the table had to be J. Willard McIntosh, chairman of the board and former president of NEMECO. The aristocratic woman had to be the last member of the founding Cranmer family on the Board, the spinster Marion A. Cranmer. I could tie faces with names for a couple more. There was Lieutenant General Maxwell J. Hettinger, USAF (Retired), because I'd seen him years before. Winthrop G. Dykmann of Dykmann and Roberts, members NYSE, had a very expensive look. I knew who was Saul M. Rothstein of Rothstein, Rothstein & Feinmann, attorneys at law, New York City. Obvious as well was Diogenes Konstantinos Generales, the head of Aegean Trading Corporation. I knew who these people were, but the others had used photos that had been taken when they were younger.

Halden was at the opposite end of the table from McIntosh, and Hay Newcomb was next to Halden. Behind them both sat Bill Osbourne.

"Please excuse the intrusion, ladies and gentlemen." I interrupted the complete silence that greeted our entrance. "I knew that we'd want to talk together sooner or later. And, since we just thwarted an attempt to either kill us or kidnap us, Tammy and I felt we should get over here right away."

Grant Halden arose from his chair smoothly. "Welcome, Tammy. And you, too, Mike! I didn't expect to get with you quite this soon and under quite these circumstances. But perhaps it's just as well because the Board was discussing the situation you've put us into . . . and we therefore might as well talk about it together." Grant Halden looked fatigued, and I knew the strain he'd been under since Sunday night because I'd created that strain with great care. But, in spite of it all, Grant Halden remained a gentleman.

Tammy and I were introduced to everyone around the table. They were polite—not always friendly, but polite. This was not a group of people who interacted every day with the rank and file of the human race; they operated on their own level far above everyone else, turning the crank that ran the world. I knew it. I could sense it. And I knew from Tammy's face that she knew power, too, when she saw it. But now she seemed unafraid of it.

It was a *big* table, the same that the few of us had sat around during Sanatella's infamous marketing presentation. So there was room for Halden to have the two of us seated on one side of him without requiring any director to move an inch.

I knew they'd been here all day. There were plastic cups on the table. They'd had coffee and sweet rolls earlier at mid-morning; the coffee urn and the crumbs were still on the linen-covered table on one side of the room. They'd had lunch sent in because I got a glimpse of the contents of a wastebasket.

It was obvious why the other shoe hadn't dropped yesterday. One cannot get people like those on the NEMECO Board to drop what they're doing at the moment and run up to Bridgeport for a meeting. In fact, it was rather amazing that Halden had managed to convene them by Tuesday! That told me we'd done a superb job of throwing a great deal of it into the fan.

"You mentioned something about an attempt to kill or kidnap the two of you," Halden said. "Would you explain what happened?"

I gave them the details and told them that it had happened before with the same goons . . . I thought.

"They tried to get me then because of what I'd learned about the sky hook. They tried to get Tammy and me now because we both knew a great deal about it. One of them is the chief kingpin of an extensive industrial espionage operation. The police will hold them temporarily, and I expect a phone call shortly. We know how the NEMECO sky hook data got to Universal American AeroSpace. The agent is a loyal NEMECO employee who was threatened under unbelievable circumstances and will fully cooperate with you. With the arrest of the chief of this operation and with our notebooks and lab records, the Universal American AeroSpace theft of the sky hook data will clear the complete patent rights matter in NEMECO's favor. There's one condition: the agent requests full pardon. There are more than twenty NEMECO employees who will vouch for her . . ."

"Her?" Grant Halden asked.

I started to say something, but Tammy stood up. "Yes! Me! I'll give you all the details of what I did! I'll tell you what they did to me! I'll tell you how they tried to kill my husband . . . and then me! I'll tell you how they forced me to work against the only people who've ever cared for me at NEMECO Corporate Research labs. I'll work with you to put these thieves in jail where they belong. I'll help you set up a counter-intelligence system that can't be penetrated. And I'll testify against Universal American AeroSpace so that any interference action they take will collapse in their faces. In the meantime, I'll program computers and fly sky hook machines the way only one other person in this company can: my husband, Mike Call, who had the guts to walk in here and face all of you to get the truth to you before it was too late." There were tears in her eyes, but they were the fierce tears of emotion, of defiance, of a complete woman I knew had been Tammy all the time. "I'll cooperate fully, but I want to keep working for you. However, I have learned from my current husband not to put up with being bullied . . ."

There was dead silence in the board room. Tammy sat down, proudly. Grant Halden looked at her kindly and said, "Mrs. Dudley-Call, I accept your offer with its conditions. Since it's an operational matter, we'll discuss it later. No need to involve the Board members unless they wish to become involved. And, thank you, Tammy!"

Newcomb spoke up. "Grant, perhaps we'd better arrange for the personal security of Mr. and Mrs. Call."

"Thank you, Hay," I put in at once, "but Tammy and I are perfectly capable of taking care of ourselves." I didn't want to find myself suddenly sequestered by NEMECO. I didn't think that the NEMECO president would do such a thing, but Tammy and I were in the lions' den, literally and figuratively, and I didn't know what some of these other people were capable of doing to us.

I only knew that we had to be very, *very* careful.

I was amazed at my wife and at Halden's reply, but we still had to complete Plan A. We had a couple of very good hole cards. I didn't think they knew where *Two To Tango* was. And they hadn't summoned us; we had instead bluffed and blustered our way in, literally forcing their hand. I was gambling that they hadn't made up their minds yet what to do about us or with us because of their protracted silence. The news media must be hounding them, to say nothing of the Wall Street analysts.

"Nevertheless," said John van der Hayden, the NEMECO secretary, "we can't have thugs molesting our employees, Grant. I'll have a chat with the Bridgeport Police about this."

"Please do, sir," I told him. "They're holding the espionage boss right now."

I could see Tammy blink at this. It would take her some time yet to become a real American—a person who dislikes cops but who is damned glad they're there.

"Be that as it may," Willard McIntosh broke in, "let's get on with the primary reason for our meeting." The chairman of the board removed his glasses, wiped them with a white handkerchief he removed from his breast pocket, and looked at me as he said, "Mr. Call, according to the records of the Federal Aviation Administration, you made an aircraft flight on Sunday."

"My wife and I made a flight in our plane from Waterbury-Oxford Airport. It was a nice Sunday afternoon once we got above the clouds."

"Mr. Call," McIntosh went on, "we have reason to suspect that you and your wife utilized proprietary NEMECO information and equipment to propel your aircraft during that flight."

"No sir, we did not!"

"Damn it!" Emory C. Mather exploded, getting to his feet. He was president of Consolidated Industries, Inc., a large conglomerate that included Great Western Aircraft, a highly respected aerospace firm with a fine reputation stretching back several decades to the years before World War II. He pointed a finger at me, obviously not used to taking any guff whatsoever from employees, as was typical in even the best aerospace firms. "We've been told that you and several unknown accomplices stole experimental equipment from the NEMECO Corporate Research Center Laboratories and installed it in your airplane without permission from your supervisors and without the knowledge of the NEMECO officers. You then proceeded to operate your airplane far above its absolute ceiling using that equipment. We have incontrovertible proof of this! Van der Hayden, play the tapes . . . that part over Albany!"

Somehow, they'd gotten a copy of the FAA tape recordings of the air-to-ground communications during our encounter with the American Airlines 727 over Albany at 36,000 feet. "Grant," I broke in, "that's unquestionably the tape recording of our air-to-ground communications during our flight. But, tell me: The FAA routinely records this sort of thing for their own use and for possible use by the National Transportation Safety Board in case of an accident. How'd you get a copy?"

"Young man!" General Hettinger rumbled, "Don't you believe that some of us might have a few friends around Washington?"

"Oh, undoubtedly, General! However," and I looked at Emory Mather, "you've made some very strong and possibly damaging statements against us, Mr. Mather. Can you prove your contentions?"

"No Cherokee can possibly fly that high! Bill Piper would have been delighted to know that it could! You stole and used what Dr. Newcomb and Dr. Osbourne have described to us as a 'sky hook' that you helped develop at the NEMECO laboratories!"

I maintained a polite, mannered voice and appearance. "Do you have proof that we had NEMECO proprietary equipment in my airplane?"

"Young man, you're being very immature!" It was Generales of Aegean Trading Corporation, a man who was at the top of the world transportation industry but with little known about exactly how he managed to get there. "We know that you've done this, and you've placed the corporation in a very difficult position because of your dramatic actions and youthful dreams without thought of the way the real world has to work . . ."

"Mr. Generales, if the real world works the way it did about an hour ago when my wife and I were openly attacked in public by goons bent on violence, I'm proud to be immature enough to believe it can and should be changed!"

"You're naive," Generales remarked, imperturbably. "Such an attempt as you described is only done by small men . . ."

"Yes, Mr. Generales, but big men can hire small men to shoot dogs for them no matter where."

"I assure you that NEMECO doesn't use such methods," the Greek transportation tycoon reminded me. "I believe that both Willard and Grant are trying to deal with you as any of us here would deal with one another. But you're showing extremely immature judgment, which appears to be your prime weakness."

"You must remember that I'm an idealist. General Hettinger will tell you I'm like my father, whom I'm certain he remembers because I remember a *Captain* Hettinger visiting us a long time ago." I looked around the room. "You have many idealists working at NE-

MECO. Bill Osbourne, Hay Newcomb, my wife, myself, and a group of people you know only as NEMECO Corporate Research Center Laboratories are idealists doing what we were told to do and what we enjoyed doing. Our dreaming and 'immature' judgment gave you the sky hook which means the Solar System and perhaps the stars themselves. Somebody in your company decided that NEMECO shouldn't take what was being offered. So the whole project was simply canceled. I know the decision was *not* made by this Board. NEMECO middle management people were the ones afraid to take the slightest risk. Through corporate political maneuverings, they forced your president to cancel it. The details are too tawdry to drag into the open now. Their middle management credo is: Play it safe, it's too new, it'll change things, it's too risky! Well, Tammy and I were willing to take some pretty hairy risks not only with my airplane but with our lives to show what the sky hook could do . . . If that's immaturity, we probably need a whole hell of a lot more of it!"

"Mike, where *is* the airplane?" Hay Newcomb suddenly asked . . . and I knew I had them! "As I'm certain you anticipated, we obtained a search warrant and went looking for it yesterday . . . and it wasn't at Waterbury airport. Where is it, Mike?"

"Hay, it's my airplane. I own it outright. It's properly licensed, certificated, and inspected. I can store it wherever I please, and I don't have to tell *anybody* where it is—not under these circumstances. It's *my* airplane!"

"Yes, but it has equipment belonging to NEMECO in it," Newcomb said. His voice was level and controlled. He, too, had been under a lot of pressure, but NEMECO couldn't have had a better executive VP capable of standing up to pressure the way he did.

"It does not!" I interjected and turned to Bill Osbourne. "Bill, you gave instructions to Len Marshall and myself to cancel the laboratory's Dynamics Systems project under which we were developing the sky hook. Right?"

"That's right, Mike!"

"You told us to cease work on it and surplus all equipment, right?"

"Those were the orders I was given, and I relayed them to you."

"You also told us that NEMECO had no further interest in the sky hook because of two things. One: Universal American AeroSpace managed to steal the sky hook right out from under us and beat us to the Patent Office with applications, thereby putting NEMECO into a possible interference which you told me NEMECO was not prepared or anxious to contest. Two: You were told to do this with the justification that an internal NEMECO marketing report said that there was absolutely *no market* for any device that produced a unidirectional, reactionless force . . . a classical sky hook, in other words."

Bill Osbourne looked around the room, brightening as he suddenly realized what game I was playing. "That's precisely what I told you and precisely the reasons I was given for the action!"

I stood up. I don't stand very high, but I stood up anyway. "I did install a sky hook in my personal airplane. My wife and I flew my personal airplane, shut the engine off when climbing through twenty-three thousand feet, and climbed to thirty-six thousand feet under a legal ATC clearance, propelled *only* by the sky hook device." Then I said very slowly, "Since I was informed by my superiors that NEMECO did not choose to fight for something that had been stolen from it and which they therefore had no further interest in, I didn't steal a thing!"

I looked at Saul Rothstein, one of the top corporate lawyers in America, a man who had come from the death camp of Belsen without a penny after World War II, one who had survived the Holocaust because he was a survivor type, and a man who was where he was solely because of his brains. "Mr. Rothstein, *can there be theft if there is nothing of value taken?*"

I didn't wait for the answer. I knew what it was. I sat down and added, "If NEMECO is really interested in the sky hook after all, I'll be more than happy to remove that equipment from my airplane and return it to you. Maybe I can go back to work on it then, and maybe we can turn NEMECO into the General Motors of the Solar System. But that's up to you here! I still work for you, and I'm a loyal employee because, of all the companies and organizations I've ever worked for, NEMECO has treated me like a human being instead of someone to be exploited and thrown away when his usefulness came to an end or when the money ran out. I've hidden the airplane and its equipment *not* from you, but from other organizations who might like to find out exactly what's in it. If NEMECO is not interested, there are academic organizations interested in scientific research into the basic nature of the Universe . . ."

Grant Halden sighed. "Mike, why did you put us under all this pressure by telling the FAA to have the press contact me?"

"Grant, I signed an agreement when I came to work for NEMECO that says that I can't make statements of any sort to the news media without the approval of the NEMECO chief executive officer. That's you. You know what the FAA tapes contain. I was unprepared for any attention from our nation's news media since they appear to be ignoring technology these days. Under the NEMECO agreement, I had no recourse but to tell them to get in touch with you so that you could give me permission to talk to them . . ."

"Why didn't you call me about it?"

"Sir, you're a busy man with a seventy-five-million-dollar company to run. I felt that you'd call me if the press contacted you. If I was wrong about that, I apologize. But that's the way I read the agreement." I looked directly at Halden. "It was not my intention to cause you any problems and I don't want to make trouble. If NEMECO still maintains its interest in the sky hook, I contend that Tammy and I made our flight Sunday with the understanding that NEMECO was *not* interested. The worst we felt we might have to confront was Universal American AeroSpace when and if their stolen patents issue to them . . . and neither Tammy nor I felt that You-Ass—pardon me, Universal American AeroSpace—would be upset over the resultant publicity of two people doing something on their own that had never before been done. At least, we felt there would be as much approval for what we did as for the people of *Double Eagle II* and the *Gossamer Albatross.*"

I sat back in the big leather-covered chair. Tammy was looking at the Board members, waiting, pride shining on her face—a most unusual expression for her. I looked up that long table to Chairman McIntosh. "There you have it—all of it, as straight as I can tell it to you. I'm still your employee, and you're still my employer. I don't intend to say one further word about this whole matter; Tammy and I can manage, on our own, to drop well out of sight if you wish for a few days or a few months, as long as necessary for this to blow over . . ."

"Do you think you can get away with this by a simple apology? You've caused us a lot of trouble, Call!" That was Humphrey A. Jackson of Ajax Steel Company. "We could make things very difficult for you."

"Probably! But I don't believe that we did anything wrong. And I won't be bullied any longer! I'll fight and I'll win because we're two ordinary people against a corporation. I don't mean to threaten you with that statement . . . although you *did* threaten me!"

It was Grant Halden who put in hastily, "Now, let's not waste our time talking about threats and recriminations, Hump! Let's get a solution to our problem, since Mike and Tammy are cooperative. It appears that because of a number of rather small and innocuous decisions, internal political maneuverings at middle management level, and poor data, we may have almost thrown away the most important product development in the company's history. Mike has taken a great risk to bring this fact to our attention in a highly dramatic fashion. I'm curious, though. Mike, why did you do it?"

"Grant, I'm an astronomer and a pilot. I'm also a dreamer. I want to see us go to the stars. It can be done *soon*. NEMECO can do it and make a lot of money doing it. All of you in this room can make a lot of

money in the process. As a matter of fact, each of you
with any NEMECO stock is at least twenty-five percent
richer today because of what Tammy and I did Sunday.

"Or NEMECO can sit back and watch somebody get
rich because of what they *really* stole from us: the
whole Solar System and *everything* that's in it! There
was only one way to get these facts to the attention of
the Board of Directors of this company, who could do
something about it. And we did it."

I'd played my hand. I could only hope that I'd
played it properly. I felt I knew these people, and I felt
that they were honest and human. A company like NE-
MECO—and there are thousands of them in America—isn't the fat, greedy J. Pierpont Morgan caricature,
interested only in money at the expense of people. Not
at this level. Not these days! Maybe lower down in NE-
MECO among people like Sanatella and Destry, but not
at the top . . . not in a company more than a hundred
years old that had the guts to try to do something different with a bunch of crazy inventors called the NE-
MECO Corporate Research Center Laboratories.

And I was right.

"Mr. Call." It was the quiet and cultured voice of
Marion A. Cranmer. "Your enthusiasm encourages me.
I'm glad to know that there are still people like you and
Tammy who are willing to work and take risks for a
dream. My forefathers had a dream, too, you know;
they worked hard and they took risks, and we're sitting
here today because of that legacy. Perhaps we on the
Board have been far too insistent upon immediate re-
turns and a bigger dividend, most of which ends up as
taxes in Washington anyway. Perhaps it's time we
looked as far as you are presently seeing . . ." She
shifted in her chair and turned to the chairman. "Willard, there's been too much incrimination and suspicion
here today to suit me. That doesn't make a business
grow. I'd like us to spend a little time this afternoon
looking into the circumstances that forced good men
like Grant Halden and Dr. Newcomb to make the decision to abandon this sky hook thing . . . a device
which sounds impossible to me, except for the fact that

Tammy and Mike apparently made it work very well indeed. I'd like to see this report that says there's no market for such a device. Why, I could think of a dozen myself! And I'd like to meet the people who talked Grant and Hay into this course of action. Then, perhaps tomorrow after a good night's rest—we have a great deal of work to do, it seems to me—we should let Dr. Newcomb, Dr. Osbourne, Tammy Dudley-Call, and Mike Call tell us what we might do to keep NE-MECO in business twenty-five years from now . . ."

J. Willard McIntosh adjusted the glasses on the bridge of his thin nose. "You know, Marion, you've always had that admirable trait of being able to get right to the important heart of the matter. Mr. and Mrs. Call, I invite you to stay as our guests. I think you along with Dr. Osbourne may be able to advise us on a few matters. Now, my fellow directors, I've been with the New England Mill Equipment Company since 1935, and I've seen many things happen here and in other companies. It sounds to me as if we have a classic case of covert internal corporate politics epidemic in this company at the moment . . . and we weren't aware of it—and no fault of Grant's in this regard, by the way. I suggest that we follow up on Marion's suggestion and authorize Grant to cut this cancerous growth out as quickly as possible. Ambition to achieve, excel, and succeed is an admirable and desirable thing to have in middle management, but it can get completely out of control unless we, as the Board of Directors responsible for policies, take action to bring it under control as it's always been in this company. I've also found that the only way to get an accurate picture of what's going on is to ask the people down in the working levels of the company who are most affected by such political maneuverings. Mr. Call, would you tell us what you believe led to the decision to cancel the sky hook?"

Chapter Twenty

Neither Tammy nor I was really prepared for the press conference in the main ballroom of the Waldorf the following Friday night.

Two To Tango sat in the middle of the stage where Guy Lombardo used to make "the sweetest music this side of Heaven" on New Year's Eve because it had flown closer to this side of Heaven than any other Cherokee in the world. My blue-and-white plane was illuminated by brilliant spotlights, and in that environment, it didn't look very big at all. Its wing spanned only 30 feet. As I looked at my airplane there, I wondered to myself if I'd *really* flown it across America and taken it up to 36,000 feet as well. It's such a simple *little* machine to have permitted me to do that!

It came apart with nuts and bolts, and it had been easy to move it down from Meriden and reassemble it inside the ballroom. Brinks' guards were posted around it. Photographers and reporters were allowed to look and photograph anything they pleased, but *no one* laid a finger on that ship! Not only was this at the insistence of NEMECO, but I didn't want my airplane torn apart by souvenir hunters.

The whole NEMECO Corporate Research Center Laboratory staff was there (including Mac Roston because Tammy Dudley-Call, NEMECO's counter-intelligence chief, said he was a good machinist and harmless to have around because he didn't *know* that he'd blown his cover).

The NEMECO Board of Directors and the complete roster of NEMECO executive officers and division managers were on hand.

Phil Sanatella was not present. To this day, I don't know where he went.

Naturally, Dr. Theodore Mayan was there, relishing every moment. Professor Serge Korsinski had in tow the officers of the New York Academy of Sciences. The presence of highly respected scientists did a great deal to prevent people from snorting, "Impossible!" Even without them that would've been very difficult, however, because NEMECO's public relations firm had located the crew of American Airlines Flight Six Nineteen, who were there as NEMECO's guests in addition to the controllers from New York and Boston air traffic control centers who'd worked our flight that Sunday afternoon. Of all the people present, the airline crew and the controllers were the most interested in the little, inexpensive, low-powered general aviation sparrow that had flown up there with the professional jet-powered eagles. (I got some guff out of the FAA, who claimed that Wimpy and I had exceeded our authority in certifying the airworthiness of *Two To Tango* with the sky hook installed; but they had two things going against them: we were heroes, and Hettinger had friends in high places.)

It helps to be a hero.

For the sky hook, it was just the sort of glaring public exposure that was necessary.

Bill Osbourne was right: you can do anything and get away with it if you're able to move faster than the system can react. That's the philosophy I'd used in Plan A. And the principle was also used by NEMECO in Washington. At first, the bureaucrats believed our flight was a hoax because it was "impossible." Then, they decided to send a scientific review board to look into the matter in a few weeks. Friday afternoon before the NEMECO press conference to which General Hettinger invited the Secretary of Defense while Diogenes Generales invited the Secretary of Commerce, somebody panicked and tried to ram a secrecy order through. But the secretaries had gone home by the time they got everything coordinated, and there was no one to type it up! It took them four days to "staff it," and by then it was too late.

NEMECO put out far too much information far too quickly for the government to put a lid on it. The general details, the basic principle of operation, and the photographs were in the papers on Saturday with big Sunday spreads that followed.

But, as Len Marshall once observed, just because you know what it looks like doesn't mean you can duplicate it and make it work. There were a couple of things we *didn't* reveal or talk about and things that I don't ever discuss because they're keys to highly proprietary NEMECO products. Some later aspects of our work are government secrets, and they have to be . . . like how to put a gravitational lid over a city, and a couple or twenty or so other goodies that make science-fiction movies and TV shows look old-fashioned to those of us who know. Like any technology, the sky hook bred both peaceful and military applications. Until we manage to expand further into space, it looks like we will have to put up with such dichotomies because Earth continues to produce "men on horseback" who would rather take it than make it. My esteemed colleague Victor Aboud gave it to us straight that day in the lab, and unfortunately that's the way a lot of the world thinks and operates. We've *got* to do something about that! In the meantime, we're prepared to fend off the bullies.

It was a very good party . . . and Tammy and I were at the center of it. Or, I should say, Tammy was, because when she gets gussied-up for an occasion such as that, she's a real knockout. I don't mind taking a back seat to a gorgeous wife. After all, even though we could do many things in common, she was also busy at the moment doing something she alone could do . . . and it didn't show, being only two months along.

Tammy had been prepared to go to the figurative gallows when we sat down after the Board meeting to talk with Grant Halden. We were both surprised when the entire Board wanted to hear the full story and sat in along with Bill Osbourne. Tammy told her story, and she did it proudly with head held high, unafraid and undaunted. Everyone listened, often stupefied. When it was over, there was only one thing that Grant Halden could do: set a spy to catch spies. Besides, no company president in his right mind could or would fire, reprimand, or discipline someone like Tammy Dudley-Call, who not only had the whole Corporate Research staff behind her but who was about to become the darling of the world's press as well. (Things were worked out with the immigration authorities, quietly and privately because of Tammy's family. It pays to be a heroine, too. And to have Friends In High Places.)

I was handed two surprises at the Waldorf press conference. I didn't have time to check over all the press releases and backgrounders and stuff that the NEMECO PR firm had put out about me.

The first surprise came when Dr. Theodore Mayan stepped up to me before the press conference began and handed me an envelope on which was written: "To Dr. Michael Cochran Call." The letter was very short. The Board of Regents said it was honored to inform me of their award of a degree as a Doctor of Philosophy in Physics.

Looking at it, I said to a broadly grinning Ted Mayan, "I feel like the little dog chasing the big diesel switch engine down at the railroad yards."

"How's that?" Mayan wanted to know.

"Once he catches that switch engine, what's he going to do with it? Now that I'm Doctor Call, what am I going to do that's different? Seriously, thanks, Ted!"

"Oh, you'll use it!" Mayan replied, unoffended because he was the sort of person who could not be offended anyway. "When you get through flying things all over hell and gone with sky hooks, you can always get a job . . ."

"In an astronomical observatory . . . I know!"

The second surprise came during the formal news briefing. Grant Halden introduced me as the new "Chief of the Aviation Division of NEMECO with an additional special assignment as head of experimental flight operations for the sky hook." I hadn't read the NEMECO press releases, and it served me right for not doing my homework!

I managed to get through my portion of the presentation and all the news media questions, including the stupid ones from reporters who could probably never solve a simple equation much less understand what keeps the Moon from falling. And I did it without losing either my temper or my composure.

But I did approach Grant Halden and Bill Osbourne privately after the party started to wind down. Bill knew what my question was going to be. "I'm glad I hired you, Mike. But you're a lousy research employee because you think you know more than the Director of Research. I'm going to be much more comfortable working with you as a division head."

"I don't really know which of us is going to be more comfortable!" I kidded him back. Then I turned to the NEMECO president. "Grant, thank you, but what happened to Jake Stock?"

"Oh, I suspect you didn't hear about it in all the fuss. Jake, our crusty old pelican, failed to pass his First Class physical . . ."

"That's too damned bad! . . ."

"No, he can still fly, but not as our Chief Corporate Pilot. He's got a Third Class medical certificate, so he isn't out of the air. He's going out to Airborne Controls Division in Tempe for about six months, then he'll take over that division when we move Vern Bates up to the Trumbull operation."

"Well, is Bob Destry moving up to corporate level, then?" I wanted to know.

Grant Halden's face was totally emotionless. "Mr. Destry is no longer with us."

I blinked and changed the subject. "I'll have to re-staff and reorganize the Aviation Division, then. I'd like to have two special people as my assistants, Grant. Wimpy Winfield's the best pilot I've ever known, and he's being wasted as a mechanic. Wendell Stone won't fly—yet—but he's one hell of an engineer . . . and I'll need them both!"

"Mike, it's *your* show," Grant reminded me. "Run it your way!"

Bill Osbourne and I found ourselves alone in a corner shortly thereafter. The research director pulled at his bushy moustache and quietly remarked, "Mike, I don't think anybody but Len and I recognized the superbatteries in *Two To Tango* . . ." And nothing more was ever said.

The relativists claim that it'll take years to get to the stars. They're right. But we'll probably make the trip in a few weeks when we go. No technology can come to fruition overnight. The breakthrough—such as the original sky hook hanging there as a ballistic pendulum totally displacing itself from the vertical—is only the beginning. It takes years of hard work to get from that point to having a mature technology working for you the way you want. Once the romantic research and development work is done, the elegant experiments are carried out, and the exciting trials are complete, it's a matter of grinding numbers and fiddling for months or years to get the preproduction units to work the way they're supposed to. Then production problems arise, followed by problems in the field. Wendell Stone had a better idea of what was to come than all of us dreamers at NEMECO Corporate Research Center Laboratories. As Vic said one day in complete exasperation, "If I had to do it all over again, I'd do it all over somebody else!" There are set-backs, things that don't work out the way you'd hoped or theorized or checked out in the lab. There are slow-downs because the company has to make a buck on prosaic, everyday products to pay for the far-out stuff. And there are still those who try to grasp and connive and steal. But Bill Osbourne, Vic Aboud, Len Marshall, Wendell Stone, Tammy Dudley-Call, and myself didn't worry about them because we knew how to handle them.

Osbourne was fond of quoting from Kipling's *The Mary Gloster*:

"They copied all they could follow, but they couldn't copy my mind.
So I left 'em sweatin' and schemin', a year and a half behind . . ."

We're going to the stars.

It's inevitable now.

We don't know yet whether the sky hook's progeny will be able to propel anything faster than light. All of Vic's field equations say "maybe," but Ted Mayan says Vic missed the equivalent of a decimal point, a "small error" that Mayan claims will raise the ultimate velocity of a gravitation charge to more than 30,000 times the speed of light. Korsinski argues with him, but Serge is interested in what goes on at the other end of the universal scale where he's working on a theory of the quantization of time that has its roots in our work. Between Mayan with his grand view of cosmology and Korsinski delving into the basics of matter itself—two doors that were opened by Bill and Vic—we'll get the answer someday. And "someday" isn't an indeterminate time in the far future; I'm betting on no more than ten to fifteen years before one of Mayan's or Korsinski's graduate students makes that trip to Stockholm. Any of us would be proud and honored to be a laureate, but we don't have time for all the scientific papers and meetings that lead up to a nomination; we're far too busy putting the sky hook and its various modifications to work. We know how bread is made, and if we're going to go where we want to go, NEMECO has to make lots of bread. It will. The stock just split for the fifth time, and it was up to 215 before the split. There are a lot of ways to make money. As Dr. William D. Osbourne once said, "Do not bind the mouths of the kine who tread the grain!"

With luck and gerontology, I *might* make it to the stars. But Wendell Victor Call has a much better chance. And, because his son will probably be born in space, my grandson will be a natural-born starman who never knows planetary gravity except during brief visits.

But I've come further than I thought I would. We all have. I went through what might be termed a changeover point and Tammy did too.

It was a change-point for Dr. William D. Osbourne, as well. When I first met him, I felt I was seeing only the tip of the iceberg that was Osbourne. We were much

alike, fellow dreamers and schemers for the future. I'd
been running without considering why I should have
fought for that job in Flagstaff. And Osbourne had been
running from the Sidewinder that went up his F-4's tail
pipe and the people who had chased him out of his military profession. The difference came when I learned at
NEMECO to stop running and fight for what I knew
could be done. Bill eventually became a very good professor of physics in the academic environment of NYU
where, because of NEMECO's success with the sky
hook, he finally stopped running, stood firm, fought for
what he had done, and years later got the Stockholm
trip he certainly deserved.

Because of his weakness, he made me overcome
mine. He was a much better teacher than a leader . . .
and taught me a great deal.

Len Marshall changed, too. He became a leader
when the vacuum was created by Bill's demoralization.
It sucked him right into the position where he was the
obvious Director of Research long before Bill left for
his professor's chair.

As for Vic, he just kept right on having fun.

And this old ag pilot never thought he'd routinely
cruise above a million feet with something resembling a
cluster of glowing fluorescent lights in the rear cabin.
Star Driver I carries N1422T on her tail because the
Cherokee now rests in retirement at Silver Hill, Mary-
land, in storage with the National Air and Space Museum.

At a million feet, which is good orbital altitude,
there's beauty in the sunset over the Earth's rim, and
there's beauty in the not-so-distant stars that shine both
through the windshield and the optically flat ceiling
panes where Brad Johnson occasionally makes measurements because we can now get up there quickly and
cheaply. That's the outward-looking beauty.

Tammy says I've changed greatly. She may be right.
She usually is. She says I once thought of nothing but
astronomy and airplanes but have since discovered
something else. I know that Tammy looks outward into
the universe as we both see it from *Star Driver I*, but

she and I together have learned to see inward into ourselves as well. If I have changed, so has she, but always for the better.

I'll probably never be able to combine my talents as a star gazer with those of an airplane driver to become a star driver. But, since I got things started, perhaps it isn't as vitally important for me to do it as it once seemed when *nobody* believed we would *ever* do it!

Tammy, my inward love who shares my outward loves, understands this. If there's a chance we aren't going to be around long enough to go to the stars in a future *Two To Tango*, we came to the conclusion that there was only one thing that the two of us could do about it:

We could make star drivers.

It's more fun, anyway.

About the Author

This is Lee Correy's fourth science-fiction novel, but the first he's written in over twenty years. Better known under his real name, G. Harry Stine, he's a rocket pioneer, a futurist, an expert in space industrialization and high-technology marketing, and the author of or contributor to more than twenty books on science and technology. He uses his pen-name "Lee Correy" for fiction to separate it from his nonfiction.

He's been the director of an industrial research laboratory and marketing manager for a small industrial company. He is an instrument-rated private pilot with over a thousand hours, owns his own Cherokee (N95439), and is an aerospace historian and a consultant to the National Air and Space Museum.

He lives in Phoenix, Arizona, with his wife, a cat with twenty-four toes, and three Golden Retrievers.

Exciting
Space Adventure
from
DEL REY